PRAISE FOR *THE FORTUNE QUILT*

"Quick humor." —*Booklist*

"A beguiling twist on ..." —*Reviews*

"This vibrant novel from Rich shows that chick lit can deal intelligently with fate, family issues, and romantic relationships." —*Publishers Weekly*

"Mystical quilts, a hunchback toad, and a wisecracking heroine ... what else could you ask for from a book?" —Whitney Gaskell

"Funny and completely involving. Carly is the rare character who is both appealing and confused enough to actually fit in with the rest of your friends." —Jane Espenson

———

...AND FOR THE OTHER NOVELS OF
OF LANI DIANE RICH

"I love Lani Diane Rich's thirtysomething heroine.... Fast, funny, and always true to herself, Wanda is one of those heroines you want to have lunch with." —Jennifer Crusie

"A sparkling debut, full of punch, pace, and wonderfully tender moments." —Sue Margolis

"Terrific and absolutely hilarious ... with a thoroughly delightful and original heroine." —Melissa Senate

continued ...

"This effervescent debut novel will strike a chord with every woman who has ever been tempted to give her life an extreme makeover." —Wendy Markham

"A warm and funny story. A perfect read for a rainy afternoon. Or *any* afternoon." —Karen Brichoux

"Rich has managed to skillfully blend serious topics with humor, and readers will love her for it." —*Booklist*

"Sprightly dialogue. . . . A fast, fun read, especially for those who enjoy the quirky characters of authors like Jennifer Crusie and Eileen Rendahl." —*Library Journal*

"Wacky characters, nonstop action, riotous dialogue . . . the merriment keeps the pages turning." —*Publishers Weekly*

NOVELS BY LANI DIANE RICH

The Fortune Quilt

A Little
Ray of Sunshine

Lani Diane Rich

NEW AMERICAN LIBRARY

New American Library
Published by New American Library, a division of Penguin Group (USA) Inc.,
375 Hudson Street, New York, New York 10014, USA • Penguin Group (Canada),
90 Eglinton Avenue East, Suite 700, Toronto, Ontario M4P 2Y3, Canada
(a division of Pearson Penguin Canada Inc.) • Penguin Books Ltd., 80 Strand,
London WC2R 0RL, England • Penguin Ireland, 25 St. Stephen's Green,
Dublin 2, Ireland (a division of Penguin Books Ltd.) • Penguin Group (Australia),
250 Camberwell Road, Camberwell, Victoria 3124, Australia (a division of Pearson
Australia Group Pty. Ltd.) • Penguin Books India Pvt. Ltd., 11 Community Centre,
Panchsheel Park, New Delhi – 110 017, India • Penguin Group (NZ),
67 Apollo Drive, Rosedale, North Shore 0632, New Zealand (a division of Pearson
New Zealand Ltd.) • Penguin Books (South Africa) (Pty.) Ltd.,
24 Sturdee Avenue, Rosebank, Johannesburg 2196, South Africa

Penguin Books Ltd., Registered Offices:
80 Strand, London WC2R 0RL, England

First published by New American Library,
a division of Penguin Group (USA) Inc.

First Printing, February 2008
3   5   7   9   10   8   6   4   2

NEW AMERICAN LIBRARY and logo are trademarks of Penguin Group (USA) Inc.

LIBRARY OF CONGRESS CATALOGING-IN-PUBLICATION DATA:
Rich, Lani Diane.
A little ray of sunshine / Lani Diane Rich.
p. cm.
ISBN: 978-0-451-22296-1
1. Single women—Fiction.   2. Angels—Fiction.   3. Reconciliation—
Fiction.   4. Domestic fiction.   I. Title.
PS3618.I333L58 2008
813'.6—dc22   2007029763

Set in Janson Text   •   Designed by Elke Sigal

Printed in the United States of America

For Sweetness and Light, my own little angels

Acknowledgments

I loved writing this book. Usually, at some point during every book, I want to find a blunt object and beat myself to death with it just to end the misery of my swift and certain failure. Then everything turns out okay. (Writers. Drama queens, each and every one of us, I'm telling you.) This book was different, though. I loved every minute. Because of that, I'm hoping it's special, so my first debt of gratitude is to you, its reader. Thanks so much for completing this process with me. I hope it's as much fun for you as it was for me. Or, at any rate, worth whatever you shelled out for it.

To Samantha Graves, Robin La Fevers, Alesia Holliday, Michelle Cunnah, Whitney Gaskell, Eileen Rendahl, Beth Kendrick, Jennifer Crusie, Anne Stuart, Cate Diede, and Rebecca Rohan—I can't imagine a funnier, sharper, more supportive group of women to have by my side through all the insanity. I must have done something very good in a past life to deserve you, because it's for damn sure I haven't done anything near good enough in this one.

To the Glindas, for suffering through many revisions of the awful duck joke—I'm forever in your debt.

To Stephanie Kip Rostan, the Best Agent Ever, for being the Best Agent Ever. You are the Ella Fitzgerald of agents, and don't you forget it.

To Kara Cesare, Editor Extraordinaire, for loving this book as much as I did, for being so damn *good* at what you do, and for being so delightful as you do it. It's the lucky author that gets you for an editor.

To Fish, Sweetness, and Light, who sacrifice hot meals and a clean house so I can do what I love, there's no expression of gratitude that even comes close to what I owe you. Except maybe cooking and cleaning—but the truth is, although I do like to blame it on the writing, I probably wouldn't have cooked and cleaned anyway. So really it's a wash.

A Little
Ray of Sunshine

Chapter One

The night the angel found me was pretty much like every other night at the Quik 'n Go. The air smelled like moist cardboard beer boxes, lemon-scented Lysol, and cinnamon-tainted coffee; the *National Enquirer* I attempted to read under the humming fluorescent lights was full of crap and yet, still oddly fascinating; and the customers were few, far between, and uncharacteristically inclined to talk to me. Case in point: Middle Eastern Guy, who I blame for starting this whole thing, because it was he who jerked his head toward the plate-glass window and asked, "Are you going to go help her or what?"

I flipped down one corner of my *National Enquirer* to find him raising an expectant eyebrow at me. This was highly unusual behavior for Middle Eastern Guy (midthirties, five foot eleven, short dark hair, light blue windbreaker jacket; you work in a convenience store for a while, you start to see people in police description-ese), who had never spoken to me directly before, and I wasn't a fan of the sudden switch. His eyes flickered toward the front window, then landed back on me.

"You should go help her."

He had no accent. No accent on a Middle Eastern guy in northern New Jersey. Forget that he was probably raised in America, I got that, but this was northern New Jersey. Even the crickets had accents. I'd only been there for two months and was already pronouncing the word *coffee* as though I had a mouth full of marbles. I put the tabloid down and glanced at the register.

"Pump number four, right?"

His eyebrows did that little twitchy thing that happens when someone's not sure if you're socially challenged or just being rude. I didn't fault him the wondering. People skills have never been my strong point.

"You should go help her," he said again, but slower this time.

I followed his eyeline. Outside, there was a blonde— late twenties, five foot six, denim jacket, khaki pants, medium-length hair shooting out from behind her ears in two girlish ponytails—staring at the hood of a beat-up white Toyota. About five minutes prior, I had rung her up for a bottle of Snapple Diet Raspberry Iced Tea and a box of Whoppers.

I looked back at Middle Eastern Guy. "Your total comes to twenty-seven eighty-four. Will that be cash or are you going to put this on your Quik 'n Go card?"

We were supposed to do that—presume that everyone has a Quik 'n Go card, make them feel like they're missing out if they don't have one. It's in the manual. You can check—page thirteen. We were supposed to use their names, too, if we got a credit card or a check, so that the customer would feel like they were in a chummy, personable locale rather than a cold, lifeless turnpike convenience pit.

Next time, I thought to myself, *I'm getting a job that doesn't make me deal with the public.*

Of course, I knew I probably wouldn't, as those kinds of jobs usually require skills, or a degree in something other than Beer Bongs 101. No one with aspirations wants to work with the public for seven bucks an hour, so it's nomads like me that usually get stuck doing it.

"She needs your help," he said, motioning toward the blonde with one hand as he gave me his cash with the other. "Go help her."

I opened my mouth, but nothing came out, because I didn't want to say what I was thinking, which was that I couldn't help her if I wanted to. She was staring at her car, which indicated her car wasn't working, and I didn't know squat about cars. Best I could do would be to go out there and say, "Hey. Dig that. It's not moving," which wouldn't be terribly helpful. Plus, her legs appeared to be in working order. If she needed help, she could come in and ask to use the phone. Tap on the glass. Wave me over. Whatever. But because explaining all this seemed like too much trouble for too little pay-off, I just said, "I can't leave customers alone in the store."

"What customers?" he asked, looking around. "There's just me."

I cleared my throat to indicate my annoyance. "Here's a thought. Why don't *you* go help her?"

"Because I'm a guy," he said. "She's stranded and alone at a convenience store at midnight. I don't want to freak her out. Just go, and I'll go with you." His eyes locked on my name tag, and his eyebrows knit. "What does that stand for? EJ?"

I glanced down. "It's my name."

"It doesn't stand for anything? You're just . . . EJ?"

"Yep." And in the grand tradition of defense by offense, I shot back, "Where are you from, anyway?"

He looked surprised. I kept my expression flat and expectant.

"Springfield," he said finally.

"New Jersey, Illinois, or Missouri?"

"Ohio."

I pulled his change from the till. "Too damn many Springfields."

I gave him his money and picked up my *National Enquirer.* He didn't leave, though, just stood there watching me with a look that told me our interaction wasn't over. I sighed and looked out the window.

Ponytails still hadn't moved. She just stared at the hood of her car, which left me with two choices. I could be stubborn and wait Springfield out until Edgar came in to take over at midnight, which was exactly seventeen minutes away by the official Quik 'n Go clock. But, the way it looked, Ponytails was still going to be standing there when I got off my shift, and I knew I wouldn't be able to ignore her out of spite. I was a lot of unflattering things, but spiteful hadn't made the cut up from the jay-vee team.

Which left me with door number two. I could take thirty seconds, get both Springfield and Ponytails out of my hair, and spend the last quarter hour of my shift reading the tabloids, the way God intended.

"Okay," I said finally. I glanced up at the store security camera and gave the hand signal for "All is well, assisting customer in need." This was so that if my boss reviewed the tapes the following morning, I wouldn't lose my job. Not that it was a great job, but it was mine, and I wanted it until I didn't want it anymore.

I pulled my keys out with a flourish so that the camera would catch me dutifully locking the door, then followed Springfield out to Ponytails and her car. Springfield stopped a few feet away from her and motioned for me to go on ahead. I stepped forward.

"Everything okay out here? You need me to call for a tow?"

She looked up at me with an expression so perplexed you would think the car hood was a calculus textbook.

"My car broke down," she said simply, her voice surprising me with its lightness and lack of frustration. Had it been me, I would have expressed that sentiment with a few strategically placed expletives and maybe a kick to the tire. Ponytails just looked around as though trying to solve a puzzle in her head.

"Why here? What's here?" she mumbled to herself.

Her focus switched from the car to Springfield, locking on him with a hopeful expression. "Oooh. Maybe it's you. Can I help you?"

"Um, no. Thank you." He glanced at me, then, when I remained silent, sighed and looked back at her. "Do *you* need help?"

She ignored him and looked at me. "Is anyone here in trouble?"

"Think so," I said, glancing pointedly at her car. "Do you need a tow?"

"No, I mean . . ." She paused, her face scrunched up in thought for a moment. "I mean, it was fine until I pulled up here and then it just died. There has to be a reason, right?"

"Well . . . ," I said slowly, coming to the conclusion that Ponytails wasn't firing on all cylinders, so possibly neither was the car. "Did you put gas in it?"

"Pffft," she said with a giggle. "Of course. No, it was fine. Then I pulled in here, and it just . . . stopped."

Springfield stepped closer and held out his hand, palm up. "Would you like me to try?"

"Thank you, but I doubt you'll be able to do anything," she said. "It won't start until I do what I'm supposed to do."

He smiled at her. "Well, then, it can't hurt if I try, right?"

She shrugged and handed him her keys.

"Do you know anything about cars?" I asked, but Springfield shook his head in my direction; his radar had apparently detected some crazy, too. He slid into the front seat and stuck the keys in the ignition. Pony-tails's eyes drifted down to my name tag.

"EJ," she said softly, a light smile on her face. "That's nice. It's funny how names like that can be ironically feminine, isn't it?"

"Sure." I shuffled to the left a bit, putting a few more inches between us. Springfield pushed himself up out of the car.

"Didn't even click," he said. "My guess is the battery. Maybe your alternator."

Ponytails released a sigh of acceptance. "No, it's fine. It's me. Thanks anyway." She smiled at him as she took back her keys. "So, then it's down to you two. Sir, are you sure you don't need any help with anything? Nothing I can do for you?"

Springfield and I exchanged a look and he said, "Noooooo, but maybe I can drive you somewhere. Like, maybe, to a hospital . . . or something?"

"Oh, no," she said, not seeming to take the slightest offense at the fact that he basically had just called her crazy to her face. "Thank you. I'm fine." She crossed her arms over her chest and stared at Springfield hard for a minute, then gave a brief nod and turned to me. "I don't think it's him. It must be you, then."

I'll admit, this took me by surprise. "What must be me, then?"

She held out her hand for me to shake, and I reflexively took it.

"My name is Jess. I'm an angel." She said it as though she were telling me she was a Pisces, or a paralegal. "And when things like this happen to me, it's because I have a job to do. EJ, I think you're it."

Springfield patted my shoulder. "Okay. If you've got this under control, I'll just be going."

"Thanks so much for the help," I said with a bite in my voice, then turned back to Jess. "Let's go call you that tow."

I pulled my keys out of my pocket and headed back for the store. Jess followed, chattering at me the whole way.

"So, you need to tell me everything about yourself, even if you don't think it matters. You'd be amazed how many of these things are resolved when I find out something that my assignment thinks is unimportant."

Assignment? Hmmm. I yanked the yellow pages out and let the book thunk on the counter with the heavy weight of purpose.

"I'll call you a tow and have them bring it to Busey Brothers. It's on the edge of town, but they'll do a good job and probably won't rip you off too bad."

"Do you have a husband or a boyfriend? Are you fighting? That's usually my specialty." She grinned. "I'm something of a cosmic relationship mender."

"If you stay at the Super 8, that's within walking distance of Busey's." I picked up the phone. She took the receiver from my hand and replaced it in the cradle. I'd never seen anyone actually do that in real life, so instead of smacking her hand and picking the phone up again, I just stared at her, my head cocked to the side, making me feel like a curious dog whose owner had just done a strange jig in the middle of the sidewalk.

"Oh, no," she said. "I really should stay with you. I need to see how you live, get to know your family and your friends. I can't help you if I'm staying at a motel."

"I don't need any help," I said. She watched me, a beatific smile on her expectant face, as though she were waiting for more. I decided to speak clearly and slowly, much the way Springfield had spoken to me earlier. "You cannot stay with me."

"Oh, don't worry. I'll earn my keep. I make these blueberry yogurt pancakes that are truly amazing, if I do say so myself. Oh—and I also have a lot of basic carpentry skills. Does anything in your house need fixing? I can make you a bookshelf."

"I live in an Airstream," I said. "You know, the motor homes?"

Her face lit up. "The ones that look like big silver hot dogs? I love those!"

I didn't know how to respond to that. What I was thinking was that even the stray cats that eat out of the garbage cans at the RV park don't want to come home with me, that I'm not the kind of person people attach themselves to. Even crazy people. I was also thinking that I didn't want to be killed in my sleep, and while Jess didn't seem violent at the moment, it wasn't really a chance I cared to take.

Instead I said, "I'm just gonna call Busey's."

She watched me, her eyes narrowing in thought, then finally nodded toward the phone. I picked up the receiver and dialed Busey's. I waited the five rings for the answering machine, then punched in "9" for emergency so it would transfer me to Vince Busey's cell. As I arranged for Vince to come and tow her car, Jess fiddled absently with my *National Enquirer,* then leaned forward after I hung up the phone.

"You don't believe I'm an angel, do you?"

I stared at her. I wanted to tell her that no, as a matter of fact, I didn't believe in angels at all, because angels weren't real and she was obviously in dire need of some sort of medication. I wanted to tell her that even if angels were real, which they were not, they certainly wouldn't come find me. I was no George Bailey. I was just plain old Emmy James, and I lived in a trailer and I worked in a convenience store and I was simply not the type of girl that drew angels to her.

Instead, I said, "Cab should be here in just a few minutes," and waited out the rest of my shift in silence.

You have to understand that by the time Jess found me, I was pretty set in my ways. I liked my Airstream. I liked living in RV parks and working temporary jobs. I liked the fact that, at any time, I could decide that I'd had enough of one place and just pick up and go someplace else. In the six years I'd been nomading it, I had lived in over twelve places. Rolla, Missouri, was my record shortest stop, clocking in at just over two days. Billings, Montana, was my longest; I was there for almost a year. I had worked as a waitress in South Dakota, a car washer in San Diego, a dog walker in Fort Lauderdale, a seasonal customer service rep for a financial software company in Tucson, and an ice cream vendor on the boardwalk in Atlantic City. It worked for me, and I liked it.

What I didn't like was the pity. Every now and again, I'd get to talking with someone, and when we got to any of the details of my life, the conversation would usually go a little something like this:

Them: So, you live alone?
Me: Yes.
Them: In a trailer?
Me: Yes.
Them: And you just keep moving to different places whenever you want?
Me: Yes.
Them: Don't you have family?
Me: No.
(That's a lie. I have family; I just don't like to talk about her.)
Them: And you're . . . happy?
(There was always a pause before "happy." Always. As though it was so unbelievable that I might actually like my life that it took extra effort just to get the words out.)
Me: Yes. I'm. Happy.

That would pretty much kill the conversation every time, and then I'd end up feeling like there was something wrong with me. Which, well, obviously there was, but still. I didn't want to have it thrown in my face. I knew I was socially disabled; I didn't need their looks of pity to remind me. So that night, as I sat in my trailer eating Frosted Mini-Wheats Strawberry Delight for dinner and watching my DVD of *North by Northwest*, I gently fumed. Who was this Jess, anyway, to decide that *I* was the one who needed *her* help? She was the crazy one. If anyone needed help, it was her, okay? And how could she be so sure it wasn't Springfield whose life was such a big fat mess that she had to be sent from Heaven above to come clean it up? I mean, he bought five packs of Doublemint and a tank of gas in cash every Tuesday night. If that wasn't a cry for help, what was? And I liked my life. I was doing great. I was . . . okay, *fine*, I wasn't exactly happy, but who's happy?

No one. That's who. And who cared what one crazy angel thought anyway?

Not me.

I pushed myself up from the foldout table and continued to steam as I took the three steps to my kitchen. I washed out my bowl and spoon and stuck them in my tiny dish rack, then stared down into my tiny, tiny sink as the familiar wave of emotion slammed into me.

Here we go.

I closed my eyes and breathed slowly, trying to calm my heart rate as I rode out the episode. In a powerful whisper, I heard the voice, my own voice, tell me what I already knew.

It's time.

When I opened my eyes, my lashes were wet with tears, which was weird, because I had no memory of actually crying. With a shaking hand, I reached up and swiped at my face. That one had been stronger than the last one, which had been stronger than the one before it. Seemed a bad trend. Not that it mattered much, though, because in the end, they all meant the same thing.

Wearily, I made my way to the door of my trailer and stepped out into the balmy June night. I walked barefoot over the warm gravel to my truck, stuck my head through the open passenger window, and reached for the glove compartment.

Minutes later, I was back in the Airstream, my AAA United States map tacked up on my corkboard, my trusty red dart at the ready. I closed my eyes, said my prayer, and hurled the dart. When I opened my eyes, I could see that the dart had landed somewhere in Colorado. It didn't really matter where; I'd figure out the specifics later. I had a direction now—west—and that was all I needed. Suddenly I felt overwhelmed with exhaustion, and my mind whirled with all the tasks I had before me. Give my notice at the Quik 'n Go. Get a prorated rent refund from the RV park for the remainder of the month I wouldn't be using. Unhook the Airstream and latch it onto my truck.

And then . . . go.

I glanced up at the television to see Cary Grant scaling Mount Rushmore with Eva Marie Saint, gunmen on their heels.

Maybe I'll check out Mount Rushmore on the way, I thought as I picked up the remote and clicked off the television. *Nobody at Mount Rushmore thinks twice about a girl living in a trailer.*

"So, how exactly does this angel thing work?" I asked when Jess opened her motel room door. I was glad to see she didn't wear froufrou floral cotton nightgowns to bed; she was respectably clad in a University of Arizona

Wildcats sweatshirt and a pair of black yoga pants with her hair pulled back into an off-kilter ponytail. I was dressed in my best pair of dark jeans and a shirt I'd had to iron, and I'd actually washed, dried, and curled my hair. And put on mascara.

It was sad. So very, very sad.

"I brought coffee." I lifted up the cardboard drink carrier in my hands, trying to look as if I hadn't been up all night obsessing over what exactly the crazy angel lady thought was wrong with me.

Jess took a moment before stepping away from the door to let me enter. "You didn't have to bring me coffee, but thank you. It's very thoughtful."

There it was, an open zone for me to pitch my big, fat lies into. I went for it.

"Well, it's the least I can do, considering that I'm waking you up at the crack of dawn. But, see, I've got a busy day ahead of me and it occurred to me, you know, before I fell asleep last night, that you might be an interesting person to talk to." I took the coffees out and set the cardboard tray on the motel dresser. "You know. For my book."

Her eyebrows raised as she sat on the edge of one double bed, motioning for me to sit on the other. "Wow. You're writing a book?"

"Yes," I said overbrightly, putting one of the coffees in her hand. "I'm writing a memoir of my travels. Young woman on the road, occupational . . . adventures. Kind of. The people I meet, that sort of thing. And it occurred to me that I may have dismissed you a little . . .

abruptly last night. You know, because even though I'm just fine and don't need your help, I thought that maybe you might be an interesting person to talk to. You know. For the book."

I took a sip of my coffee; it was too hot, and I tried to mask my cringe as it scorched its way down my gullet. *Liar, liar, esophagus on fire*, the smug voice of reason inside me cooed.

"Wow," Jess said. "You're writing a book. I'm honored you would think of me for it."

"Oh, of course." I added a small "pffft," as though it were an obvious choice and absolutely no big deal. Which it wouldn't be. If there really was a book. I extracted the fresh notebook I'd just bought from my bag and flipped it open.

"So, tell me about yourself," I said. "Where are you from? What brought you to New Jersey? Are you from this area originally, or do you travel?"

She took a thoughtful sip of her coffee. "I'd rather learn more about you. You know, I had a feeling about you the moment we met. And . . . this may sound crazy, but . . ." She paused and I wondered what she was going to say that could possibly top "I'm an angel" in the crazy department. "I feel like I know you already. You just seem so familiar."

I thought briefly about dodging, but Jess seemed the junkyard dog type; once she got into something, my guess was that she didn't let go easily. So, I shot straight. "I look a lot like my mother. She used to be kind of famous."

"Really? That's fascinating. Who's your mother?"

I tried to hide my internal cringe as I dropped my mother's name. "Lilly Lorraine. She used to play—"

Jess squealed, her available hand flailing in the air by her face, making her look like a teenager who'd just walked outside and found a brand-new car with a big bow on it. I sat up straighter and pulled back a bit.

"Twinkie!" she screeched. "Oh, my God, you're Twinkie's *baby!*"

I'm pretty sure my face registered stark horror at this description, but Jess didn't seem to notice. She giggled some more and reached forward to give my knee a playful slap of excitement. "Oh, my God, I *love* your mother. They play *Baby of the Family* all the time on Nick at Nite, and I've seen every episode at least twice. Your mom was *so* adorable. I loved the way she did the—"

Jess rolled her eyes skyward, donned an angelic expression of innocence, and shrugged with her hands up. The gesture had been my mother's "Whatchoo talkin' 'bout, Willis?" and if I had a drop of water for every time someone had performed it for me, I'd have drowned by the age of two.

Jess released the pose and grinned. "Wow. Lilly Lorraine. How is she doing?"

"I have no idea." I lifted my pen. "So, tell me, how long have you been an angel? Are you born that way, or was it something you were, um"—I cleared my throat, searching for words that would make me sound like I had the slightest idea how to interview someone— "called . . . to?"

She crossed her legs yoga-style in front of her and gave me an appraising look. "You really don't like talking about yourself, do you?"

"Well, you know how we"—*What was the word? Journalists? Memoirists? Sad, sad fakers?*—"writers are."

She smiled. "Yes." She watched me for a moment, and then sat up straighter. "Okay. We can start with me. My name is Jess Szyzynski . . ."

"Szyzynski?" I jotted in my notebook dutifully. "Can you spell that?"

She smiled and obliged. "I was born in Gulfport, Mississippi. I think."

"You think?" I asked.

She gave a small smile. "I moved around a lot as a kid. It's probably how I got the bug for my kind of work."

"Yes." I pointed my pen at her. It seemed a journalisty thing to do. "Speaking of which, how exactly did you end up in this line of work? I mean, it's not like there's a big angel corporation or anything. Unless . . ." My eyes widened and I glanced around at the motel room. "Do you work for some kind of *Candid Camera* show?"

She laughed. "Oh, no. No. And the angel thing . . . well, it's not so much work as, like you said, a calling."

"Oh. Okay. So, what's your day job?"

"I don't have one."

I raised an eyebrow. "So, where do you get money? You don't charge for your . . . angeling, do you?" Jess didn't seem like the scamming con artist type, but I guessed the best scamming con artists were the ones who didn't look like scamming con artists.

"Oh, no, I don't charge. I don't need money. I mean, I need it, everyone needs it, but I have money from—" She stopped, her face registering a quick flash of something that was gone before I could read it. "I mean, I have enough. I don't need much. Kind of like you, I guess."

"Okay. So, how does one get called to your kind of work?"

"Well . . ." Her thin fingers rubbed absently at the cover on her to-go cup. "I don't know. You just wake up one day, and you *know*. You know?"

"No."

She leaned forward. "Well, how did *you* end up traveling around alone?"

I felt a prickle of annoyance. "We were talking about you."

"We still are. I'm just trying to show you that you and I . . . maybe we're not that different."

Of course we're different, I thought. *You are certifiable, whereas I am merely quirky and interesting.*

I flipped my notebook shut. "Well, thank you for your time. I really need to get going. Like I said . . . busy day."

Jess smiled. "Yes. It's almost seven. Where has the time gone?"

I stood up and headed for the door, crazy angel lady on my heels.

"Thank you so much for coming by, and thank you

for the coffee," she said. "Although we've hardly even scratched the surface. Maybe we can talk again. Later today, if you have time?"

I pulled the door open, then turned to face her. "Well, I don't know. I mean, you know. Busy day."

"Surely you can find a half hour to slot me in. For the book. Books like that can't possibly have enough colorful characters, and I am nothing if not colorful. How about twelve thirty? I can make my pancakes for you."

"I don't know . . ."

"Then one o'clock. I'll bring all the ingredients. Do you have a skillet and a spatula, or do I need to bring those as well?"

I glanced at my watch. "I really have a lot of stuff to do . . ."

"Six o'clock. I'll come by and make them for dinner. You haven't lived until you've had my pancakes for dinner, I'm telling you. Yogurt and blueberries and just a touch of vanilla. Oh, they melt in your mouth."

I stared at her. She sure was pushy for an angel.

"Well, I won't take no for an answer, so it's settled." She held up her finger and ran to the desk, pulling a pen and notepad out of the drawer. "How do I find you?"

With great reluctance, I told her. There was only one trailer park in town, and only one big silver hot dog in it, and I had a feeling that this woman would track me down if it came to that. And hell, I could maintain the charade through some pancakes. Maybe my willingness to endure her company would be sign enough that I didn't need any help from an angel. I was just fine as I was.

"We're all set, then." To my complete surprise, she pulled me into a hug, not seeming to mind that my arms hung unmoving at my sides.

"Thanks so much for the coffee, EJ," she said after releasing me. "I'm so glad you came by. I'll see you to-night."

She shut the door. I stared at it for a full minute before realizing that I had been completely and totally played. By an angel.

"Hmph," I huffed as I turned on one heel. It would serve her right if I wasn't there when she showed up at six.

But I knew I would be. She hadn't admitted outright yet that she'd made a mistake, that I didn't need her help, that her car had broken down because of Spring-field, or because it was old and there's no meaning in the universe and maybe she'd be better off temping. I wanted to hear her say it, at least the part where she was wrong about me, because she was, and if it meant having blue-berry pancakes for my last dinner in town, then that was fine by me.

Simon flew into a rage when I told him I'd scheduled an abortion. No matter how rationally I explained it to him, he couldn't get it through his head that yes, I had agreed to get pregnant, but no, I'd never thought it would actually happen. Somewhere deep inside, I truly believed I couldn't get pregnant, for the simple reason that I wasn't fit for it. For example, God allows horses and donkeys to make mules, right? But mules can't get pregnant, because they're not fit for it. I thought that God, of all people, would know that I was a mule. I could agree to try for Simon's sake, but what kind of God would ever allow someone like me to have children?

Well, He did, and I discovered His betrayal not two days before an audition for my first starring role since Twinkie. I mean, an abortion was the only thing that made sense, right? As a director who would die a bloody death before casting a pregnant woman for his *hit show, I thought Simon would understand. He didn't. He badgered and cajoled me until I agreed to go through with the pregnancy. The argument that finally convinced me, ironically, was that the life experience of having children would better my chances of getting the more mature roles I'd been craving my whole life.*

What a steaming pile of manure that turned out to be.

—from Twinkie and Me:
The Real-Life Confessions of Lilly Lorraine

Chapter Two

For the cost of a twelve-pack of beer, I got Burly and Unemployed from lot 1B to help me hook the Airstream to the hitch ball on my truck. It was a damn bargain. I'd spent the day running errands (quit my job at the Quik 'n Go, printed out a route to Colorado Springs from the library computer, bought a twelve-pack of beer to lure the unsuspecting Burly in to help me) and was just too wiped to do it myself. As I watched Burly and Unemployed retreat back to 1B with the box of Coors tucked under one tremendous arm, I considered walking to the store on the corner and getting another twelve-pack.

After all, *someone* was going to have to unhook my water and electric tomorrow.

I crawled inside the Airstream, threw myself down on the foldout bed, and checked the clock. It was five forty, which gave me twenty minutes before the angel would be knocking down my door with pancake fixin's. I closed my eyes, wondering what the hell I'd been thinking when I'd told her where I lived. Maybe I could call in the twelve-pack payoff and get Burly and Unemployed to unhook everything now, and just drive off. Unfortunately, as I was pondering this very idea, there was a knock at the door. I glanced at the clock again.

The angel was fifteen minutes early.

"Who is it?" I yelled, expecting to hear Jess's bubbly tones rattling happily about how the early bird gets the worm, or something similarly upbeat. Instead, a male voice tentatively called out, "EJ?"

I shot up, my heart exploding in my chest in response to the sudden rush of adrenaline, causing everything inside me to hurt.

It couldn't be. It was impossible. But the voice jarred me to my core, and my body hummed with a deadly cocktail of dread, panic, and hope.

"Luke?" I whispered the name, trying to prepare myself for the possibility that it was his fist banging on my door, his presence causing my flimsy blinds to quiver. I tucked two fingers between the slats and peered out. His back was to me, but the hair was blond, short, and jagged, and there was a small hole in the shoulder of his worn black T-shirt. I released a breath.

Digs.

My heart shrunk back down to its regular size, but my insides throbbed with residual ache on every beat. I walked slowly to the door and pulled it open.

Digs was tall and lanky like Luke, but he'd gotten a

bigger share of their mother's Scandinavian genes. His bright blue eyes locked on me, and I wasn't sure if he was going to kick my ass or yank me into a big hug, so I just braced my hands against the tiny doorway and awaited his verdict.

Finally, one edge of his lips curled up slightly, and I knew I was safe. For the moment, anyway.

"Hey, there, kid." He took one last drag on his cigarette, tossed it to the ground, and stamped it out with the heel of his workboot. "What, aren't you happy to see me?"

"I think I will be, when I get over the shock." I shook my head, trying to get a grip on the moment. Of all the times I'd imagined someone from my past hunting me down, I'd somehow never thought it would be Digs. "It's been a while, huh?"

"Since you skipped town in the middle of the night?" he said, his eyes darkening a bit. "Yeah. Six Christmases. No card."

"Are you mad?" I asked quickly, biting the inside of my cheek in response to my sudden awareness of how much I had riding on his answer.

"Hell, yeah, I'm mad." He held one hand out to me, palm up. "Now come down out of there and let me beat the crap out of you."

I kept my eyes on my feet as I took his hand and stepped down to the ground in front of him. He looked at me for a while, as if inspecting me for damage, then pulled me into his arms, hugging me tight. I had to work hard not to break down into a blubbery mess all over him. His left arm went around my waist and his right hand cupped the back of my head, and he squeezed me the way an older brother would, as though curling invisible blankets of protection over me until it felt like only my eyes and nose were showing through. After a long moment, he gave me a gentle smack to the back of my head and released me. I stepped back, tucking my hands into my back jeans pockets so he couldn't see them shaking.

"So. Wow." I bit the inside edge of my bottom lip as hard as I could without drawing blood. The shaking muted a bit, and I was able to smile. "So, um, how's"—*Don't say Luke. Not Luke. Don't talk about Luke*—"your dad?"

"Funny you should ask." Digs pulled a pack of smokes out of his back pocket and tapped one out. "He's the reason I'm here."

My face must have gone white, because Digs paused with the smokes and gave my shoulder a reassuring pat.

"Relax, he's fine. Actually, he's great. But, damn . . ." He chuckled and shook his head. "I've got a hell of a story for you." He held the pack out to me. "You still quit?"

I nodded. "Seven years. So, what's up with Danny?"

Digs lit his smoke and took a drag before meeting my eye to answer. "He's getting married."

A joyful whoop escaped me. Luke and Digs's mother had died when they were very young, and for the last twenty-five years, Danny Greene had lived the sad, quiet life of a widowed father. In all the summers I'd spent with Danny and his boys while growing up, I'd never seen him so much as date. His whole world revolved around his boys, and me whenever I was around. Who in the world could have broken through—?

And that's when my train of thought came to a screeching halt. My eyes went wide and I shook my head. "No."

The edge of Digs's mouth twitched, and his eyes lit with an even mix of irony and amusement. "Yes."

My mind reeled, looking for something solid to grab on to. "What about Glenn?"

"Hell, EJ. They split up years ago, a few months after you disappeared off the face. You didn't think she'd make it to a wooden anniversary, did you?" Digs chuckled on a smoky exhale. "Bright side: they say the eighth time's a charm."

My stomach turned. This couldn't be. It just couldn't be. As bizarre as it would have been to have seen Luke pounding on the door of my Airstream, this news was a thousand times crazier. I blinked and leaned against the cold metal of the motor home. Digs held up his pack again.

"You sure you don't want one?" he said gamely.

"Ugh!" I held my hand out, irritation running through me because, at that moment, I really did want one. "Seven years, Digs. Back off. Jesus!"

He shrugged, tucked the pack into his pocket, then pivoted and leaned against the trailer next to me, both of us staring out into the simmering metal jungle of a New Jersey RV park. I tried to picture a world in which this could possibly be happening, but it would require flying pigs. Hell freezing over. The four horsemen tramping into town to catch a steak dinner before the planet exploded in a fiery maelstrom.

"Hey, there!"

I glanced up and saw the angel walking toward us, her arms full with paper grocery bags. In the summer sun, her blonde hair actually gave off a halo effect. It was disconcerting.

"You made a friend?" Digs asked, not bothering to mask the surprise in his voice.

I ignored him, just pushed myself off the side of the trailer and took three shaky steps to meet Jess.

"Um, hey," I said. "Look, I'm sorry. I think I might have to cancel tonight."

Jess's smile didn't waver. "Why? What's up?" She glanced past me and grinned at Digs. "Hi, I'm Jess."

"Oh, this is an old friend of mine, David Greene."

Digs ambled up behind me, and despite the fact that I couldn't see him, I could feel him wink at her, and I sighed. Digs and blondes were a lethal combination.

"You can call me Digs."

"Nice to meet you."

Digs shot me a look; I gave a brief shake of my head. Jess hefted the groceries in her arms. "I hope you like blueberry pancakes, Digs, because I brought enough to feed an army."

I put my hand on her arm. "Look, Jess, I'm sorry, but I just got some bad news and I'm not sure I'm up to having company tonight, so . . ."

Jess's smile flipped into an expression of deep compassion. "Oh, no. I'm so sorry. What happened?"

Digs snorted. "Her mother is getting married."

I resisted an urge to elbow Digs in the ribs as Jess gasped and her grin returned. "Oh! But that's wonderful news! I'll make the pancakes, we'll celebrate!" She turned her grin on Digs. "So, Digs, how long have you known EJ?"

"Oh, let's see." He glanced upward. "Somewhere around twenty-five years."

Jess's eyes widened. "That's wonderful! I've been trying to get to know her, but she's kind of dodgy when it comes to questions. Maybe you can fill me in." She shifted the bags in her arms again, and Digs reached out to relieve her of a bag.

"Oh, thank you . . ."

I grabbed the bag from him and held it out for Jess. "Yes, thank you, Digs, but she can't stay."

"Oh, sure I can!" Jess said. "We're celebrating your good news!"

"And I happen to love blueberry pancakes," Digs said, taking the bag from me and starting back toward the trailer. "So, Jess, how long have you known EJ?"

Jess followed along behind him, and I reluctantly brought up the rear.

"We met last night. I'm her angel."

Digs glanced over his shoulder at me. I hadn't seen him this happy since the time he'd found two cases of grape soda at the dump when we were kids. "You're her angel?"

"It's not—," I started, but Jess talked over me.

"The Universe sent me to help her," she said, as though this were an even remotely sane thing to say.

"No, it didn't," I said. "Because I'm fine."

"Oh, sure you are," Digs said, then turned his attention to Jess. "And you make pancakes?"

Jess's head bobbed up and down. "The best you've ever tasted."

"Wow." Digs pulled open the trailer door. "A pancake-making angel. Now this I gotta see."

I don't drink often, so after searching the entire kitchen, all I was able to come up with was a dusty fifth of Jack Daniel's they'd given to all the employees at the liquor store in New Mexico where I was working last Christmas. I nabbed two plastic cups before Jess took over the kitchen area and sent Digs and me to the dinette table. I slammed down one shot and poured a second before Digs had even touched his.

"So," Jess said as she ducked her head into all my cupboards and drawers, looking for utensils, "why isn't it good news that your mother is getting married?"

"It's complicated." I slammed down the second shot and reached for the bottle, but Digs was faster, and he moved it just out of my reach.

"As the first object in your puke zone, I get administrative rights," he grumbled, then spoke louder in Jess's direction. "It's Lilly's eighth wedding, and my dad is the victim."

Jess's lips twitched as she shot a look at Digs. "You mean the . . . the groom?"

"Yeah," Digs said, cutting me a quick look. "That's exactly what I mean."

"So, how do you all know each other?"

"Heh heh," I said. "That's a complicated story."

"My father and her mother were best friends in middle school," Digs said.

"Oh!" Jess said, clapping her hands. "Childhood sweethearts!"

"Just friends," I said. "Even by the tender age of ten, my mother knew better than to fall for anyone who wasn't 'in the business.' She always said that sex without career advancement was a waste of a clean set of sheets."

Digs shot me a look.

"What?" I said. "You were there that Thanksgiving."

"Anyway," Digs went on, focusing on Jess, "my dad's family moved up to Oregon, and Lilly stayed in LA, but they remained close. EJ used to spend summers with us when her mom was working."

"Or when she was drinking, or when she was chasing a man, or when being a mother cut into her spa time too much." Both Digs and Jess went quiet, and I raised an eyebrow at Digs. "Hey, if you hadn't taken the booze, I'd be drinking instead of talking. Your fault."

"Well," Jess said, her expression bright and cheerful, "it has a happy ending, anyway. After all these years, they've found each other again and are getting married! How romantic!"

"Just warms the cockles." I turned my focus on Digs. "So, what's up? You came all the way out here. It has to be more than just spreading the good news."

"Smart girl." He looked at me, then shrugged. "Might as well tell you now. Lilly says she won't marry Dad unless you're at the wedding."

I sat up straighter. *Wow. That was easy.*

"Done." I nudged my cup toward him to fill. "I've just saved your dad from a horrible fate. I'm a hero. Pour."

Digs nudged the bottle even farther away. "Dad paid a private detective four thousand dollars to track you down, then he spent a week dogging me until I agreed to come out here and talk to you in person. I'm flipping a property out in Hillsdale that's worth almost two million, and I've already missed two days on the site. Pack up, kid. You're going."

"Well, of course she's going."

I looked up, surprised. I'd almost forgotten Jess was still there. She stood, an unbroken egg hovering in her hand over a bowl, and gave me a look that was an equal mix of kindness and blind determination. I would learn later to take that look seriously, but at that moment, I just scoffed.

"No, I'm not." Even I could hear the quiver in my voice, so I cleared my throat and repeated firmly, "No. I'm not."

Digs sighed, grabbed the bottle, and poured me two fingers.

"The wedding is on Friday, June twenty-ninth, at the county courthouse—"

I held up my hand. "Wait, wait, *what*? The county courthouse? You want me to believe that my mother is going to have a quiet little ceremony at the county courthouse?"

Digs gave me a blank look, cleared his throat, and continued. "You will be in Fletcher no later than ten in the morning on the day. There will be a private party afterward. You can leave the next morning if you want, but you will be there. Considering that for six years you haven't found it within yourself to send so much as a fucking postcard to let us know you're alive, this is the least you can do, okay?"

I cringed and lowered my eyes. Digs was about as laid-back as anyone I've ever met; when he's pissed off, you know you've screwed up but good. And I had always known that I'd screwed up—I could just never figure out a way to fix it, so I never tried. It wasn't a good excuse, but it was all I had.

"I had my reasons," I said finally. I could hear the sound of the egg cracking as Jess regained animation.

"That's your business," Digs said softly. "And if this was the first two years, I would have come out here to tell you not to come back. But Luke's over it now, and it's time for you to come home."

My brain latched onto "Luke's over it," and a thousand stupid questions jockeyed for position. Was he over it like he'd forgiven me, or over it like he'd just moved on and still hated me? Was he with someone else now? Was he *married*? Good God, did he have *kids*? If I did go to this ridiculous wedding, would he talk to me, or would he pretend I didn't exist, the way I'd done to him for the last six years? Or, worse, would he be polite to me, as if none of it mattered anymore? Oh, God. Did it not matter anymore?

My heart seized. I'd hit the far edges of my ability to think about Luke. Panic slithered cold streaks over my arms, and I downed the two fingers.

"I can't go," I said, my voice roughened by the liquor. "I'm sorry. Tell Danny I'm sorry, and that I love him, and that I'll send a card—"

"He doesn't want a goddamn card," Digs said. "You think you can't face Luke? Fine. You don't want to see your mom? Fine. But Dad wants you out there and you're going, if I have to wrap you in a fucking sack and drag you there myself."

The panic was quickly outpaced by an anger so familiar that I embraced it like an old friend. "See? This is what she does. She won't marry him unless I'm there, and suddenly, I don't have any choices anymore. She doesn't even ask me if I can make it, she just assumes—"

A bright voice broke in from the kitchen. "Well, how *could* she ask you?"

I looked up to see Jess staring down at me. For the second time that night, I had managed to be surprised by her presence.

"You don't know anything about this, Jess," I said, not bothering to keep the sharp edge out of my voice.

"I know that you haven't spoken to your mother in years," she said, her tone light and even. "I know that these people went to a lot of trouble to find you, and I guess that was quite a chore considering that your home is on wheels. I can tell that Digs here loves you very much, and it sounds like there are some other people who do as well." She opened up a carton of plain yogurt and dumped a dollop into the mixing bowl. "It's time to go home, EJ."

I turned suspicious eyes on Digs. "Did you put her up to this? Is she some kind of mole you sent to coerce me?"

Digs shook his head. "I don't have that kind of initiative."

"Honestly, EJ," Jess went on, "do you really think it's a coincidence that the Universe sent me at the exact same time She sent Digs?" She held the bowl to her stomach and turned to face me, shaking her head as she mixed. "No matter how many times I see it, it still amazes me how hard some people will work not to see the obvious."

"The angel makes a good point," Digs said.

Jess poured some batter onto the griddle. It sizzled heartily and filled the small area with a heady, fruity scent that I found both comforting and oddly anxiety-producing. I put my forehead down on the cool Formica dinette table and groaned.

Digs patted me on the back.

"Huh," he said. "I think we broke her."

When one grows up under the bright lights of a Hollywood soundstage, it's hard to imagine childhood any other way. Don't all children memorize scripts every night? Don't all children have fans chasing them down at shopping centers? Don't all children spend more time with adults than with kids their own age?

A mother without a normal childhood cannot be expected to understand her child. It's simply asking too much.

—from *Twinkie and Me:*
The Real-Life Confessions of Lilly Lorraine

Chapter Three

The pancakes were that special buttery kind of delicious, the kind where even when they're in your mouth, you still can't believe how good they are. I ate slowly, because even an angel's pancakes are questionable after three shots of whiskey. The conversation relaxed, and Digs filled me in on the last six years, during which he'd dated inconsequentially and gone into business with Luke flipping houses for fun and profit. I filled him in on my life—in which the only interesting thing that had happened was being adopted by an angel. Jess asked us question after question about our childhood, and we kept her entertained with stories until Digs glanced at his watch.

"It's almost ten," he said. "My plane leaves at midnight." He gave me a quick nudge with his elbow. "I gotta run."

"You know what?" Jess pushed herself up from the dinette and grabbed the plastic bag of garbage from under the sink. "I'm gonna take this out for you."

"You don't have to—," I said, sliding out from my seat, but she *pshaw*ed me and was out the door. I turned to Digs.

"Well," I said.

"Yeah," he said.

"Thanks for coming. It was good to see you." I breathed in deep and chewed the inner edge of my lips, blinking hard. Stupid whiskey.

He chucked me under the chin. "So you're gonna be there, right?"

The very thought of attending yet another one of my mother's weddings made my heart seize up in impotent fury and terror. The fact that wonderful, sweet, kind, loving, innocent Danny was the victim only intensified the sensation that the world was whirlpooling into disaster. I couldn't even think about seeing Luke again without my stomach turning cartwheels in my gut. There was no way in hell I was going to that wedding. I wouldn't survive the first fifteen minutes. But I knew Digs wouldn't leave until I told him what he wanted to hear.

"Yeah," I said. "Of course. I'll totally be there. I mean, it's Danny, right? How can I not be there for Danny's wedding?"

"Right," Digs said, watching me. "June twenty-ninth. That gives you almost two weeks."

"Plenty of time," I said. "I'll just finish up my business here, and I'll be right on my way."

He raised his eyebrows. "So you'll be there early?"

"Sure," I said. "Or on time. Whatever."

"But you'll be there."

I nodded emphatically, hoping he'd leave before I burst into tears right there. He pulled me into a hug and kissed the top of my head, and it wasn't until that moment that I fully felt how much I had missed him. "It was good to see you again, kid," he said.

He released me, gave a short wave, and headed out the door. I stared at the door for a long while, hating that I'd just lied through my teeth to Digs. But even worse would be going to that wedding, and I had no intention of putting myself through that.

Besides, I thought as I ran my fingers over my eyes, *it's not like I'm going to have to face Digs again, anyway.*

The door opened and Jess stepped inside, her smile fading as she caught the look on my face.

"EJ?" she asked, putting her hand on my elbow. "Are you okay?"

"I'm drunk, I think." I grabbed a tissue off the counter and blew my nose.

"Yeah, I think maybe," she said, guiding me toward my bed in the front of the trailer.

"I had no choice," I muttered, closing my eyes as she pulled the sheet up to my neck.

"I know," she said softly.

Then all went black, and the next thing I remember is opening my eyes to the bright light of day flickering over my face as the curtains by my bed shimmied back and forth. At first, I thought it was just the world's worst hangover, because the reality—that my Airstream was moving down an unknown highway at high speed—was too much for my feeble brain to wrap around at that moment.

I sat up and put my feet on the rumbling floor and tried to think of a possibility, any possibility, other than the obvious one, which was that Digs had kidnapped me. He'd known I was lying about going to Fletcher, and he'd kidnapped me, the bastard. He'd said he would drag me if he had to, and he did.

"Bastard," I muttered. I stood up, but between the hangover and the movement, it took me a while to properly search the Airstream. My cell phone was not in it. I must have left it in the cab of the pickup the night before. I was truly helpless, although he would have to stop for gas eventually, and when he did I'd get my keys back, kick him to the side of the road, and keep heading west.

To Colorado Springs.

I crawled back onto my bed and pulled open the curtains on the front window, which looked right into the back of my truck, and almost fell off the bed.

It wasn't Digs who had kidnapped me, not unless he'd grown his hair out about five inches and pulled it into two telltale ponytails.

I'd been kidnapped by the angel.

I swished the curtains shut and thumped back down on the bed in disbelief.

"You've gotta be kidding me," I muttered to myself, putting my hands over my eyes as I waited for the trailer to stop moving.

The Airstream pulled to a stop about an hour later, at a gas station off I-80, somewhere in the middle of Pennsylvania. Jess was at the door ready to greet me when I burst out of the trailer.

"What the hell do you think you're doing?" I sputtered. "This is kidnapping, you know. And, and, and . . . *theft*. And carjacking. And lots of bad, bad things. You're lucky I don't press charges. I might. I could. I could send you to jail. Are you *crazy*?"

A trucker passing by snorted into his coffee cup. I pushed up my sleeves, about to launch into another tirade, when Jess put one hand calmly on my shoulder.

"The keys are in the ignition," she said, "but the tank is still filling up. I put it on my credit card, and you're free to drive off wherever you want to go when it's done. You were going to go where? Colorado Springs? Well, you'd be headed this way anyway, right?"

I opened my mouth, but only managed to release an impotent squeak.

"This will be what it will be," she said. "If you send me to jail, then that just means there will be something for me to do there, someone I need to help. If you leave without me and go on to Colorado Springs, then maybe I'll meet the person I'm supposed to help in that little diner next door. But"—she crossed her arms and watched me, smiling—"for the last couple of hours, you thought you were going back to Fletcher, right? How did that make you feel?"

"It made me feel like I was being kidnapped." I

pointed my index finger at her. "You? Are insane. How does that make you feel?"

She squinted in the bright daylight. "You're at a crossroads here, EJ. You have the opportunity to make a choice. I'm going to get some coffee and donuts inside, and if you're not here when I get back, I'll understand. If the police come to arrest me, I'll understand that, too. Still, I'm so glad we met. I don't think I'll forget you soon. You're very . . ." She stared at me for a long time, as though searching for the right adjective, and I waited for something vague and uncondemning. *Interesting. Unusual. Special.*

". . . sad," she said finally.

I blinked, not sure how to respond. *Sad?* That was an insult, right? She wrapped her arms around me and gave me a hug, then released me and nodded to indicate the duffel bag and backpack sitting next to the truck.

"Don't run over my stuff," she said on a wink, then turned and headed toward the mini-mart.

"Oh, my God," I muttered, racing to the side of the truck to stop the pump and hang up the nozzle. I wasn't going to call the cops, I decided, but damned if I was going to let some crazy woman who fancied herself as one of God's winged army drag me all the way to Oregon. I hopped into the driver's seat and put my fingers to the keys in the ignition, then paused and cursed. I let my forehead drop against the steering wheel.

I couldn't leave her. She was totally certifiable, but mostly harmless, and completely helpless. There was no way I could abandon this woman at a gas station. She needed a hospital, or family, or something. At the very least, I had to bring her back to her car at Busey's. I ground my teeth, reminding myself that she'd kidnapped me and thus had given up her rights to my assistance, but it was no good. Whether I liked it or not, she was mine until I could pawn her off on someone else. I closed my eyes, took a few deep breaths, then pulled the keys out of the ignition and tucked them in my pocket.

"Hey, you're still here," she said, grinning as she held up a green and white donut bag. "I'm so glad. They have Krispy Kremes here, can you believe our luck?"

I tossed her duffel bag into the Airstream and locked it, then handed her her backpack.

"What the hell were you thinking?" I asked her. "If I wasn't such a nice person, you'd be going to jail right now, you know that?"

"Well, you're supposed to go to Fletcher, and you weren't going to go, so I did what I had to do. I knew you'd be mad, but you have to understand. This is what I was sent to do."

"To kidnap me? To inject yourself into my life, which is none of your business, by the way, and—" I paused and straightened. "How did you know I wasn't going to go? I said last night I was going. I told Digs that I'd be there."

"Really?" She crinkled her nose. "Hmmm. He told me you weren't going."

"But I told him I was."

"Well. I guess he didn't believe you."

"*Whatever*," I said. "That doesn't give you the right to—"

"I don't have the right. I have the responsibility. The Universe directed me."

"Oh, hell," I said. "Not this crap again."

"I came by this morning to check on you," she said, "and this big guy from the lot across the way comes out of nowhere and asks me if we need help disconnecting the water, electric, and sewer."

"Oh, hell," I said. "He just wanted more beer."

"Then I came in to check on you, but you were passed out. And your keys were right on the counter next to a map with directions out west."

"To Colorado Springs," I growled.

Jess threw her hands up in the air. "Look, maybe the Universe has to hit you over the head with a brick before you hear Her talking, but I don't need that."

I rubbed my hand over my face, trying to remember that I was dealing with a woman who'd anthropomorphized the Universe and made it a girl. She thought she was an angel. I could not expect her to be rational. I set my voice to calm, and spoke in strong, even tones.

"Okay. Look. Here's how it's gonna work. I will bring you wherever you need to go. Either back to Busey's and your car or I can drop you off with family or friends or—and here's my vote—a mental health institution. Angel's choice."

"Really?" She beamed. "Anywhere I want to go?"

I sighed in relief. No arguments. Happy expression. She clearly had a place in mind. This was going to work out just fine. Everything was going to be fine.

"Yes," I said. "I will take you wherever you need to

go. Just tell me where, and who I'm dropping you off with."

She reached into her purse and withdrew a large white envelope, then handed it to me. I looked down at the elegant calligraphy, stunned. Leave it to Lilly Lorraine to have official invitations printed up even for a small courthouse wedding. I looked up at Jess, who was grinning so wide I had sympathetic cheek pains.

"Digs invited me to be his date," she chirped.

I waved the invitation in the air. "When did he give you this?"

"When I took out the trash, and he was leaving. We talked a little bit." She giggled and bounced on her heels. "I'm so excited. I'm going to Twinkie's wedding!"

She tossed the backpack over her shoulder and hopped into the passenger side of the truck. I walked around to the driver's side and got in.

"That was a dirty trick." I turned the key in the ignition.

"You said anywhere."

"I *meant*—"

"But you *said*—"

"*Fine!*" I clenched my fingers around the steering wheel. "Fine. I will take you with me to Colorado Springs—"

Her eyebrows knit. "But the wedding's in Oregon."

"—and I'll put you on a plane to Portland from there."

"Oh, so we're flying from—?"

"No. *You* will be flying. *I'll* be staying in Colorado Springs, investigating local dive bars where I can drink away all memory of this entire episode."

"But—"

I held up my hand. "Some ground rules. One, no talk of the wedding." She opened her mouth. I held my hand up higher. "Ah-ah-ah. No. Talk. No trying to convince me to go. No making me feel bad about lying to Digs. None of that. Do we have a deal, or am I leaving you here?"

Jess's eyes narrowed in thought for a moment. "I don't know. What are the other ground rules?"

"What?"

"Well, ground rule one was no talking about the wedding, which related directly to everything you said after that, so I assume there's a two. What's the second ground rule?"

I white-knuckled the steering wheel. "No counting my ground rules."

She smiled and held out her hand, and we shook on it. I started the truck, figuring that if the Universe told Jess to kill me in my sleep, it'd be my own damn fault anyway.

In the middle of the night, in an RV park on the western edge of Ohio, I found myself staring up at the ceiling of my Airstream, unable to sleep. Jess was snoring lightly from the twin bunk at the back of the trailer, but after six years of RV park living, I was under no illusions about what I was capable of sleeping through. The snore of a deluded angel was not powerful enough to keep me up on its own.

I threw my legs over the side of my bed and stuffed my feet into my sneakers, then quietly opened the door and slipped outside. I took a moment to stare up at the clear, black sky, peppered with stars, and breathe in the smoky fragrance of a distant campfire in the warm summer air. It had been an RV park much like this one that had gotten me hooked on the things in the first place. Of course, most of the parks I'd lived in during recent years had been nothing like this. Places like this were too far out in the middle of nowhere, and it was almost impossible to get any kind of viable employment within a reasonable distance, except during the occasional lucky summer when the park itself needed extra help. I glanced back at the private little nook where I'd parked the Airstream under the protective bulk of a giant willow tree, far enough away from any neighbors to provide a decent sense of privacy. I liked this park.

Maybe, someday, I'd come back.

In the distance, from the direction of the rec center, I could hear music playing, the sounds of people laughing, the erratic *conk-plink*s of two people playing Ping-Pong at the outdoor table. This was a family place, where moms and dads took their kids for long weekends and let them stay up late drinking sodas and feeding quarters into the jukebox. When I was twelve, Danny had taken Digs and Luke and me to a place like this for the summer while my mother did a TV movie-of-the-week for NBC and snared husband number three, a talent agent who, as it turned out, had no talent for agenting. But that's another story. Anyway, Luke and I had piled our jukebox quarters together and gotten a pack of menthol cigarettes out of a vending machine, then walked down to the lake and tried to smoke them, to horrendous but predictable results. Eventually we traded the remaining fifteen cigarettes to Digs in exchange for his silence and a pack of Bubblicious bubble gum.

I turned and walked back to my truck. I pulled open the passenger-side door and reached underneath the seat to withdraw the wooden stationery box I'd bought at a paper crafts fair not long after I left Fletcher. It was squat and wide, allowing it to double as a writing surface for people like me who had no room in their lives for a real desk. The sides were accented with dried daisies that had been glued on and then shellacked within an inch of their lives. Nested inside was a shallow, flat drawer that held my pens, stationery paper, and envelopes. I crawled into the seat and set it on my lap, then flipped the top off and pulled out a sheet and a pen. I set the top back on, situated the box on my lap, flicked on the cab light, and started to write.

Dear Luke,

I stared up at the dim cab light, thinking carefully about what I wanted to write next. Finally hitting on just the right thing, I smiled and put pen to paper.

A duck walks into a bar and orders a beer.

"We don't serve ducks," the bartender says.

"Yes, but I'm special," the duck says. "I can sing." And the duck belts out a perfect aria.

"Oh, he's cute," the blonde sitting at the next stool says. "Give him the beer."

"No," the bartender says. "We don't serve singing ducks." And he throws the duck out.

The next day, the duck comes back and orders a beer.

"Forget it," the bartender says. "We don't serve ducks."

"Yes, but I'm special," the duck says. "I can dance." And the duck waddles over to the blonde and dances with her, twirling her in her seat with his wing, then goes back to his spot at the bar when the song ends.

"Oh, how sweet!" the blonde says, laughing. "Come on, give him a beer."

"We don't serve dancing ducks, either," the bartender says, and throws the duck out.

The next day, the duck comes back and orders a beer. "I told you," the bartender says, "we don't serve ducks."

"But I'm special," the duck says. "I can—"

The bartender picks him up and throws him out.

"Fucking duck," he mutters as he comes back to the bar.

The blonde gasps. "Who told you?"

I read it over again and laughed to myself. Luke had always had a soft spot for bad duck jokes.

I signed my name at the bottom, folded up the

paper, and tucked it inside an envelope. I wrote *Luke Greene* on the outside, then lifted up the panel and set the envelope inside, with some fifty of its unsent brothers. I tucked the box back under the seat, flicked off the cab light, and went back into the Airstream, where I continued to toss and turn until the sun rose.

I have been married seven times, and am so glad to be on my last one! Glenn is everything I've ever wanted or needed in a friend and companion. He is my light and my hope, my compass, my best friend. I am his world, and he is mine, and we need nothing else besides each other. It is such a blessing to be so fulfilled by one person that, even if everyone else on the planet were to disappear, you wouldn't really mourn them.

—Lilly Lorraine, quoted in "The Real Lives of Forgotten Child Stars," by Rebecca Wade, *Women's Day*, 12 March 1997

Chapter Four

I don't remember when Luke and I started communicating through jokes, but then I don't remember a lot of specific moments between us. I remember our first kiss—age thirteen, broad daylight, in the middle of Danny's pool, after which Luke dunked me under and we never spoke of it again—but most of the other stuff happened so naturally that it just seemed like it had always been that way. I can't say when I fell in love with Luke because I can't remember ever not being in love with Luke. It's the same with the jokes. They started during one of the many summers I spent there, sometime between that first kiss/dunk and when I went away to college out east. I remember being upset about something—a boy, a fight with a friend, I don't know—and Luke told me a joke that involved a penguin and a bowtie, and ever since, whenever we had anything even remotely serious to discuss, we told jokes. It was just what we did.

It was actually a joke that finally got us together. After college, I'd moved to an apartment in Fletcher just to be near Luke. Never did get up the nerve to tell him I was crazy in love with him, though. I was too scared he'd never see me as anything other than an old family friend. Or worse, a sister, the kiss in the pool notwithstanding. Well, about eight months of that torture was all I had in me to take, so when a friend asked me to move to New York City with her, I agreed. When I told Luke, he hugged me and wished me well and didn't seem too sad to see me go. I cried for two days. Then, finally, the night before I was going to leave, the levee broke.

"So, two guys walk into a bar," Luke had said as he taped up the last box of kitchen stuff. It was late and we'd been packing all day, and I was giddy from the tension of all the things I'd been unable to say, so I started giggling immediately.

"I'm not done yet," Luke said, crawling over to sit next to me, our backs against the wall as we stared out at my empty apartment. He looked at me, smiling—Luke was never not smiling—and raised an eyebrow in mock irritation. "Can I continue?"

"Yeah," I said quietly, my heart pounding as I stared up at him, wondering how I was ever going to survive life without that smile. "Go ahead."

"Thank you. So, the first guy says, 'Drinks are on

me! I just asked the woman I love to marry me!' And everyone cheers and claps him on the back."

And there, Luke stopped talking, his eyes locking on mine, making my breath rush out as my cheeks flamed hard.

"And the second guy?" I prodded quietly.

His eyes trailed down to my lips. "Hmmm?"

"The second guy. In the bar. What did he say?"

"Oh, yeah." Luke let out a small chuckle, then his smile faded. "He said, 'Good for you. The woman I love is moving across the country and I'm too much of a fucking coward to ask her not to go.'"

My heart pounded painfully in my chest as I tried not to read this the wrong way, searching for the punch line that would make me feel like an idiot for even thinking Luke was trying to tell me something. Finally, I cleared my throat and said what I was thinking.

"That's not funny."

He reached up, took a strand of my hair in his fingers, and shook his head.

"No," he said. "It's really not."

That night, we had sex for the first time, on the floor of my apartment, and the next day, I called my friend to back out of New York. Later that week, we moved all my stuff into his apartment. And the rest, as they say, was history.

Until I blew everything up in a life implosion so powerful that even six years later, the sharp edges of my personal impact crater were visible to everyone around me.

My point is, if you were Jess, you'd be asking, right? *What the hell happened, EJ? Why are you a misanthropic wreck? Why do you choose to live alone in a big tin can rather than near the people who love you?*

Of course you'd ask. Any sane person would be too overwhelmed with curiosity not to ask.

Jess didn't ask a thing. Three days we'd been on the road, and the endless barrage of questions I'd been expecting about Digs and Luke and Danny and my mother never came. For three days, I stared at endless lengths of highway pavement, forming my evasion tactics for when she finally did come at me, curiosity swinging, but she never engaged in anything more than idle chitchat. Waiting for the shoe to drop wore me down and finally, in a diner somewhere between Kansas City and the fifth ring of hell, I broke.

"Okay," I said. "Fine. You win. Ask me anything."

"Mmm?" she said, sipping her coffee.

"No games. I'm too cranky, and too tired. We're gonna be in Colorado Springs in another day or so, and then you'll be going off to meet my mother, which is like sending a lamb to the slaughter, by the way. This is your last chance to be duly informed. I'm an open book; ask me anything."

"I don't have any questions." She paused. "Well, that's not entirely true. I have questions, but I don't like to ask direct questions unless I have to. That's not how I work." She poked at her pancakes, her expression dubious. "These are from a mix. What self-respecting diner owner charges five ninety-five for pancakes from a box?"

"One with a firm grasp of basic capitalism," I said. "So, how do you work?"

"Mmm?" She dumped the fork and the pancake and smiled at me. "Oh, yeah. Well, I find that when I ask direct questions, people tend to directly lie, so mostly, I observe. I watch you and get a feel for what you're about, and then when the opportunity comes where I can help, I do what I can. Like when I kidnapped you."

"Ah. I see. Well, it all makes sense now, because that was very helpful."

"But to be honest," she went on, "I usually don't have to do much. In the end, it's entirely up to the person I'm assigned to. If she doesn't want to help herself, there's not much I can do for her."

"Well," I said, "*that* was thinly veiled."

She smiled. "Subtlety's not one of my gifts."

"So . . ." I nudged sausage around on my plate casually. "What have you observed about me?"

She sighed and sat back, the red vinyl of the diner booth making unflattering sounds for which she was oddly unapologetic. "Well, you have a lot of maps."

"So? What, are maps some kind of spiritual metaphor for being lost or something? What is that supposed to mean?"

"I think it means that you live on the road and you need to know where you're going."

I raised an eyebrow. "Insightful."

"Insight *is* one of my gifts."

I nibbled on a sausage. She took a bite of her pancake. The tinny diner sound system played a Muzak version of Billy Idol's "Rebel Yell," which was wrong on a lot of levels.

I threw down my fork.

"That's it? Three days, and all you've noticed is that I have a lot of maps?"

"No, that's not all. Did you want everything?"

I played with my coffee mug. Did I really want to hear everything?

No.

"Yes."

"Okay." She smiled and leaned forward, pushing her plate away with one elbow. "You don't have a computer, and you only have one notebook, which creaks when you open it, so I don't think you're really writing a book. Which means that for some reason you wanted me to think you were, which means you care what people think."

"Wait a minute. I could have a great memory. I could be one of those photographic people. I could be writing a book from memory. You don't know."

"You didn't abandon me at that gas station in Pennsylvania," she went on, as though I hadn't spoken, "which shows me you care about other people, period, despite what you'd like people to believe. You exist on as little as possible, and when you sleep, you breathe very shallowly. Either you don't think you deserve the space and air you need, or you're waiting to disappear into nothing, to become totally invisible." She watched me for a minute, tapping her fingernails on the linoleum surface of the table. "I haven't decided which."

I huffed. "Wow, you are so far off—"

She held up her hand. "I'm not done. You don't have any books, television, or newspapers. That speaks to invisible; you're retreating from the world. But at the same time, you don't shy away from the people who seek you out. The other night, with me and Digs, you were fully engaged, fully there." She gave a curt, decisive nod. "I'm going with unworthy. And, yes, I do wonder why. But I'm not going to ask, because even if I do ask, you won't tell me the truth, which may be an unfair assumption, but based on my experience—"

"I killed a man," I said quickly.

She froze. "Really?"

"Yep," I said. "With a salad fork. So you see why I can't go back to Fletcher now."

Her shoulders relaxed. "Yeah. I can see how that would be a problem for you."

"Well, yeah. I'm a killer. I kill people all the time, usually with some sort of kitchen utensil, although in a pinch, a tire iron will do. You might wanna sleep with one eye open."

She kept a straight face. "Well, I'm sorry I misjudged you by assuming you'd make something up."

I lifted my coffee mug in salute. "You'll want to be careful about that in the future. I'm not the kind of girl you want to tick off. Especially not when there are spatulas around."

"Thanks for the heads-up."

We shared a smile and, despite all reason, I found myself warming up to Jess. A little.

The waitress slid the check onto our table and Jess grabbed for it. I would have argued, but outside of that first tank of gas, I'd picked everything up so far. Jess swiveled as though she was about to get up, then turned to face me.

"I have something," she said. "Digs gave it to me, and told me to give it to you when you sobered up, but I didn't feel like the time was right. I think now, maybe, the time is right."

"What is it?"

She reached into her coat pocket and pulled out a long, sealed letter envelope. On the front, in Luke's chicken-scratch hand, was simply *Eejie*. Even if I hadn't recognized Luke's handwriting, I would have known it was him. He was the only person to ever call me Eejie.

"I'm gonna go pay this," Jess said, sliding the check under her hand as she rose from the table. I think I mumbled something at her, but mostly, I just stared at the letter in my hands, unable to figure out if it was a nice gesture or a dirty trick. Either way, I wasn't going to read it. I didn't need to. I knew what was inside. On the first line *Dear Eejie*, followed by some joke, probably one about a wedding, a sly way to encourage me to come and see my mother, to tell me in our own private shorthand that he was fine with my coming and that life was too short for me not to mend things with Mom, because that was the kind of guy Luke was. It didn't matter, though. He may have survived the big train wreck intact, which I was glad for, but I was still hunched over and hobbling, and in no shape for a big reunion. I traced my fingers over the space where he'd scribbled my name, then folded the envelope in half and tucked it in my back pocket before going up to meet Jess at the register.

"So," she said, shooting me a sideways glance as she handed the cashier a twenty, "what did it say?"

"Nothing," I said. "Just an inside joke."

She nodded, told the cashier to give the change to our waitress, and tucked her hand in the crook of my elbow, guiding me out of the diner.

"I think we need to have some fun," she said.

"This is your idea of fun?" I asked, staring down at the cardboard tray in my arms as Jess stepped in front of me, her head darting from side to side like a dousing stick looking for water. The sickly sweet smell of five bags full of sausage McGriddles wafted up from the tray, and I turned my head.

"It's harder to find them in the small towns," she said as she hurried down a side street toward a large park.

"You know, it's early, but I'm sure we can find a bar or something," I said, shuffling behind her, raising the box over my head and inhaling the fresh air.

"Alcohol is a depressant," she said, marching down the road. "Random acts of kindness are a natural mood elevator. Like exercise. And better than any of those damn pills they're putting everyone on lately."

"Okay," I said, thinking that maybe now was not the time to argue for the pills, although I had no doubt that at least one of us, if not both, could seriously benefit from a prescription or two.

The sidewalk ended, just like that, and we found ourselves walking on the dusty shoulder of a two-way road. To our right, across the street, was a park where harried mothers yelled at their children to stop kicking dirt in the faces of the other harried mothers' children, and to our left, an abandoned VFW hall that looked like it had seen far, far better days.

Jess clapped her hands together. "Perfect!"

My arms got tired and I was forced to lower the tray again as I followed her around the back of the abandoned VFW.

"Jess, this is how nice girls like us get killed," I said, but she ignored me, so I continued mumbling to myself over the crunch-crunch of our Keds on the gravel. "Oh, yes, God. Thanks so much for sending your angel to get me hacked to pieces while committing random acts of hello-Mr.-Serial-Killer—"

"Yay!" Jess hopped up on her toes and turned to me and snatched a bag off the tray, her eyes alight. "Watch! This is so much fun!"

I peered around the back of the building. Dumpsters. Of course, it had to be Dumpsters. The bottom half of the world's skinniest man poked out of one, and Jess ducked with agility as a crumpled beer can whizzed past her head and straight onto a pile of recyclables forming about two feet away.

"Good morning!" she called out.

The man hopped up out of the Dumpster, landing

on his feet. He looked warily from Jess to me, then back again.

"What do you want with me?" he growled.

"Nothing. Sorry. Our mistake," I said, taking a step back.

Jess moved toward him, holding out the bag. "We thought you might be hungry."

"I don't need no handouts," he said, nodding toward the worn-out bicycle resting behind the Dumpster. Behind it was a very sad-looking wagon fashioned from warped plywood and chicken wire which held clear plastic bags full of recyclables. "I make my own way."

"Of course you do." I shifted the tray onto one arm, stepped forward, and snatched a handful of Jess's denim jacket in my hand. "He makes his own way. Let's go."

Jess eyed me until I released her, then stepped closer. "It's not for you. It's for us. My friend and I have been having a bad couple of days, and we really need to do something kind for someone. We've been all over this town, and there's just no one who needs us, and the sandwiches are getting cold. It would really help if you'd take one."

He watched us for a long moment, the eyes in his haggard face narrowing to slits. I was pretty sure he was going to pull out a knife and fillet us both, and I was going to die unmourned behind a VFW somewhere between Kansas City and the fifth ring of hell. When he reached into his pocket, I squealed and jumped back.

He stared at me, hand still in his pocket. "What's wrong with your friend?"

"Bad couple of days," Jess said. He watched me with suspicious eyes as he pulled a dirty quarter out of his pocket and handed it to Jess.

"I pay my way," he said.

Jess smiled, took it gratefully, and handed him the bag. "Thank you so much. We really appreciate it."

"Yes, thanks so much." I grabbed her elbow and pulled her around with me until we were safe in the sunlight on the dirty shoulder of the road. "So, where does the natural high come from? Is it like a bungee-jumping thing, you work off the adrenaline your body produces when you narrowly escape getting strangled to death with chicken wire?"

She laughed. "He wasn't going to hurt us. Most of the truly dangerous people in the world have jobs."

I couldn't argue with that. I was too focused on the fact that we had four bags left, and not another homeless person in sight. I glanced across the street at Harried Mom Park.

"Lots of hungry moms. We can unload the rest of these and get on the road. Let's go."

I stopped when I felt Jess's hand on my arm. "But they're not . . . I mean, they've probably already had breakfast."

"Are you kidding?" I said. "Moms never have time to eat. This will be a huge act of kindness. Plus, we wandered for a half hour and only found one homeless guy. I don't think this is a homeless-guy kind of place. Let's just unload these and—"

"No," Jess said, her voice quiet but determined. "I'm not going over there."

"Okay," I said, a little startled by her vehemence, but unwilling to give up that easily. "That's fine. You can wait here. I'm unloading these things."

I dashed across the street to the park before she could say any more. When I arrived at the picnic bench, a frail, redheaded harried mother shouted, "Hannah! Don't put that in your mouth!" then turned to look at me. "Hello." She sounded even warier than the Dumpster guy.

"Look, see that woman across the street?" I turned and waved at Jess, who gave a small wave back. "It's a really long story, but she's making me give away Mc-Griddles and I was just hoping you guys could act like you're hungry. Or . . . something."

Red sniffed and turned up her nose. "Do you know how much saturated fat is in one of those things?"

"I'm not saying you have to actually *eat* them," I said through clenched but smiling teeth. "I'm just asking you, as a favor to me, as a random act of kindness on your part, to pretend that you're hungry and grateful."

Another harried mother, who seemed blissfully unaware of the spit-up on her collar, said, "Who are you again?"

I closed my eyes and sighed. There were times in life when a girl had to do what a girl had to do, dignity be damned. I opened my eyes again and smiled. "Have you ever seen *Baby of the Family*?"

The redhead looked confused. I didn't blame her. "What, that sitcom from the sixties?"

"Yep." I cleared my throat. "You know Twinkie?"

Spit-up's eyebrows knit. "Was that the dog?"

"No," I said. "The daughter. The adorable little blonde girl who did this"—I did the beatific shruggy thing—"all the time?"

Another mom, a pudgy woman with hair in long Laura Ingalls braids, approached and glanced at the McGriddles. "What's going on here?"

"I'm her daughter," I said.

"Whose daughter?" Braids asked.

Red shaded her eyes with one hand and squinted up at me, then smiled. "Oh, wow. You do look a bit like her."

"Thanks," I said, trying to bear the comparison as a compliment. "But back to that woman who's forcing me to hand out food to strangers—"

"Twinkie's daughter!" Spit-up Mom clapped her hands. "Oh, my God. What are you doing all the way out here?"

"You wouldn't believe me if I told you. Now, if you could please just—"

"Wait!" Spit-up reached into her purse and pulled out a pen, then continued rifling through her bag. "Does anyone have any paper? I want an autograph."

I had to raise an eyebrow at this. People rarely wanted Mom's autograph unless she was at an opening for a mall or something. These west-edge-of-the-fifth-ring-of-hell people must have been truly desperate for celebrity. Lucky for them, I was desperate, too. I reached into a McGriddle bag, pulled out a sandwich, unwrapped it, and set it in front of Spit-up. Then I pulled out a napkin and took her pen.

"Make it out to Sandra," she said, giggling.

"Who are you?" Braids asked, then turned to Red. "Who is she?"

"She's Lana Lorraine's daughter," Red said. "You know. Twinkie, from *Baby of the Family*. Can you believe it? All the way out here!"

I didn't bother to tell her the name was Lilly, not Lana. I didn't care. I was already knee-deep in the muck of my mother's faded celebrity; I wasn't going any deeper by pretending I had pride. I scribbled my name on the napkin and handed it to Spit-up. "Okay, so, McGriddles for everyone, right?"

"Wow," Braids said, reaching to shake my hand. "Lana Lorraine's daughter."

"'Sandra, all the best, Emmy James,'" Spit-up read, then glanced up at me. "Who's Emmy James?"

I forced my smile. "I am. But you can call me EJ. I go by EJ."

Red looked up. "So, your last name isn't Lorraine?"

"No," I said. "My father was a director. His name was Simon James. He left when I was two. And even if I didn't take my father's name, my name still wouldn't be Lorraine, since my mother's real name is Wilhelmina Gwartney."

Dead silence as three sets of mommy eyes stared me down, blinking in disbelief or surprise or just sheer exhaustion from being mommies. I was stuck. There was no getting out of this without significant sharing.

So I shared.

"Since my father moved to Spain to get away from

her, my mother has remarried six times. *Six times.* Now you tell me, what kind of woman needs to get married seven times before she realizes she's just no good at it? I mean, shouldn't the first three or four times be a solid clue? I only had to forget to feed one hamster before I realized that rodents were not my thing."

Braids and Red exchanged a glance, then looked back at me and made awkward noises of reassurance.

"Anyway," I went on, "she's about to snare number eight in Oregon. I'm not going to the wedding, because I don't speak to my mother, because she kind of ruined my life. I live by myself in an Airstream trailer, and at the moment, my closest friend is a woman who thinks she's an angel, and who is forcing me to ply you with the deadliest food known to man. Now, I'd really appreciate it if you all would smile and wave at me as I leave, as though we've had some kind of pleasant interaction here. Can you do that for me?" I clasped my hands in front of my heart in a gesture of total supplication. *"Please?"*

Spit-up was the first to smile. "Sure. You bet."

She reached in the bag and handed a McGriddle to Braids, who stared at it dubiously, then smiled at me.

"My mother was a piece of work, too." She opened up a McGriddle and took a bite, then said, loudly, "Thanks so much!"

I smiled, mouthed "Thank you," and turned to walk back to Jess, the cheers of the Harried Moms ushering me on my way.

Dedication:
To all my fans, who have been so faithful and loving to me,
giving me strength when I felt weak, and making me laugh
when I needed cheering. You all have meant so much to me
through the years; you have kept me going.
And to Emmy.

—from *Twinkie and Me:*
The Real-Life Confessions of Lilly Lorraine

Chapter Five

"EJ?"

I opened my eyes. In the dim shaft of rest area light that came through the curtains, I could see only the faintest detail of the Airstream's ceiling. "What?"

The twin bunk squeaked as Jess shifted in her bed. "You should read the letter."

I closed my eyes. "What letter?"

"The letter Digs gave me. The one I gave you at the diner."

"I told you," I said. "I read it. It was just a joke. Good night."

"If it was important enough for Digs to bring all the way from Oregon, then it's important enough for you to read."

How did she always know when I was lying? That

was getting really annoying. I sighed and pushed myself up on my elbows. "It's the middle of the night, Jess. I'll read it in the morning, okay?"

More noise, and then Jess stepped into the dim shaft of light coming through the curtains near the dinette table. "We're less than fifty miles from Colorado Springs. Tomorrow you're going to be rushing to get me on a plane. Now's your last chance. You have to read it now."

"I don't want to read it now."

"You have to. I'm thinking about it so much I can't sleep, which means the Universe thinks it's important. You have to read it now."

I sighed and sat up in bed. "We need to discuss your deluded relationship with the Universe."

"Do you really want to point fingers about delusions?" she asked.

I glanced up at her. She stood with her arms crossed over her stomach, looking fairly threatening, the pink camisole and blue capri sweatpants notwithstanding.

"You know, for an angel, you can be kind of mean sometimes."

"I'm just trying to communicate with you in a way you'll appreciate. Now get off your ass and read the damn letter."

"Wow." I sat up, stretched to the far edge of the bed where I'd thrown my jeans, and whipped the letter out of the back pocket. "You're a mean angel."

Jess flicked on the lamp by the dinette table and sat down. I unfolded the letter in my hands and stared at it.

It's just a joke, I thought. *Just read the damn joke and get some sleep.*

Still, my fingers wouldn't move. A joke from Luke was never just a joke. Once I opened it, I knew I'd spend the entire night tossing and turning, looking for the hidden meaning. Shaggy dogs meant he was angry, and elephants were forgiveness, and "two men walk into a bar" meant we needed to talk, and . . . hell. I'd forgotten what the priest and rabbi ones meant.

"Do you want me to read it for you?"

I glanced up to see Jess looking down at me, kindness in her eyes. I handed her the letter and rested my head in my hands, listening as she tore the envelope open and unfolded the paper inside.

"'Dear Eejie,'" she read. "'Enclosed please find a check for two hundred and thirty-three dollars and eighty-two cents, which is your prorated rent refund for that last month. I wanted to be sure you got it just in case you decide not to come to the wedding. Best, Luke.'"

I raised my head to find Jess turning a check over in her hands. She looked mortified, but it was mortification on my behalf, which made it a thousand times worse. Her face cleared as she realized I was watching her, and she tucked the check back into the envelope.

"Well," she said, "that was very thoughtful of him."

I stood up and snatched the envelope from her, pulling out the check and the letter.

"'Best'?" I said. "What the hell does 'best' mean?"

Jess smiled. "It means he sends you his best regards. It's affectionate . . . kind of. And it's better than being all angry and bitter, right?"

"'Best' isn't affectionate. 'Best' is what you write when you don't care enough to say 'drop dead.' 'Best' is"—I swallowed—"ambivalent."

Jess clasped her hands together. "You know what? Why don't I make us some tea? We can sit and talk."

I stuffed the check and the letter into the envelope. "'Best.' He can bite my ass for his 'best.' Thinks I need his stupid two hundred and thirty-three dollars after six years? And prorated, no less. Jesus. I'm surprised he didn't calculate interest. What kind of guy, after six years, sends a prorated rent refund check?"

Not Luke, I thought. *Luke would never, ever . . .*

Except he had.

"So . . . ," Jess said, motioning vaguely toward the stove, "tea?"

"No," I said. "Thank you. We've got a long day tomorrow. I'm gonna—" I interrupted myself with a forced yawn. "I'm tired."

"Okay." There was a long moment of awkward silence, and then Jess shut off the lamp by the dinette and scurried back to her bunk. I clutched the envelope in my fist, crawled back into bed, and stared at the ceiling of the Airstream until the sun rose.

"This looks like a nice place," Jess said as I hopped back into the cab of the truck, which was parked in the lot of an RV park off Route 24, just outside of Colorado Springs. "Do you think you'll be here long?"

I held up the receipt in my hand. "Just paid for a month in advance."

She paused. "Is that a long time for you?"

I sighed, staring at the hanging wooden sign by the road that read GOLDEN ACRES CAMPGROUND, the letters carved out in that faux burned-in style that many RV parks out west were fond of.

"It's nice here," she said in sunny tones. "I think you'll like it here. It has a nice country atmosphere. Do you know where you'll be working?"

"I keep reading 'Golden Arches,'" I said, pointing to the RV park sign.

She leaned forward to get a better look at it. "Oh. Yeah."

"Doesn't help that the letters are painted yellow."

She sat back. "It looks like a pretty place, though. I like the log cabin lodge thing they've got going on with the rec center—"

I twisted in my seat to face her. "So, you fix people, right? I mean, that's what you do?"

"Well, not really." She cocked her head to the side. "What exactly are you asking me?"

"I just want to know what you do. I mean, when we met, you said you help people, right? You fix them. That's part of the whole angel thing, isn't it?"

"No." Jess cleared her throat. "I don't really fix people. It's not like a surgery. I just do what the Universe tells me. I help the way I'm guided to help. I don't—"

"But if you went there," I said, frustrated, "and someone was obviously broken, then that could be the reason why you went. Right? Like, to fix him."

"I'm not sure you're hearing me. I don't fix people. I can't change who they are, or interfere with their free will. It doesn't work that way. I just . . ." Jess watched me in silence for a while, then shook her head. "What are we talking about?"

"When we met, you said everything happens for a reason, right? You met me, and that's why you're going to Fletcher now." I leaned my head back and stared at the ceiling of my truck cab. For someone who tagged herself as insightful, Jess was being particularly obtuse at the moment. "I mean, maybe you're meant to help someone there. Someone who writes weird letters and sends them with his brother. Someone like that."

She shrugged. "I know you're bothered by that, but it was just a rent refund. It was thoughtful of him to remember after all these years."

"Thoughtful, sure. But not funny. Not warm. I know I haven't exactly earned funny and warm, but if Luke were stuck in a waiting room with Hitler, he couldn't *not* be funny and warm. It's just who he is." I sighed. "Or who he was. Trust me, the Luke I know is not the same guy who wrote that letter."

Jess nibbled one edge of her lip. "Has it occurred to you that maybe it's not *my* destiny to help Luke?"

I huffed and threw my hands up in frustration.

"Well, if it's not yours, then who—?" I broke off, and she raised an eyebrow at me. I shook my head. "No. Trust me. I'm not a fixer. I—" I cut off, my mind pushing against the memory of stupid things my mother has said to me. "I'm a breaker."

There was a long moment of silence. "You really believe that?"

I shrugged. I had believed it enough, once, to make the biggest mistake of my life, so . . . "Yeah. Sure."

"Do you think you broke Luke?"

A sharp pain shot through my ribs at her words, and I realized I'd hit my limit on this conversation.

"You know what?" I said, reaching for the gear shift. "Let me get this thing parked and set up, and we'll get you to the airport."

"He's not broken," she said, her voice soft.

I sat back, leaving the car in park, as the core of my being roiled with emotion I struggled to keep below the surface. "I really don't want to talk about this."

"I know you don't. But I think it's important for you to know that Luke isn't broken."

"How would you know? You've never even met him."

Jess stared straight ahead at the lodge, but I could tell by the misty look in her eyes that her head was somewhere else. "If he was really broken, he wouldn't have been able to send you any letter at all." Her voice was strange and distant, and her eyes blinked slowly as though she could hardly bear to look at whatever pictures her mind was putting in front of her. Then she blinked hard, and turned her focus to me. "Whatever it is, it's reparable. It's not too late. He can be who he was again, and he probably will be, if it's his natural inclination. But he's not lost."

For the first moment since I'd met Jess, the thick fog of my self-absorption lifted, and I could see that she wasn't talking about me, or Luke. Not entirely, anyway.

I was suddenly overtaken with curiosity about her past, but I didn't ask any questions, mostly because she hadn't asked me any, and she seemed like a "do unto others" kind of girl.

I cleared my throat. "I'm just gonna get the Airstream set up in my lot, and then we can get you to the airport."

She flashed a smile. "Sounds great."

I put the truck in gear and started down the path to my section of the park. "Or, you know, I *could* drive you to Denver. I mean, it's only another seventy miles, and it's a bigger airport up there. You can get a direct flight to Portland and it'll be cheaper."

"Well, sure," she said. "That'd be nice. Thank you."

We drove in silence for a short while.

"Or," I said, "I *could* just drive you all the way to Fletcher."

I kept my eyes on the dirt path ahead of us, but even not looking at her, I could hear the smile in her voice.

"That you could."

"I mean, I've paid for the full month. I could just park the damn trailer here and get over myself and go to my stupid mother's stupid wedding. I mean, I owe Danny that much, right? The few good qualities I have are because of him. I can just think of it as Danny's wedding, and put up with her for his sake."

"That's an interesting perspective."

"Okay. So we'll just park this thing and pack up and be on our way."

A wooden sign nailed to a tree marked my lot and I

pulled easily into it. I shut the engine off and turned to face her. She glanced at me, not working too hard to hide her victorious grin.

"Stop smiling," I said, reaching for my door handle. "Nobody likes a cocky angel."

The so-called feud between Shelley Fabares and myself, like many Hollywood stories, has been wildly overreported, and never accurately portrayed. I would like to take this opportunity to clear up some points:

1. She did not win the part of Mary Stone on The Donna Reed Show *over me. Obviously, given that Shelley is somewhere between ten and fourteen years my senior (no one has ever been able to pin down her actual birthdate with any precision), this would be impossible. I will say that the producers were, at one point, thinking about adding a younger sister to the cast, and my name was bandied about.*

2. I have no proof that Shelley requested that there only be one Stone daughter, and threatened to quit should I have been added to the cast. That is hearsay. And my source, while reliable, shall remain anonymous.

3. It is patently untrue that I snuck onto the set of Girl Happy *and put hot pepper flakes in Shelley's bikini bottom. That could have been any number of girls on the long, long list of people who didn't like her, of which I am only one.*

4. As to the rumors that I named my daughter Emmy just so I could say I got an Emmy before Shelley ever did . . . well. She still doesn't have one, now does she?

—from Twinkie and Me:
The Real-Life Confessions of Lilly Lorraine

Chapter Six

As we hit the first stoplight on the outside of Fletcher, I gripped the steering wheel so tight my fingers went numb. We'd driven almost nonstop for two days, and I was exhausted. While the driving was easier and faster without the trailer hitched up, I found myself in an elevated emotional state for most of the drive. If I was scared of going home, I was terrified; if I was happy about seeing the people I loved again, I was giddy. I couldn't maintain a level state of mind, and found myself spiking into hyperactivity whenever I wasn't fighting to keep from bursting into tears. Jess, for her part, had handled me well, distracting me with crossword puzzle clues and reading aloud from her Agatha Christie novel.

Now, less than five minutes away from Danny's house, I was beyond even her powers to calm.

"Okay," I said, my chatter matching the pace of my racing heart, "here's the thing. Danny's a big sweetheart. He's big and cuddly like a teddy bear, and he'll make you feel at home instantly."

The light turned green and I hit the gas. "He's got a big, soft heart and at some point during the visit, I almost guarantee he'll adopt a three-legged stray or save a whale or something. It's just Danny. He's an architect, and he does pretty well for himself, so the house might be a little intimidating at first, but he's got a great, warm style and—"

I paused as we passed by the old second-run movie theater where Luke and I used to go every year for the Humphrey Bogart festival. At the top of the marquee, in all caps, was PETE'S FEED AND HARDWARE with *Sweet Crimped Oats and all hammers 20% off til June 25* in smaller, mismatched letters underneath. The knowledge that the Lyceum had sold out to become a feed store shot a weird panic through me, and I stopped breathing for a second.

"EJ?"

I snapped out of it and glanced back at the road, my heart still hammering. I took a left onto Wingdale Drive.

"Right. Where was I? Oh, yeah. You need to be prepared for my mother. She's probably already living there. I mean, she's getting married in a week for the eighth time, why be precious about it, right? So. My mother." I heaved out a long breath. "I don't want to say she's evil, but I find myself at a loss for a more fitting word. First of all, she wears pearls and diamonds and dresses all day long, even at breakfast. Her hairstyling habits alone have probably contributed to half the hole in the ozone. The second we get there, she's gonna start in on my hair, then my clothes, then my shoes, then my weight."

"Your weight?" Jess said. "You're kidding. What are you, a size eight?"

I shot her a look. "In Hollywood, the fat girls are a size six. But that's okay; the physical critique will only last an hour, tops. By then, she will have moved on to my disappointing character traits, such as how I have no appreciation for making a good first impression, and how my unwillingness to participate in the latest gossip about her fading Hollywood D-list starlet friends constitutes an ignorant disdain for current events and popular culture. She won't even notice you until probably day two or three, at which point she will quote-unquote 'kindly' offer to take you to the salon to fix either your hair or your nails or your skin, whatever feature she feels is less than acceptable. Whatever you do, don't buy into her bullshit. You're fine the way you are."

"Thank you."

"Oh!" I snapped my fingers in the air. "Also, whatever you do, do not mention Shelley Fabares." I swallowed hard as we took a right onto Kotter Drive.

"Shelley Fabares?" Jess asked. "The lady from *Coach*?"

"Oh, crap. You know who she is. Yes, it's the lady from *Coach* and also she was on *The Donna Reed Show* and she starred in a movie with Elvis and my mother is completely obsessed with her for reasons that are way beyond my comprehension."

"Didn't she also have a hit song in, like, the fifties?"

"'Johnny Angel.' Nineteen sixty-two. You hum one bar of that song, my mother's head will twirl around, she'll start speaking in tongues. It's crazy. Just to be safe, don't mention Shelley. Not that you would, I mean, you're smarter than that, but . . ."

I released a long breath as the road wound its way toward Danny's house, which sat at the end. I pulled my foot up from the accelerator and let the truck slow down to twenty miles per hour.

"Um . . . EJ?" Jess's voice was thick with worry, but I couldn't take my eyes off the road. "Are you okay? You look kind of pale."

"I'm fine," I said, forcing out a weak and thoroughly unconvincing laugh. We wound around a curve and I could see the edge of Danny's roof through the huge firs that flanked the edge of the property. I slowed down to a crawl and turned into the long paved stone drive.

"Whoa," Jess breathed as we closed in on the house, a four-thousand-square-foot craftsman Danny designed himself back in the seventies. The exterior was the same familiar smooth stone, the overhung roof made of the same natural wood. The interior used to be simple and understated, white walls with natural blond wood trim over hardwood floors, everything natural, simple, comfortable, just like Danny, but I shuddered to think what my mother had done to it. She had the decorating tastes of Zsa Zsa Gabor on methamphetamines. She was probably having the back deck plated in gold at the very moment we pulled up.

I edged the truck over to the side of the circular driveway and parked it, then leaned forward and stared at the house through the windshield.

"I wonder if they're even home," I said. But before I could finish, Jess said, "Is that Digs?"

It was. He stepped out from the porch and then paused when he saw us. Our eyes met, and, very slowly, he smiled. I smiled back and he approached, walking around to Jess's side of the truck first and opening the door for her.

"I have to apologize," he said, holding his hand out to help Jess. "I didn't think you'd be able to do it. I have obviously underestimated your divine powers."

"It wasn't easy," Jess said. "I had to kidnap her."

"Way to think on your feet, angel." Digs shut the door, and then walked around to my side. I kept my hands firmly gripped on the steering wheel, and as the door opened, I asked the question on my mind. "Who's home?"

He gave one gentle shake of his head: *Luke's not here.* "I'm helping Dad fix some planks out on the back deck, and Lilly's in the kitchen, making lunch."

I glanced up. "What? You're letting her *cook*? Are you insane?"

Digs chuckled. "She cooks now. And knits."

I gave him a hard look. "Okay, now I know you're full of shit."

Digs kept a straight face. So straight, I almost

thought he might not be kidding. "Things are different now, EJ. I could have warned you if you'da called first."

I shrugged and stepped out of the truck. "I wasn't sure I'd make it all the way here. I'm still *thisclose* to turning around and going back."

"Ah, just as well," he said, "because this is gonna be fun to watch."

I had just shut the door when I heard the deep, rumbly, genuinely joyous laugh that could only come from one source: Danny Greene. I tucked my hands in my pockets and watched as Danny walked toward us. His thick hair had thinned a bit at the temples, and gone from his old salt-and-pepper look to mostly salt, but his grinning, ruddy face was exactly the same as it had always been.

"EJ," he said softly. His face didn't hold even the slightest note of reproach or anger, despite the fact that I'd earned it in spades. He simply smiled and reached for my hands, holding them out from me as he surveyed me from head to toe. "Just as beautiful as ever."

My eyes filled as he pulled me into a hug, but I bit the inside of my cheek and blinked the tears away. Danny released me and put both hands on my cheeks.

"How have you been, sweetheart?" he asked.

"Good," I said, choking on the word and blinking harder. "I'm sorry, I would have called, but—"

"Oh, you know better than that. You never need to call first. I'm just glad you're here." He lowered his hands and reached one out to Jess. "Hi. I'm Danny Greene."

Jess stepped forward. "I'm Jess Szyzynski, a friend of EJ's. It's so nice to meet you. EJ's told me so much I feel like I already know you."

I cleared my throat. "We were just going to get set up at the Grande, but I thought we should let you know we were here—"

"You're not going to any hotel," Danny said, then turned to Digs. "Get their bags, David. I'll show these lovely ladies inside."

"Danny, really, we can—," I began, but he grabbed my hand, tucking it into the crook of his elbow.

"There's plenty of room, and you know the rule: No arguing allowed on my property." He held one elbow out to Jess. "Humor an old man. It might be my last chance to escort two gorgeous young women into the house. I'm getting married, you know."

Jess grinned and took his arm while Digs grumbled behind us as he tried to dislodge Jess's duffel bag from the narrow space behind the cab seats.

I heard her before I saw her, that familiar, lacy voice calling out, "Danny, who's here?" and my stomach tightened with tension as I awaited the oncoming assault. Then a moment later, as she appeared in the driveway, I was too stunned to feel much of anything.

She was wearing jeans. *Jeans.* And a green cotton turtleneck. And an apron—check, a *dirty* apron—on which she was wiping her hands. Her hair was pulled back in a demure, white-blonde ponytail that gave her a fun, youthful appearance. Her bright blue eyes stared out from lashes clear of mascara and lids sans eyeshadow.

Her cheeks held only a natural blush, and her pale pink lips were lightly glossed. There was not a diamond nor a pearl in sight.

She froze as she came around the porch. I let go of Danny's arm and stopped where I was, staring at this creature as though she'd just been beamed down from a passing spaceship. In my peripheral vision, I could see Danny step aside and whisper something to Jess, who nodded, but I couldn't hear anything. My blood was roaring in my ears and I felt like I was about to fall over.

This woman who looked vaguely like my mother put her hand to her mouth and I think she said something, but I couldn't hear it. Then she opened her arms and ran to me, throwing them around my neck and hugging me with a warmth I had never experienced in the twenty-four years we'd actually been speaking to each other.

". . . can't believe you're here, sweetheart," I heard her weepy voice saying when my hearing returned. "Oh, Emmy, darling, I've just missed you so much." She stepped back and put her hands on my face. They were still cold and bony, the only thing about this woman that was even remotely familiar. Her eyes glistened as she smiled at me, a full smile that allowed for crinkling at the edges of her eyes, something I'd never seen her do before. "You look wonderful. A little on the thin side, but I'm making paninis. We'll get you fed."

I opened my mouth but was too stricken to talk. Digs came up behind me and put his hand on my back as if he were concerned I might fall over. I turned and looked at him, and he watched me with a mixed expression of amusement and guilt.

"Okay," he said. "Maybe I should have told you."

My original shock started to transition into annoyance somewhere around the time paninis were served on the back deck. I was unable to figure out which emotions were which, and what I was and was not entitled to feel considering that I wasn't within a country mile of blameless here, so I kept my smile on and engaged in polite chitchat while we all angled to see each other around the five-hundred-pound gorilla sitting on the center of the circular deck table, feeding off our unasked questions. For instance, I did not ask who this nice woman was and what she had done with my mother. My mother, for her part, did not ask if Jess was just a friend or my lesbian lover, although that was obviously the question rattling around in her head. Danny, smiling despite the fact that he had every right to be seriously pissed off at me, did not ask where the hell I'd been all these years and why I'd forgotten how to use the phone or write a letter. The only people who seemed to be completely comfortable with each other and themselves were Digs and Jess.

"So," I said, poking at my panini with a fork, "you really cooked this? All by yourself?"

The stranger pretending to be my mother smiled. "Yes. I've learned to cook. Can you believe it? I never had the patience before, but now I've figured out a thing or two in the kitchen and I really enjoy it."

"A thing or two?" Danny leaned forward and put his hand on hers, giving her a smile. "She can make a gourmet meal out of a can of kidney beans and a bag of pasta."

"Wow." I had an odd urge to throw the panini at her head, but reminded myself that such an action would probably be frowned upon. "The place looks great, Danny. The same, actually. Mom, you *are* living here, right?"

She nodded and smiled girlishly at Danny. "Going on five years."

Five years? Five years and no hideous abstract murals on the walls painted by some crappy but popular artist whose name looked better than the art? Five years, and she hadn't disrupted the lake view with a hot tub and sauna and a circus tent? Five years and—

"Blink," Digs whispered, giving me a gentle poke on the leg under the table.

"So, Jess," Danny said, turning his warm smile on her, "how long have you known our girl?"

She looked at me, seemed to do the math in her head, and then smiled at Danny. "I guess about eight days."

My mother reached for her wineglass and took a generous sip. I put my hand on Jess's shoulder.

"Yeah, we just hit it off from the start," I said, enjoying the sight of the woman I barely recognized as my mother rending at the napkin in her lap, tortured at the thought that her only daughter had turned gay, thus seriously complicating her shot at grandchildren.

Serves you right, you big faker.

"Jess was there when I went out to visit EJ," Digs said. "She didn't get a chance to warn Jess against me, so I was able to sucker her into being my date for the wedding."

Mom released a breath in a manner she probably thought was subtle, then grinned at Jess. "Oh, how wonderful! You two will make such a handsome couple."

"Yes, they will." I sat back and shot Digs a look.

"Well, don't be shy," Danny said, motioning toward the plates. "Eat up. It's good stuff. Our Lilly is a master at paninis."

I watched as everyone else took bites—except my mother, of course. Interesting. I waited for the chokes and gasps, but each of them just smiled and made yum noises as though it were possible those sandwiches weren't the most deadly things ever created at the hands of a mortal. I knew better, though. I'd been there for the Great Pot Roast Disaster of '86. Jess took a healthy bite, touched her napkin to her lips daintily, and grinned at my mother.

"Lilly," she said, swallowing, "these are wonderful! What's in them?"

"Oh, nothing really, you wouldn't believe how simple. A little sliced turkey, caramelized onions, and some fontina, and then you just layer it all between thin slices of sourdough, and—you won't believe this—actually wrap a brick in tin foil—"

"Caramelized onions," I snorted. I didn't realize I'd verbalized the thought until I looked up to see four pairs of unamused eyes watching me. "I mean . . . you can't . . ." I blinked at the blank faces, then looked to

Jess and spoke under my breath. "Can you caramelize onions?"

Jess gave me a stern look, then dropped her eyes to my sandwich and raised them back to me, arching one eyebrow to tell me I'd better take a bite of that sandwich or risk losing a hand. I sighed, leaned forward, and took the smallest bite I could, my free hand reaching for my glass of ice water to help me choke it down . . .

. . . except it was good. *Really* good. I put it down, said, "Mmmmm," and smiled. My mother glanced happily at Danny, as if she had ever in her life given the slightest crap about my approval. What the hell kind of *Twilight Zone* reunion was this? Where was the contempt, the disdain, the recrimination? Who was this woman?

"So, Jess, where are you from?" Danny asked, his head politely angled toward the poor, poor guest.

"Oh. Um, I've kind of lived all around, actually," she said, then turned her grin on my mother. "Lilly, I can't tell you how exciting it is to meet you. I have been a fan of *Baby of the Family* since I was a little girl, and to get to meet you in person is such a thrill!"

Oh, God. Here we go. Despite the fact that any normal human being would be sick to death of talking for nearly a half century about what they did between the ages of six and ten, Lilly Lorraine thrived on it. I zoned out for a bit, staring at my sandwich while trying to work up the strength to listen, once again, to the story about the time she accidentally fed chocolate to Rex, the dog that played Skipper, thus making him puke up Hershey's all over the second assistant director.

". . . don't you think, Emmy?"

I raised my head. "What? Huh?"

My mother smiled amiably. "I was just telling Jess how lovely the path around the lake is at dusk, and how it makes such a nice after-dinner walk. Don't you think so?"

I blinked. No Rex story? How was this possible? I sat up straighter. "Yes. It's really"—I met my mother's eyes—"lovely."

The thing about being annoyed with someone is that, if you add guilt at your own horrible behavior to the annoyance, it blazes straight into anger. White-hot anger, as a matter of fact. Just a hair shy of rage. As I watched everyone at that table accept my mother's pretense of being a decent human being, I began to fume. Then the guilt piled on as I grudgingly noted she'd been nothing but nice today. And the paninis were really good. By the time the discussion had turned to the unusually sunny weather they'd been having, there was only one way for me to vent the steam building in my gut without exploding all over the table.

I started humming "Johnny Angel."

Digs was the first to notice. He shot me a look, but that didn't stop me. I just hummed louder.

"Is that . . . ?" Jess said, but she stopped and her eyes got wide, and she mumbled, "Oh, no."

Still I continued humming, turning my focus on my mother, whose face was starting to show some real color now. Her eyes glinted with anger, and she curled her napkin up in her fist. Finally, there she was, the Lilly Lorraine I recognized.

"Emmy," she said quietly, "I think you've made your point."

"It's EJ," I said, "and I haven't even begun to make my point."

"EJ." Danny's voice was sharp and serious. "That's enough."

"It's okay, Danny," Mom said, putting her hand on his. "She has every right." She turned to Jess and gave her a sad smile. "I'm so sorry, Jess. There's a very complicated history here."

I shook my head and sputtered, "Complicated history? Is that how you'd describe it? Who *are* you?"

"Sweetheart, you have every right to be upset. I sometimes forget how much I've changed, and I understand this might come as something of a surprise—"

"A surprise? No. A surprise is coming home and finding your bedroom has been converted into a gym. A surprise is not coming home to discover that your mother has become sweet and nice and polite and not self-centered at all and has learned to cook. I mean, how am I supposed to deal with that?"

"EJ," Danny warned again, but my mother patted his hand, and he sat back and went silent.

"This has been out of left field for you, Emmy, I understand, but . . ." Mom shook her head and sighed. "I've changed."

"No shit."

Danny shot me a warning glance, and I shrunk back a little.

My mother, seeming not to notice this exchange, kept talking. "After you left, I went down a very destructive path. Glenn and I got divorced. I started drinking way too much, and there was one night . . ." She swallowed, and her eyes glistened with tears, and Danny put one arm around her shoulders. She smiled at him, tightened her grip on his hand. "Danny saved my life. He came down to California, sold my house, brought me back here. He took care of me. He got me in touch with an excellent therapist—oh, I would never have survived the past few years if it weren't for Dr. Travers. It's been a long road, and it's required a lot of work, but finally, I feel . . ." She breathed in deep and dabbed at the corner of one eye with her napkin. "I'm happy. I'm healthy."

"You're healthy?" I tried to give the idea a moment to sink in, but it just wouldn't. "You're *healthy*? So, you're saying that the woman who made me go on a grapefruit diet at the age of seven because I'd crept up to the seventieth weight percentile for my age . . . you're telling me that woman is healthy?"

She sighed. "Emmy, that was a long time—"

"Not done!" I held up a hand to silence her. "Give me a minute here. So the woman who assigned her driver to take me to the mall on my fifteenth birthday while she ran off to France to marry a man she'd known for three days . . . *this* woman is healthy?"

A deathly silence came over the entire table. Mom raised her eyes to mine and we connected, and I knew she knew exactly what I was thinking.

So the woman who called me the day after my engagement to tell me I'd never make a decent wife, that I'd ruin Luke's life as well as my own, that Luke deserved better, that I wasn't cut out for marriage and that the best way I could

*show Luke I loved him was to drop out of his life that minute
and never show my face again . . .* this *woman is healthy?*

I shifted my gaze to Danny, focused on him and how
much I loved him and wanted him to be happy, and the
rage inside started to calm.

"I'm sorry," I said. "It's been a long week for me, and
I'm really tired. Does anyone mind if I just go on up and
take a nap?" I glanced at Jess. "You'll be okay?"

She smiled and nodded. I dropped my napkin on my
plate and forced myself to meet my mother's eyes.

"Thank you," I said tightly, with as much sincerity
as I could muster. "The panini was very good."

Although there were a lot of ugly truths about that last
conversation I'd had with my mother six years ago, the
ugliest was this: Nothing that resulted from that conversation was her fault. She didn't put a gun to my head
and make me leave Luke's ring on the kitchen table in
the middle of the night. I did that all on my own. My
mother hadn't created a situation out of a pure vacuum
and injected it into my life; she'd just poked a bear that
was already sleeping in my head. When I came to my
senses some ten months later in a trailer park in Utah
and realized I'd made the biggest mistake I would ever
have the opportunity to make, I'd blamed her, of course.
And some of that was justified, I guess. But when it
comes right down to it, the truth was that I had done it
to myself.

And that infuriated me more than if she *had* put a
gun to my head.

After finding my way to my old room, I threw

myself down on the bottom twin bunk and stared up into the support bars that held up the top bunk, much as I had through so many summers and holidays when I was a kid. Many hours were spent staring at those supports, hardening my heart against the things my mother did or didn't do, what she said or didn't say, and here I was, at it again.

Just like old times.

A knock came at the door and I called out simply, "Come in," not really caring who it was.

"Hey," Jess said, closing the door behind her and pulling the desk chair over next to my bunk. "How are you doing?"

"Fine," I said, still staring up at the supports. "I'd say I'm sorry, but you're the one who kidnapped me, so you're really just getting what you deserve."

She laughed lightly. "Is there anything you want to talk about?"

I shook my head.

"Okay."

We sat in silence for a while. I wondered how long she planned on sitting there, but lacked the energy to ask. Finally, the last of my strength to hold it all in left me, and I started talking.

"Part of me wanted to come, you know," I said. Jess barely moved, but I knew she was listening, so I kept talking. "When we stopped at that first truck stop, you asked me how I felt when I thought we were heading to Fletcher. You know what? I felt relieved. I've been thinking about coming back for a long time, but I couldn't bring myself to because . . . Well. It doesn't matter. But when I was stuck inside that Airstream, barreling down the road, and it wasn't my choice anymore, I felt relieved."

"That makes sense," she said quietly.

"I wanted to come here for a lot of reasons, but a big one was to show her how great I was without her in my life. Show her how happy I'd been. How little I needed her. Even if it was a lie, I wanted to show her." I let out a bitter laugh. "And now, the woman I came all the way here to show up doesn't even exist anymore. I mean, how is that fair? It's like she gets to twist the knife one final time and I just have to suck it up and deal with it because the woman pretending to be my mother is kind and sweet and 'healthy.' And I'm . . ."

I trailed off. I wasn't sure exactly what word best described me, but I knew what it wasn't.

It wasn't "healthy." And it for damn sure wasn't "happy."

Jess sat there in silence as afternoon rain clouds closed in, darkening the room. She sat as the storm started with gentle pitter-pats on the window, and then as it raged, pummeling the roof and the walls. She was still there when I fell asleep, but when I woke up briefly in the middle of the night, the chair was empty, and settled back into its spot next to the desk.

So many of my friends have entered treatment of one kind or another. I have to say, I don't understand it. Not that you shouldn't ask for help if you need it, but just the sheer number of people in my acquaintance deciding they're addicted to drugs or alcohol or sex or money . . . it's shameful. How bad have we had it, really? We've had food to eat. We've had luxury. We've had fame. Millions of people worldwide look to us for guidance and role modeling. And what message do we send? That we can't handle the good life? That our good fortune is somehow a curse? I'll tell you what—all these quote-unquote unfortunates should have to starve like those children in Asia. Or Africa. All of these so-called unfortunate Hollywood success stories should be banned to an A-country, that's what I think.

—Lilly Lorraine, *The Dick Cavett Show*, 1982

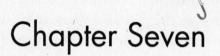

Chapter Seven

"Emmy, darling? Time for breakfast!"

I opened one eye and glanced at my watch, then put my pillow over my head.

"You've got to be kidding me," I muttered.

Knock knock knock knock.

"Emmy? I'm counting to five, then I'm coming in!" she called through the door. "One!"

I threw the pillow down on the floor. "What the . . . ?"

"Two! Three!"

"I'm not four years old!" I threw my feet over the side of my bed. "Come in if you're gonna come in!"

The door flew open and my mother—the new version, Lilly 2.0—stood in the doorway, dressed in a white cable-knit sweater and jeans with her arms crossed over a green apron. "Four-five. Okay, get up. Family meeting, downstairs, right now."

"Family . . . what?" I looked at my watch again. "It *is* six thirty in Oregon, right? I mean, I set my watch—"

"Yes, it's six thirty, and we have a lot of things to address, so you and I are having a family meeting, downstairs, over scones and tea, like decent human beings. The day starts early here, so get used to it. Besides, you've been up here since two o'clock yesterday afternoon. It's not good for you to sleep too much." She held out one arm, ready to usher me into the hall. "Come on. Let's go."

I ran one hand through my hair and pushed up off the bed.

Mom raised an eyebrow. "Did you sleep in your clothes?"

I glanced down at my wrinkled jeans. "Looks that way."

I crossed my arms over my stomach and hunched against the cooler air of the hallway, leading the way down the stairs toward the kitchen, which was part of a big open floor plan that included the den a half step down, which in turn led out through big sliding glass doors to the tremendous back deck and lawn.

On the dark granite breakfast bar was a plate of cranberry scones, flanked by two mugs of lemon tea. I sat down on one of the stools and Mom picked up one mug and stood across from me, cupping it in her hands and holding her nose over the steam for a moment before speaking.

"The wedding is on Friday," she said. "Seven days doesn't give us much time to resolve our issues, and it's probably not realistic to think that we can. We need to establish some sort of cease-fire, however, or this wedding will be ruined, and I don't think either of us wants that, if not for each other, then for Danny's sake. I know you care about him very much, and he couldn't love you more if you were his own daughter, so we need to find a way to make this work."

"Right," I said, staring down into my mug. "You're right."

"I spent the better part of yesterday afternoon talking with Dr. Travers, and he gave me some working guidelines for establishing our new relationship. The first thing I need to do is let you know that I'm not going to apologize."

I raised my head and looked at her. "Well. That's a great start."

"Darling, I realize I have a lot to apologize for," she said, "but there simply isn't time, and I refuse to torture myself any more than I already have. All it will do is feed your anger and self-righteousness, and quite frankly, I think they're healthy enough on their own."

"Wow." I blinked and sat up straighter. "I can't believe Jimmy Carter didn't invite you to Camp David. The man was a damn fool, I'm telling you."

Her face went rigid. "Do I need to revisit that we are doing this for Danny? The same Danny who, despite the fact that he owed me nothing, practically raised you? The same Danny who paid a private detective four thousand dollars to find you? The same Danny—"

I held up one hand against the tirade. "I know. I've met him. I get it. I'm in. What's the plan?"

"The plan is this: You and I will be spending every hour together, joined at the hip, and we will not leave each other's presence until we've established a workable peace between us. If that means I have to sleep in the top bunk in your room, that is what I will do. Are those terms acceptable to you?"

"Do I have a choice?"

She pursed her lips and swiped an imaginary crumb away from her apron. "David has agreed to take Jess out and show her the town, and Danny has a project in Lake Oswego that he wants to work on anyway. If you have any commitments you need to shuffle, I suggest you do so now."

"Let me check my Day-Timer." I raised my eyes up and to the left, then let them fall back on her. "All clear."

She inhaled through her nose and puffed the air out of her mouth in what looked to be a well-practiced breathing exercise. "I will also ask that you limit your sarcasm, as it tends to block honest communication."

"*Block honest communication?* Really? Is that a trademark Dr. Traversism?" I narrowed my eyes in mock suspicion. "This guy hasn't been giving you any Kool-Aid, has he?"

She held a long, dark stare. I sighed.

"Fine. Fair enough. I'll try to keep a lid on it. Anything else?"

"One thing." She stepped forward, took a corner off

one of the scones, placed it on a napkin, and played with it as she talked. "We need a place of common ground. One that isn't Danny. Some kind of shared personal interest we can use to start the bonding process." She put the napkin with the untouched scone corner on the breakfast bar and flashed her hands over her apron. "Do you, by any chance, enjoy cooking?"

I chuckled. "Do microwave meals count?"

"No. How about, um . . . golfing?"

I gently shook my head.

"Fine." She cleared her throat and ticked options off on her fingers. "Knitting. Antiques. Nature walks. Bird watching. Clothes shopping. Spa days. Um . . ." She lowered her head and tapped her foot as she thought. "Reading's no good because we can't really do that together . . ."

"There's always Cary Grant movies," I said softly.

She raised her head. "I'm sorry?"

I shrugged and kicked my feet under the breakfast bar like a teenager reluctant to admit she still likes teddy bears. "When I was younger, we used to watch Cary Grant movies together sometimes. That was fun. Kind of." I looked up, surprised at how afraid I was of the answer to my next question. "Do you remember that?"

She blinked a few times, then nodded. "Yes."

I swallowed against the odd lump forming in my throat at the memory of those rare occasions when she'd been home and unconsumed by a job, or a marriage either on its ascent or its decline, and we had actually been able to enjoy each other.

"We could rent movies," I said. "Um, *The Philadelphia Story* is good. And then there's *Arsenic and Old Lace.*"

She smiled, her eyes misty and grateful. "*Bringing Up Baby* is one of my favorites."

We sat in silence for a long moment. I grabbed a scone and placed it on a napkin, then took a bite. It was sweet and moist and still warm, yet something about it so overwhelmed me that I had to wash it down with a large gulp of hot tea to keep it from getting stuck in my closing throat. Which was fine by me; if scorching my gullet kept my emotions in check, then scorching there would be. I might be able to form a workable peace with my mother, but no way was I going to become vulnerable to her again, no matter how much she seemed to have changed. Leopards and their spots were a cliché for a reason.

"Okay, then," she said after a while. "We can run down to Al's and get a bunch of movies. Maybe we can make popcorn. And I think there's some soda in the pantry. Oh, and Danny has a home theater setup in the den. It's pretty high-tech and I can't operate it, but I'm sure he'll walk me through it over the phone."

"Sounds like a plan." I put the scone down and pushed up from my stool. "I'd like to shower first, though, if that's okay. I mean, this joined-at-the-hip thing . . . I get to take showers by myself, right?"

She grinned. "You get a half hour. After that, I'm coming in after you."

I didn't doubt it for a minute.

The sale of the Lyceum to Pete's Feed and Hardware notwithstanding, downtown Fletcher was very much the same as it had always been. Four square blocks offering everything from coffee shops to independent bookstores to boutiques to . . . well . . . Pete's Feed and Hardware. The sidewalks were immaculately kept, as usual, and the Town Beautification Committee's love affair with bright and blooming hanging flower baskets was readily apparent. As my mother led me through the town, pointing out the places where I'd spent a good portion of my youthful summers as if I'd never seen them before, I was grateful for each and every familiarity the town had to offer.

Al's Movie Barn didn't open until ten, so Mom dragged me from shop to shop looking for a decent pair of pajamas for me, as though my sleeping in my jeans the night before was evidence that I owned nothing but the clothes on my back. Finally, after accepting a pair of silk cherry pajamas, some sunglasses, and a Hello Kitty stationery set, I was able to talk her into getting some coffee at Burgundy's, a little sidewalk café in the center of town. Yesterday's rainstorm had subsided into sunny weather, and we got a small table outside where we could at least be distracted by the occasional passerby.

"So," she said as we sat down, "tell me about your life. What have you been doing all this time? David said you were . . . traveling? Is that right?"

I picked up my menu and scanned the pastries. "You really want me to tell you?"

"Yes," she said, leaning forward. "I'm really curious."

"Okay." I put down the menu. "I've been living in an Airstream trailer, going from RV park to RV park, basically whenever the whim strikes. I've been working in convenience stores, doing temp jobs, hitting the seasonal industries, that kind of thing. Your basic minimum-wage crap work that no one else wants to do."

Her posture stiffened. "You don't have to be so abrasive about it."

I conceded. "You're right. I don't."

"Dr. Travers says that when there are moments of tension, we could try to break them by thinking of something honestly nice we can say to each other. So, I'll start." She did one of her practiced in-through-the-nose, out-through-the-mouth breaths. "I'm very glad you came. I think it shows a great amount of maturity on your part."

"Well, it's not like I had a choice," I muttered.

"What?"

"You gave Danny that ultimatum. You said you wouldn't marry him unless I came to the wedding." My eyes narrowed. "Which is classic Lilly Lorraine 1.0, by the way. If you've changed so much, what's up with that?"

She sat back. "I never gave him an ultimatum. I was sad that I'd be getting married without my only daughter there, but I never said—"

"That's not what Digs told me," I said. "Then again, there was a lot that Digs didn't tell me, so maybe he was just spinning things to get me out here. I don't know.

Anyway, it doesn't matter, because I still wasn't going to come, but then the angel kidnapped me."

"I'm sorry—the what?"

"Jess. She thinks she's an angel sent from God to drag me out here to your wedding. She kidnapped me while I was sleeping in my trailer, and that's why I'm here. So that whole thing about maturity? You might want to take that back."

Mom sat back and eyed me carefully. "Why can't you just say 'thank you'?"

"What do you mean?"

"When someone gives you a compliment, you have never been able to just say 'thank you.' You always have to come in with all these reasons why the compliment isn't valid."

I stared at her for a long time. "I don't know. Maybe it's because I'm not used to being complimented."

She opened her mouth to respond, but a waitress interrupted to take our order. I ordered a mocha and an apple turnover, then turned it over to Mom, who handed her menu to the waitress.

"I'll have a water with lemon," she said. The waitress took the menu and walked away before my mother finally realized I was staring at her and said, "What?"

"You still don't eat," I observed. "How can you cook so much and not eat? Don't you have to sample the food?"

"I eat," she scoffed, then motioned lamely toward the café. "Coffee hurts my stomach, and the pastries here are too sweet."

"Mom, you're in your late fifties and you're still a

size four," I said. "It's not natural. These are supposed to be your fat and happy years. You're getting married, Danny would love you no matter what size you are, so what's up with—?"

"It's your turn," she said loudly, her face white with tension.

I blinked. "Sorry, what?"

"It's your turn." She kept her eyes off me, neatly smoothing out the folded napkin on the table in front of her. "To say something nice to me. I may have been a terrible person for your entire existence, but I gave you life, and the least you can do is find one nice thing to say to me." She met my eye and raised her eyebrows in challenge. "So go ahead. It's your turn."

I stared at her for a long while, then sighed. "I like your new style. I like the jeans and the sweaters and the no-makeup thing. You're prettier without all that gunk."

It took a moment, but her mouth finally twitched up in a smile.

"Thank you," she said.

Involuntarily, I found myself smiling back. "So that's how you do it, then? Just say 'thank you' and shut up about it? That's the trick?"

"Yes," she said. "That's the trick."

The waitress delivered our goods, and as Mom was squeezing the lemon into her water, a tall man in a gray suit passed by behind her, talking on a cell phone, and my entire body stiffened. I glanced up, trying to process consciously what my body seemed to know on instinct, and saw only the back of his head, his hair dark and well tamed, so it couldn't be . . . except . . .

"Emmy?" My mother's voice was slightly alarmed, but I couldn't drag my eyes away from the café doors, through which the man had disappeared. My eyes were acclimated to the brightness outside, and I couldn't see in, but still, I knew. I knew his voice. I'd *heard* him.

"Emmy? You look pale." I pointed in the direction of the coffee shop. She glanced at it and then back at me. "What? Sweetheart? Are you okay? Let me get you some water."

She raised her hand to command a waitress and I leaped across the table to lower it.

"Don't bring attention to us!" I hissed, sitting back down and flipping up the paper placemat to hide my face, as though I were starring in some 1980s teen flick. "It's Luke! He just passed behind you. At least, I think it was him. I don't know. That guy was wearing a suit and his hair was all combed and . . ." I took in a deep breath. "Okay. Okay. Maybe it wasn't him."

But my mother's face only confirmed my suspicions. "I'm not the only person who has changed, Emmy."

I swallowed hard. "Oh, God. I think my throat is closing up. He's probably ordering a cup of coffee or something and will be out in a minute and he'll see you. He'll see me. Oh, my God. Mom . . ." I met her eyes. "I'm not ready."

She nodded, glanced around, and pointed. "Go. Sit with her."

I turned and looked in the direction she had

indicated. A woman sat by herself, reading a newspaper and sipping her coffee while rocking a baby stroller back and forth with her foot. I turned back to Mom and ducked lower behind the placemat.

"I don't know her," I said.

"Go. Introduce yourself. Sit down with your back to us and maybe Luke won't know it's you. Your hair is longer, and Digs told us all you weren't coming, so . . ." She glanced at the café door and her eyes widened. "Go! Go now!"

I shot up from our table and knelt-walked to the woman with the baby stroller, who froze in mid sip and stared up at me.

"Hi," I said. "My name is EJ and this is very complicated, but there's a man I need to avoid and . . . can I sit here, please? Just for a minute?"

She shrugged and nodded. I took a seat and leaned forward, talking in a light whisper. "So, behind me, the woman I was just sitting with . . . is anyone talking to her?"

She glanced up, then looked back at me. "Yes. She's talking to a tall man in a gray suit."

My heart started pounding. I looked down at the baby, who smiled back up at me with a fat-faced, toothless grin. "He's cute. What's his name?"

"Elizabeth."

"Oh." I smiled down at the baby. "Sorry, Elizabeth." I glanced up at the mom. "Are they still talking?"

The woman shifted to look past me, then nodded. "Yep."

I leaned forward and whispered, "Is he looking this way? Do you think I could look without him seeing me?"

She leaned forward as well. "Is he, like, stalking you or something? Because I've got a cell phone. We can call the police if you want."

I sat back. "No. It's nothing like that." I motioned to her watch. "That's very pretty."

"Thanks." She glanced up, then looked back at me. "I think it's safe. Go ahead. Look."

And, despite the fact that I knew it was possibly the stupidest thing I could have done, I looked.

And time stopped. It was like those scenes in the movies, the highly improbable ones where all sound and movement slows, and the only thing in focus is the man the heroine loves. And there he was. It was Luke. His hair was neatly combed down instead of unkempt and curling at the edges; his suit was expensive and neatly lined, unlike the wrinkled jeans and flannel he used to wear; and his smile was tight instead of wide and unrestrained, but it was still Luke, and it still took my breath away just to look at him.

That wasn't good.

Mom chattered on about something, motioning to my bags and making like they were hers, and Luke listened politely. Then he bent down to kiss her on the cheek, pulled out his cell phone, and headed down the street. I watched him go, grabbing on to the familiarity of his gait as he walked away—at least something was still the same—then turned to the mom and baby who had hosted my psychotic episode.

"Thank you," I said, pushing up from the table. "I know that was weird."

"Seen weirder," she said with a light smile, then lifted her coffee in one hand and her newspaper in the other. I walked over to sit down across from my mother.

"Thank you," I said.

She smiled at me. "You're welcome." Her smile faded. "You know you're going to have to deal with him sooner or later, though, right? I mean, he's going to be your stepbrother soon."

"Oh, God, Mom!" I said. "Gross! Besides, the whole stepbrother thing doesn't count with adults. You've been married so much that if it did, I'd be technically related to half the male population in America and most of western Europe. I'd have to go to Botswana to find a husband."

I didn't notice the tension in her silence until I looked up from my mocha. "What?"

"I like that"—she motioned vaguely in my direction— "design on your shirt."

I glanced down. It was a brown T-shirt that I'd accidentally thrown in with the whites, and what had resulted from the bleach was weird orange streaks throughout. I glanced up. "You're serious?"

Her left eyebrow arched in reproach. I swallowed hard and said, "Thank you. I like your earrings. Simple studs are very elegant."

"Thank you."

I took a sip of my mocha and she, for some reason I

couldn't understand, started mixing her water with her spoon. After a few minutes, I nodded to her glass.

"Good water, huh?"

"Yes," she said. "They serve very good water here."

And with that, I think we both knew it was shaping up to be a very long day.

When Emmy was little, she used to draw these adorable cartoon faces; she called them her eggheads. She'd draw an egg-shaped oval, and then somehow be able to get almost any likeness into them, with nothing more than a few squiggles here and there and some color. It was really quite amazing. I remember one Christmas when she was, I don't know, maybe ten, and she'd decorated the house with the eggheads. Everywhere I went I saw family, friends, famous faces, and some that I guessed were schoolmates of hers. I remember she asked me what I thought of them, and I told her that I loved them, and I was so happy she was going to grow up to be an artist just like me.

I never saw another one after that, and by the time she was let out of her boarding school for Easter break, she'd decided she wanted to be a doctor or some such nonsense. I was always very sad about that. I liked the idea of having something in common with my daughter.

—from *Twinkie and Me:*
The Real-Life Confessions of Lilly Lorraine

Chapter Eight

We were fifteen minutes into *Bringing Up Baby* when my mother lifted the remote control and shut the movie off.

"Hey," I said, shifting forward on the den couch to set the bowl of popcorn on the coffee table. "I thought we were bonding."

"We're not bonding," she said. "We're just sitting here in silence."

"Well . . . yeah. 'Cuz . . . the movie."

She shook her head. "It's not working. I think we need to talk."

"Okay," I said. "Let's talk, then."

"All right," she said, turning toward me on the couch. "We have a lot of issues between us. You're angry with me for maybe not being the most attentive mother in the world . . ."

"Wow, way to spin it, Stephanopoulos."

". . . and I'm very upset with you for disappearing off the face of the planet for six years without ever bothering to let us know you weren't dead in a ditch somewhere."

I shot her a dark look. She cleared her throat.

"But I think we can both agree that it would take much more time than we have at the moment to resolve all of that. So, I was thinking, maybe we should both just forgive each other."

I stared at her, wide-eyed. "But didn't you say this morning that you weren't going to apologize? You don't seem to think that you did anything wrong, so what's there to forgive?"

She shook her head. "No, that's not what I said. What I said was that there wasn't enough *time* for me to apologize for everything—"

"Do you think you even did anything wrong?" I asked, crossing my arms over my stomach.

She paused. "I think I did the best I could. And I know I'm tired of feeling badly about it."

"When? When have you felt bad?"

"The last five years—"

"I wasn't here for that, remember? I saw none of this alleged contrition. All I get is this perky, happy, healthy little pixie where my mother used to be. Meanwhile, my head is still full of your wreckage, and I'm supposed to just . . . what? Forgive and forget to make it easy for you?"

She pushed herself up from the couch and started picking up the sodas and popcorn. "What do you want?

Do you want me to have a T-shirt made, with big letters saying, *I was a bad mother*? Wear it around town? Or maybe I should just nail myself to a cross, wander down the streets of Hollywood? I don't know what I'm supposed to do, Emmy."

"You can start by not calling me Emmy," I said, following her as she brought the untouched snacks back into the kitchen. "It's EJ."

"Honestly, I don't understand that at all," she said, dumping the popcorn into the trash. "Emmy is such a pretty name."

"Emmy is an award. Emmy represents everything you wanted in your life that you never got, and it's infuriating that even my name isn't about me."

"Oh, not this again." She pulled open the refrigerator and put the sodas back. "Honestly, your obsession with—"

"*My* obsession?" I laughed bitterly. "*My* obsession! Are you kidding me? Let's go rent the first season of *Coach*, Mom, what do you say? Then maybe we can talk about obsessions."

She slammed the refrigerator door shut. "That was a terrible show! A *terrible* show and she was terrible in it, I don't care how many nominations she got!"

I caught some movement out of the corner of my eye and turned to see Jess and Digs standing at the edge of the hallway, staring at us. Jess turned to Digs.

"Did we come back too early?"

Digs grinned and stepped into the kitchen. "I'd say we're just in time."

Jess grabbed for his sleeve, but missed. "But didn't you

say there was a . . . thingy . . . museum in town? I really was interested in the . . . oh, shoot. Was it trains?"

Digs patted my mother on the back. "Hey, do I smell popcorn?"

"It's in the garbage," I said. "Apparently the key to mental health is making food you never eat. Who knew? It's gonna revolutionize the psychiatric industry."

"Oh, that's it!" My mother reached for the wood knife block on the counter and withdrew a chef's knife.

Jess stepped into the room, holding her hands up.

"Um, maybe you two should take a break from each other."

Mom twirled on her heel and threw open the refrigerator door. I smiled at Jess.

"We can't take a break. We're joined at the hip. The bright side is that if she kills me, then she has to be buried alive with me. So I can at least get in that one last dig."

Muttering to herself, my mother withdrew a block of cheese, slapped it down on the counter, cut off a chunk, and took a bite.

"There! I eat! Do you see? *Cheese*, even!" She tossed the chef's knife into the sink, and Jess shuffled over next to me and put her hand on my arm.

"Do you want me to stay?" she asked carefully.

"No, no," I said, patting her hand, "let Digs take you to the thingy museum."

"The thingy museum it is," he said, putting one arm around Jess's shoulders and guiding her back out. "Or we could get a burger."

"Burgers are good," Jess said, shooting me one last

worried look before disappearing down the hallway with Digs. I turned my attention back to my mother, who was breathing in and out, through the nose, out the mouth, with her eyes closed.

"You okay?" I asked.

She opened her eyes. "I'll be right back. I have to go to the bathroom."

"You're not going to purge that cheese, are you?" I asked. "Because if you are, then maybe I should call Dr. Travers."

"Oh!" She threw her hands up in the air and let them slap down against the kitchen counter. "Why do you have to be so hateful?"

"I don't know!" I shouted, then took a breath to calm myself down. "I don't know. But this whole thing, this trying to mend the relationship between us, it's ridiculous, Mom. It's not going to happen. You can't fix thirty years in seven days, it just can't be done. I don't see why we can't just avoid each other as much as possible and let it go at that."

She slumped against the counter and stared at the floor. "Because you're my daughter, and I love you. And I'm trying so hard but I can't go back in time and nothing I can do now is going to make a difference and . . . there's just nothing I can do."

"You can say you're sorry," I said.

She looked up, her eyes red-rimmed and tired. "Dr. Travers said—"

"I don't care what Dr. Travers said." I clenched my teeth until I got myself under control, and then looked up to meet her eyes. "I already knew it, you know."

She shook her head, her expression blank. She had no idea what I was talking about, which meant I had to elaborate. I swallowed hard and kept going.

"I knew I wasn't good enough for Luke. I had no idea how to be a good wife, and I sure as hell didn't know why he wanted me to try. You didn't plant anything in my head that wasn't already there." The memories of everything that had happened back then took their shot at me, and I had to breathe for a minute before I could go on. "But you should have thought I was good enough for him even if I wasn't. If there was only one person in the whole world who believed I was worth something, it should have been you. So if you didn't mean those things you said, if you are sorry, then a real good start would be for you to tell me that."

There was a long silence, and when I looked up she was staring at her shoes. I huffed and threw my arms up in the air. "I don't believe this."

"I just . . . I can't say I'm sorry because—"

"Because Dr. Travers said not to," I interrupted, the snotty tone in my voice so strong even I cringed from it.

"No. It's because . . ." She paused, shook her head. "If all it took to ruin everything was one phone call from me, then it wasn't going to work anyway. And, honey, take it from someone who's been there—a divorce takes a part of your soul away with it. I know I've been married a lot, and divorced a lot, and it may not seem like a big deal to someone watching, but . . ." She breathed in deep, let out a long exhale. "If I saved you from that, then I can't be sorry. As to whether I meant it or not, well . . . I thought I did at the time, but honey, you have to know that most of what people say to you has more to do with them than it does with you. I mean, obviously—"

"No," I said sharply. "Not *obviously*. You don't get to skate out of this on an *obviously*." I stared at her for a while, but she wouldn't meet my eyes. "Now might be a good time for that bathroom visit, Mom."

She released a breath. "Will you be here when I get back?"

I rested my hands on the edge of the granite breakfast bar I had watched Danny install during one of the many summers I'd spent there, and stared down at the stone floor I'd helped him pick out. "I'm doing this for Danny. So . . . yes."

She nodded and headed off down the hallway. I closed my eyes and did her trick, breathing in through my nose and out through my mouth. Took a few tries, but eventually it worked. Then I ducked around the breakfast bar, opened the refrigerator, pulled out a bottle of chardonnay, yanked the cork out with my teeth, and spit it toward the sink and missed. When my mother returned from the bathroom, she sighed.

"Oh, Emmy," she said, her voice laced with disappointment. "Drinking from the bottle?"

"Get your own," I grumbled, and lifted the bottle to my lips.

She paused, watching me for a long while, then shoved me gently away from the refrigerator.

"Out of the way," she said. "I know there's some pinot grigio in here somewhere."

There's a reason why wine has been such a popular drink for so long. It's good, powerful stuff. I'm not a big proponent of drinking your problems away, but I have to tell you, once the wine entered the picture, being joined at the hip with my mother became a much, much more pleasant experience. We'd both been so emotionally wrung out by the time we resorted to the wine that we just got silly. We made a platter of cheese and crackers and went into the den to watch the rest of *Bringing Up Baby*. We raided the wine cellar twice, and used the freezer to chill the bottles we brought back up for speed's sake, although we shared those bottles in a civilized manner, using glasses and everything, while we watched *Arsenic and Old Lace*. By the time Danny got home from work, we were out on the back deck, singing everything from Motown to '80s pop at the top of our lungs to the Oregon sky. We did Joni Mitchell's "Twisted" particularly well, as I recall.

Of course, I'm not a reliable narrator for this part. I was pretty drunk, and the night is a bit of a blur. To hear Danny tell it, Mom and I were quite a sight, out on the back deck howling like alley dogs at the sky. (His words, not mine.) I do remember coming in from the deck once it had gotten dark, Mom and me giggling like a couple of teenagers coming in after curfew, to find Digs, Jess, and Danny in the den, eating pizza and watching baseball.

"Ohhhhh," Mom said as she slid the glass door shut behind us, our most recently emptied bottle clutched in the fist of her left hand. "Did I forget dinner? Emmy, we forgot dinner."

"Whatchoo mean 'we'?" I said. "I don't cook."

For some reason, we both found this insanely funny. I don't remember the expressions Digs, Jess, and Danny were wearing at the time, but in my booze-addled memory, they thought we were funny, too.

"Why don't you girls go on up to bed?" Danny said. "We're all fine here."

"Jess." I sat down on the arm of the couch next to her. "I'm so sorry. I have been a horrible hostess."

"No," she said, smiling. "I've had a lot of fun."

"Oh, really?" I looked up at Digs, who simply smiled back. "How was the thingy museum?"

"We actually didn't make it to the thingy museum," Digs said, and he shot a sideways look at Jess.

"Oh, my God, Digs! Did you hit on my angel?" I turned to Jess. "I should have warned you. He's got this thing for blondes."

"Stop!" Jess said, slapping my arm and laughing. "We went out for burgers and we talked. That's all."

"I smell a budding romance," Mom singsonged, standing behind the couch and patting Jess's hair. "You'd better lay off the burgers and pizza, sweetheart, or you'll risk losing his interest."

Annnnnnnnd . . . the room went silent as classic Lilly Lorraine showed her true face. Digs shot Mom a hard look and Danny shook his head, smiling ruefully down at his shoes. Jess, in an act of warmth and generosity, smiled up at my mother and grabbed her hand, giving it an affectionate squeeze.

"Actually," she said, "I was just about to ask if you had any ice cream."

The tension broke and everyone chuckled. I leaned down and nudged Jess on the shoulder.

"I bet I make a lot more sense to you now," I said in low tones, then sat up and pushed up off the arm of the couch. "Okay, I'm putting Lilly to bed. Then I'm coming back down and kicking all your asses at Monopoly."

I grabbed my mother's arm and led her out, and could hear Jess ask, "Is she really coming back?" to which Digs answered, "I hope not. She's a fucking shark at Monopoly."

We were upstairs, just passing by my room, when my mother took a sharp left and went inside.

"So, do I get the top bunk?" she asked.

I stood in the doorway, watching as she put one foot warily on the bottom rung of the bunk ladder. "Not unless you've got bunk beds in your room."

"Oh, no," she said. "I'm not sleeping in my room tonight. We're joined at the hip."

"I think we're peaceful enough, Mom. I feel like we've made progress, and"—I searched my head for shrinky terms—"we're on the road to a rediscovery of our relationship . . . or something."

She stepped down off the rung and turned to face me. "Oh, stop shoveling the crap. Getting drunk together doesn't make us friends."

"Well, it's the closest we're going to get today." I

walked over to her and grabbed her elbow. "Just . . . go to your bed tonight and we'll talk about it in the morning, okay?"

She allowed me to lead her down to the master bedroom, where I deposited her just inside. Briefly, I considered going back down and starting that game of Monopoly, but I was suddenly hit with a powerful exhaustion, and detoured into my room, where I changed into a pair of sweats and a T-shirt, brushed my teeth, and hopped into bed. I was almost asleep when my door opened, and there was my mother in her silk pajamas and robe, carrying a tray with two glasses and a pitcher of ice water.

"The key to hangovers," she said, holding the tray on one hand as she flicked the light on with the other, "is water. You must drink a quart of water before going to bed. It's a rule."

I pushed myself up to sitting, and she laid the tray at my feet, then poured both glasses, handing me one. She sat down on the bed next to me and downed hers, motioning with her hands for me to do the same. I did. When we'd finished the first glass, she poured us each another.

"When you've screwed up so much in your life," she said, staring down into her glass, "the past is such an impossible thing to deal with. You look at it, and it's like this big, tangled mess of yarn you'll never unravel. The only thing you can do is snip it off and start fresh, because otherwise, you'll go insane trying to fix things that cannot be fixed."

She picked up her glass and downed the rest of her water, then set it on the tray.

"Okay," I said. "Well. Thank you for the water."

She smiled up at me, and her eyes were red-rimmed, although whether from the wine or the emotion was anybody's guess. She put one cold hand on my cheek, then leaned over and kissed the other.

"You're welcome, sweetheart."

Then she got up and put one foot on the ladder to the top bunk.

"Um . . . Mom?"

"Don't argue," she said, and disappeared onto the top bunk, which groaned slightly even under her minuscule weight. "Joined at the hip, darling. I said it. I meant it."

I put my glass down on the tray, then picked the whole shebang up and walked it over to the desk. I turned and looked up at my mother, who was curled up like a little girl with prayer-hands tucked under the side of her head. She looked so tiny and fragile, it was impossible to believe that this was the same woman who had tormented me throughout most of my life.

Well. Actually, in a lot of ways, it wasn't.

"Good night, Mom." I flicked off the light and ducked into the bottom bunk, pulling the covers up to my chin.

"Good night, sweetheart," she said, her voice dreamy, and then the gentle snores of Lilly Lorraine filled the room.

I prefer plants to children. Plants don't try to kill you in your sleep if you screw them up.

—Lilly Lorraine as Betsy Tanker in *Betsy Tanker: Runaway Mom*, NBC Movie of the Week, aired February 28, 1983

Chapter Nine

I don't think I really had a plan in my head for the first time I would see Luke face-to-face again, but I do feel pretty certain I didn't intend to be hung over. I didn't intend to have my hair up in a haphazard ponytail that looked like it had been glued to the side of my head by a preschooler, and I definitely didn't intend to be wearing a cutoff Go-Go's concert T-shirt with neon green capri sweatpants that had the words *Super Fly* embroidered in an arc over each butt cheek.

But that is, of course, exactly how it turned out.

It was a little before nine when I woke up that next morning. The top bunk where Mom had slept was neatly made, and I was too tired to be suspicious as to why she hadn't woken me when she got up. I was just happy I'd gotten to sleep in, and even happier when I traipsed out to find the entire house vacant. I padded downstairs, poured myself a bowl of Cheerios, and was just sinking into the glorious solitude when there was a knock at the door.

"Of course," I muttered, pushing myself away from the breakfast bar. I was just about at the door when it opened, and in walked Luke.

I froze in the middle of the hallway. I couldn't run; he'd already seen me. Even if I dove underneath the half-moon hallway table, it was smaller than me, so there was no refuge to be had there. I just stood there, frozen, panicked. And, as karma would have it, it was then that I started choking.

I still don't know what happened, but my guess is that the shock made my system swap breathing and swal-lowing functions, and I inhaled a little bit of Cheerio. I started hacking and turning red, mostly from mortifi-cation, and Luke rushed to me and started hitting me on the back—a little harder than I would have deemed *absolutely* necessary—and after a moment I regained my ability to breathe and stepped away from him.

"I'm okay," I gasped.

"You sure?"

"Yeah." I cleared my throat and stood up straight, looking at him. It was nine o'clock on a Sunday morn-ing. His hair was neatly combed, instead of the typical disheveled mess that always looked so cute on him. And he was wearing a suit and tie. *A suit and tie.* On a Sunday. I sputtered again. "I need some water."

I turned and headed toward the kitchen, closing my

eyes and praying to God that he was too stunned to notice the words arcing over my ass.

"Ow!" I said, opening my eyes as I stubbed my toe
on the island. I pulled a glass out of the cupboard and
stuffed it under the water dispenser in the fridge door.

"So . . ." His voice came from behind me. "You're
here for the wedding, I guess?"

I glanced behind me and there he was, standing
straight, holding a large manila envelope with one hand
and striking the edge into the palm of the other. He did
not look happy to see me.

"Yeah," I croaked, then lifted the glass to my lips and
chugged the water down, hoping I'd choke again and, with
any luck, maybe die this time. Or at least pass out.

"Funny," he said, not looking amused at all. "Digs
told me you weren't coming."

I lowered the glass, sputtered, "Changed my mind,"
and lifted it again.

"I see." He stared at me, continuing to strike the edge
of the envelope into his palm, then suddenly seemed to
become aware of it and dropped the envelope on the counter. "Lilly asked me to pick these contracts up from the
party planner for her. She told me specifically to be here at
nine to drop them off. She's not here, is she?"

I sighed and put the glass into the sink. "No. She's
not." I pulled on a tight smile, realizing now exactly why
she hadn't woken me up. "I guess she hasn't changed
quite as much as she'd have us believe."

"People don't change that much." He said the words
simply, without invective, but when I looked up, his eyes
were hard.

"You have," I said, motioning toward him, trying to loosen my smile so it wouldn't look chiseled out of stone, but suspecting I wasn't having much luck. "I mean, dig you. With the suit and the hair. You're just all growed up, aren't you?"

"Well," he said, his eyes finally rising to meet mine, "not all of us can be Super Fly."

I laughed, then abruptly stopped. "I'm sorry—was that a joke or a tag? Because if you were being mean, then I can come back with something about your Sunday morning casual wear. Tell me you're not off to Bible study. My poor heart couldn't take it."

The smallest trace of a smile graced the edge of his eyes and he shook his head. "It wasn't a tag." He self-consciously ran the palm of his left hand over his tie. "And I have a meeting in an hour."

"A meeting? On a Sunday? What's up with that?"

He suddenly straightened, and whatever trace of a smile he might have had disappeared. We stared at each other for a while, like the way you'd stare at an exotic zoo animal you'd studied but never thought you'd ever see in real life. It was strange and familiar at the same time. My gut instinct kept pushing me to jump into his arms and kiss him with every bit of life I had in me, but a thin layer of reality wrapped around me, telling me I could never do that again. I wanted to laugh, and I wanted to cry, and I wanted to run, and I wanted to grab him and hold on no matter how much he struggled to get away. I felt like I was being drawn and quartered in the town square, and just as I was about to crack down the middle, he spoke again.

"Look," he said, dropping his eyes, "if you could just make sure your mom gets these, I'd appreciate it. I'm running late."

He turned and headed toward the hallway, and the thin layer of reality broke, allowing me to feel the full weight of my desperation. I chased after him, grabbing his arm.

"Luke . . ."

He stopped, and I felt the muscles of his arm stiffen under my hand, so I let go.

"Wait," I said. "Please."

He turned to face me, his expression so tight, I hardly recognized him. "What do you want?"

"Look." I swallowed hard and forced myself to meet his eyes. "I know there's a lot of crap under the bridge for us right now, but I think maybe if we could talk—"

He shook his head lightly. "It's been six years, Eejie. If there was ever anything to talk about, that moment has passed."

"What do you mean, 'If there was ever anything to talk about'? We can hardly look at each other. That's something to talk about."

He raised his eyes to mine, and I was shocked by how humorless they seemed. I had to believe Luke was in there somewhere, though, because the alternative was unthinkable.

"I can look at you," he said. "I'm looking. Can I go now?"

"No," I said, my voice thick with petulance. "You're all weird and mad."

His jaw clenched. "I'm not mad."

"Not *just* mad. *Weird* and mad. You're just so . . . different."

"Six years will do that to a person."

"See?" I snapped my fingers. "Right there. You've got the tone. The mad tone. I've known you since we were five years old, Luke. I know the tone."

"Damn it, there . . ." He let out an exasperated huff. "There's no tone, Eejie. Are you gonna give these to your mom or not? Because I can just stuff them in the mailbox on my way out if that's going to be a problem for you."

"Admit that you're mad and I'll be happy to pass them on."

He released a breath. "I *wasn't* mad. I'm *getting* mad. Would you just let it go?"

"I can't." I lifted one hand to touch his arm, then thought better of it and let it drop. "About the night I left—"

He chuckled mirthlessly and shook his head, looking down at his shoes. "Like a damn dog with a bone."

"With anyone else, trust me, I'd have the common decency to drop it and pretend nothing was wrong, but . . ." I sighed as I stared up at him. My Luke, all abducted by the pod people. It just wasn't right. "Luke, this is us. I can't stand being like this with you."

His cheeks flushed and his head shot up. "Then maybe you should have bothered to say good-bye. Taken the time to scribble a note. Dash off an e-mail. It's a coward's way out, Eejie, to just take off in the middle of the night. It's bullshit. It's—"

He stopped, and we stared at each other in silence—

his angry, mine stunned—and then the front door opened and the happy, laughing voices of my mother, Danny, and Jess echoed down to reach us.

"I'm not doing this," Luke muttered, then stalked out of the kitchen. I stared at the floor, my heart pounding in my chest, and listened as Luke had a brief exchange with my mom, was introduced to Jess, and escaped. The door shut behind him and the only sounds were careful footsteps plodding into the kitchen. When I looked up, Mom was smiling and holding out a foam container.

"We went to IHOP," she said. "I brought you back a Rooty Tooty Fresh 'N Fruity."

I stared at her, my despair at the disaster with Luke transitioning smoothly into anger at her. "Thought we were supposed to be joined at the hip."

"You were asleep," she said, putting the container on the counter. Behind her, Danny and Jess watched quietly.

"You set me up!" I said. "I'm wearing my Super Fly sweats, and you set me up to see Luke again! What the hell were you thinking?"

"I didn't know you'd be wearing your Super Fly sweats," she said, exasperation thick in her voice. "I bought you those lovely pajamas yesterday! You could have worn those!"

"Lilly?" Danny asked, a warning tone in his voice. "What did you do?"

She huffed and slapped one hand down on the counter, looking to Danny. "I did what needed to be done, Danny." She turned back to me. "You couldn't keep ducking out forever. He's going to be my stepson, and you are my daughter, and we're going to be a family.

There are going to be Christmases and birthdays and anniversaries and funerals and the two of you need to learn to be around each other. Now the first meeting is over. That's the hardest part."

"No, the hardest part will be spending the rest of my life in jail for killing my mother."

Jess stepped forward and put her hand on my arm. "EJ. Don't say things you can't take back."

Mom sighed and turned to me. "I'm sorry if it was uncomfortable for you, Emmy. I was just trying to help."

I closed my eyes and put my fingers to my temples. In her head, of course, she was being helpful. She was Lilly Lorraine. There was nothing in the world that wasn't her business, no situation that couldn't benefit from her interference. And, to tell the truth, I was a little comforted to see the leopard's spots again. The devil you know, and all that. I took a deep, cleansing breath and opened my eyes.

"I need to do some laundry." I turned to Danny. "Do you mind if I use your laundry room?"

Danny smiled. "Sure, honey. You go ahead."

"But your Rooty Tooty—," Mom began, then cut off when I turned on her.

"I'm leaving the room without telling you what you can do with your Rooty Tooty Fresh 'N Fruity. I want everyone to witness that I am withholding my vile commentary on the Rooty Tooty Fresh 'N Fruity. I want points for that. Can I have some points?"

"Points awarded, EJ," Danny said. "Go get your laundry. Your mom and I are going for a walk."

"But—" Mom sighed and turned to Danny. "I want

points for getting her a breakfast loaded with fat and sugar. Shouldn't I get some points, too?"

Danny opened his mouth, but I held up my hand.

"Wait a minute." I crossed my arms over my chest and looked at Danny. "Hold off on those points. Did she eat anything at breakfast?"

Danny and Jess exchanged looks, then Jess laid guilty eyes on my mother, who stomped her foot like a teenager.

"I did too eat! I ordered that vegetable omelet!"

"She did," Jess said, her voice straining to be helpful. "She ordered it."

"I'm sure she did. How many bites did you have, Mom?"

"I . . . never eat much at breakfast. But—oh!" She bounced on her toes and pointed a victorious index finger at me. "I put real sugar in my coffee! And cream!"

Danny put his hands on Mom's shoulders. "Let's go for that walk, sweetheart, what do you say? Let things cool down a bit."

"No!" She wrenched out of his grip. "I want my points!"

"Fine." I walked over to the counter, flipped the top of the foam container up, and grabbed a fork from the silverware drawer. "You want points?" I handed her the fork. "Take a bite."

Her eyes widened. "That breakfast was for you."

"If it's for me, then I get to decide who eats it." I motioned toward it. "You want points? Dig in."

She grasped the fork in her fist like a weapon. "Okay. I'll take a bite. But if I eat, you eat. No points for you unless you have some of the breakfast I brought for you."

"I already got my points," I said.

"Danny! Take away her points!"

Jess put her hand on my shoulder and whispered, "EJ . . ."

I rolled my eyes, grabbed a fork from the drawer, and held it in suspension over the container. "You first."

Mom took a deep breath, cut into the pancakes with the side of her fork, and impaled a bite.

"Dip it in the fruity goo," I said. "And get a little whipped cream on there while you're at it."

She eyed me as she did it, then lifted it into her mouth and chewed, raising an expectant eyebrow at me.

"I'm not going until I see you swallow," I said.

She rolled her eyes, chewed faster, swallowed dramatically, and opened her mouth for inspection.

"Acceptable." I dug in, withdrew a bite, popped it in my mouth, and tossed the fork in the sink. "Are we done here?"

"Oh, Emmy, don't talk with your mouth full," Mom whined. "I raised you better than that, didn't I? Didn't I at least do that?"

Danny visibly fought his smile as he put his arm around Mom's shoulders and led her out the sliding glass doors. As soon as she was gone, I turned to Jess, who was watching me with her own look of amusement.

"What?"

"You and your mother are so much alike, it's kinda scary."

"I'm gonna pretend you didn't say that, since you're all divine and everything," I said, picking up the container and dumping it in the trash. "But if you say it again, you and me are gonna throw down."

I don't think what happened that afternoon technically qualifies as stalking. I mean, for that, you have to present some kind of threat, and just be generally creepy. I think I avoided both of these things, but really, you'd have to ask Luke.

In my defense, all I really did was take an opportunity that presented itself to me. Jess asked me to take her to the library, because she wanted to learn more about the history of Fletcher. Danny made Mom take a day off from the joined-at-the-hip thing, I'm pretty sure because he thought we would kill each other, and he had a point. He dangled a trip to the Leach Botanical Garden in front of her, and she reluctantly took the bait. Jess and I got in the truck and went to the library, where I casually glanced through the white pages to find Luke listed, with an address. I knew the area; it was one of the oldest neighborhoods in town. As a matter of fact, Luke and I used to dream about buying a house in that area and renovating it ourselves, back in our naive and romantic days.

I stared at the page for a long time until the letters burned themselves into my retinas, then found Jess, told her I'd be back to get her in a little while, and got in the truck.

There was no car in the drive when I got there, so I just parked on the street and stared at the place. It was a classic craftsman, not all sprawling and funky like Danny's place, but compact and charming. The siding was natural-toned cedar shingles; the landscaping simple and elegant; the front door painted a sophisticated sage green. It was exactly the house we had talked about, exactly what we'd planned. I closed my eyes and imagined the inside. Blond hardwood, to make the small spaces seem bigger. White walls. Overstuffed furniture built for comfort for when we would curl up by the fire during rainstorms. A finished attic where I could run a home-based business while taking care of the kids.

Rain started to fall in little plinks on my windshield, and I opened my eyes. Sometime during my daydream, Luke had pulled into the driveway, gotten out of his car, and seen me. The driver's-side door was still open, and he stood there watching me while the rain ruined his suit. I sat where I was, thinking that maybe he didn't recognize me, maybe it wasn't me he was looking at, maybe there was something behind the truck that held his attention . . .

The rain started coming down harder, and still he stood there, staring at me. I slowly raised my hand and placed my palm flat against the window. I don't know if it was a wave, a white flag, or a wish, but the instant I did it, Luke turned away, shut his car door, and went inside. I sat in my truck for a while, the sound of the rain echoing through my bones, until finally, I started the truck up and drove off to collect Jess.

I miss Rex. I know that sounds strange, but I do, I miss the dog. He would jump on me and lick my face between takes, and then Alice the makeup lady would get so mad, but it was worth it. Rex made me feel like a kid. I don't know if I ever would have known what being a kid felt like without him.

—Lilly Lorraine, *The Merv Griffin Show*, 1985

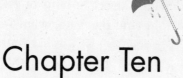

Chapter Ten

I knocked on Jess's door about five times, and was ready to go back to bed when I heard a groggy "Come in."

I poked my head in. She'd flicked the nightstand lamp on, but one eye was still closed. She didn't seem surprised to see me.

"What time is it?" she asked.

"I don't know. Three-ish. I'm sorry. I couldn't sleep."

"Mmmm," she said, waving for me to come in. I shut the door quietly behind me and sat on the corner of the bed, envying her the queen-bed guest room, which even came with its own bathroom, while I was stuck with the one in the hall. I picked at the quilt for a while, then turned to look at Jess, who had both eyes open now.

"How do you do it?" I asked.

She yawned. "Do what?"

"Fix people. You know, people who are broken."

She pulled her knees up and hugged them to her chest. "EJ, I told you, that's not what I do. And I don't think Luke is broken—"

"Did I say Luke?" I jumped in. "No. I just want to know how you do it. How did you end up in angeling? Did you answer an ad? Take a class? Are there certifications?"

She smiled lightly and shook her head. "No. Although those are very creative guesses." Her smile faded, and she stared at a spot on the wall just over my left shoulder. She was abnormally quiet, and I was beginning to wonder if she'd fallen asleep with her eyes open when she finally spoke.

"You know how I'm always telling you that the Universe has a plan? That's really hard to believe sometimes. Things happen that don't make sense. Something happened to me that didn't make any sense. So I got in my car, and I drove. I didn't know what I was looking for, or what exactly I needed, I just knew that I couldn't be in my skin anymore. I wanted to escape. And one night, I pulled into a diner in, like, Oklahoma, to get some coffee, and I started talking to this waitress. She hadn't spoken to her sister in eleven years, and her sister was sick with breast cancer, and it was really tearing her up. I ended up staying with her for a while, and was able to help her with that relationship. The sister got better, and before I moved on, she told me I was an angel and I guess that . . . I don't know. I guess it made sense."

I stared at her in silence, questions chasing each other around my head. What had happened to her? How long had she been roaming like this? Where was her family? Who had she been before? Where did she come from? And how bad could her life have been that hanging out with me and my crazy family was actually the preferable choice?

But I didn't ask any of it, because I could see in her eyes that she was close to something she didn't want to touch. I knew that feeling pretty well, so I pulled her back from the ledge by making it all about me, which, let's face it, was my default setting anyway.

"So . . . Luke," I said. "I may not have broken him, but I think I dented him a little. And now he's so weird and strange and . . ."

"Grown-up?" she said, the light smile returning to her lips.

"Exactly!" I pointed my index finger at her. "And it's not right. He's got this hard, all-business-no-play shell around him. He used to be warm, and he'd laugh all the time. All the years I knew him, I never once saw him get mad. And we were seriously dating for over two years. Trust me, there were a million times my crap should have pissed him off but good, but nothing ever got to him. And now he's all uptight and . . . with the hair and . . ." I forced myself to meet her eye. "He's not Luke anymore."

She nodded. "You mean, he's not the Luke you wanted to see."

I bristled at this. "What's that supposed to mean?"

She shrugged. "It means that he seems fine to me.

He's a grown-up, capable man with a business to run, and he's running it. I think you need to admit that your big desire to fix him is about what you need from him, not necessarily about him. Maybe you should think about what it is you need, and why."

I opened my mouth to respond and she held up her hand.

"Thinking requires at least a minute of silence." She reached to the nightstand and grabbed her watch. "Okay. The minute starts . . . now."

I inhaled deeply and thought about what I needed from Luke, why I'd come rushing back to Fletcher after reading his letter, what it was that I'd expected, and how it differed from what I got. Finally, Jess put the watch down, crossed her arms over her stomach, and stared at me expectantly.

I raised my eyebrows back at her. "What?"

"Do you have an answer?"

"Yes," I said, "and it's the same as before. He's broken and he needs fixing and I think you should hop to it."

She laughed. "You know what I really want to do?"

"Fix Luke?"

"I want to make a bookshelf for your mom. As a wedding gift. And I'd like you to help me. I think it would mean a lot to her if you made her something with your own hands."

"And in what way does that fix Luke?"

Jess smiled and shook her head. "I don't know. I had this idea in my head earlier today, and it just popped in there again, which means it's what we're supposed to do. And if it's supposed to fix Luke, it will."

I stared at her. "Really? Seriously? Luke's going to get his sense of humor back if we build a bookshelf?"

She thought for a moment, then spoke. "It's possible the bookshelf thing isn't about Luke. I'm just going to ask you to trust me on this. My internal guide says, 'Build a bookshelf,' so I think that's what we should do. We'll just have to see what happens from there. Okay?"

I sighed, then pushed myself up from the bed. "Aren't you divine people supposed to just wink or wave your hand or sprinkle some fairy dust and everything just magically falls into place?"

"I think you're mixing your mythology," she said. "Good night, EJ."

"'Night." I pulled the door shut behind me and traipsed back down the hall to my room, where I tossed and turned until the sun came up.

"Danny and I had a talk last night," Mom said at breakfast the next morning, "and we were thinking that, Emmy, it might be fun for you and Danny to have a day together, and I can take Jess out for a girls' day on the town." She reached out and patted Jess on the arm. "It's the least I can do for my new bridesmaid."

She grinned at Jess and giggled in excitement. I sat up straighter.

"What do you need a bridesmaid for? I thought you guys were getting married at the courthouse."

Mom squeezed Jess's hand. "It's my wedding. If I

want a bridesmaid and a maid of honor, I'll have them."

I glanced around the table, feeling a fist of doom squeezing down on my heart. "I assume Digs is the maid of honor?"

Mom sighed, released Jess's hand, and lifted her cup of coffee. "We'll talk about that tomorrow, darling."

I opened my mouth to respond, but Danny patted me on the back. "I have to make a trip to the Home Depot, but then I thought maybe afterwards we could go get ice cream and pretend you're still that little girl who used to smile all the time." He winked at me and grinned. "You still a fan of mint chocolate chip?"

"Always." I smiled sadly. Such a nice man, such a tragic fate.

"Oooh!" Jess hopped up from the table and grabbed a pen and a pad of paper off the kitchen counter. "If you guys are going to Home Depot, then you can pick up the stuff for the bookshelf!"

Mom perked up. "Bookshelf?"

"Yes. EJ and I want to make you guys a bookshelf for your wedding gift."

Mom looked at me, her face slack with shock. "*You're* going to make a bookshelf?"

"What?" I said, bristling. "I have skills."

Jess adopted a mixed look of happiness and regret. "We would have liked for it to have been a surprise, but it's kind of a hard thing to hide, and there just isn't time for subterfuge."

"It's a great idea," Danny said. "You can use my shop,

if you'd like. I should have all the tools you need in there."

"And then some," Mom muttered, and they shared a smile.

Jess clapped her hands in excitement. "That's so great, Danny, thank you." She shot a friendly warning look at Mom. "Can we trust that you won't come into the shop to look before the wedding?"

"Of course," Mom said. "Thank you. That's just a wonderful thing for you"—she looked at me—"girls to do for us."

Jess scribbled on the pad, ripped the page off, and handed it to me. "Just get everything on that list and we can start work tonight."

Danny put one hand on my shoulder, and I turned to find him smiling at me with something like pride in his face. Then he kissed me on the cheek and said, "You're a good girl, EJ."

I turned my head and said under my breath, "That all depends on who you talk to."

Mom cleared her throat loudly and gave me a look of reproach. For a moment, I was confused, and then I remembered our conversation at the café about taking compliments gracefully.

"Right." I turned to Danny, smiling brightly. "Thank you, Danny. I'm glad you think so."

Mom cleared her throat again.

I shifted my eyes to meet hers. "Can I get you a lozenge?"

She raised her eyebrows at me. I inhaled deep

through my nose, out through my mouth, and turned to Danny again.

"Thank you, Danny. I am sugar and spice, and all things nice."

Another eruption from Mom.

I flashed my hands into the air in frustration. "What, Lilly?"

"Just say 'thank you,'" she said, her jaw tight. "Just 'thank you.' No qualifiers, no sarcastic side comments. Just 'thank you.' Is that so hard?"

I looked at Danny, who smiled at me with that sweet face, the same face that got me through so many hard times in my childhood, and I realized that Mom was right. I owed Danny so much, the least I could do was take his compliment with a little grace. But then I thought about what he'd actually said to me. That I was good. That I had value. And I could see in his face that he'd missed me, that he was proud of me despite how badly I'd screwed up, and suddenly my throat was tightening and my eyes were filling and I could barely choke out, "Thank you."

He grinned and squeezed my hand, discreetly grabbing a fresh napkin from the pile on the table and putting it by my plate so I could dab my wet eyes. Mom started up a conversation about bridesmaid dresses, and Jess chimed in, creating a happy distraction to help me pull myself back together.

We finished the meal in relative civility, and an hour later, Danny and I headed out for our day together.

The closest Home Depot was in Troutdale, about twenty minutes away, and Danny and I made easy chitchat all along the way, never getting within a country mile of any sticky subjects. So I was a little surprised when we were in the lumber section picking out the wood that would become their bookshelf, and he said, "You haven't said anything about my marrying your mother."

I turned to look at him, and he eyed me sideways, a half smile on his face.

"Go ahead," he said. "Say your piece. I know it's in there, just struggling to get out. I'd rather you say it here than at the wedding."

I let out a little laugh. "Oh, come on. You know I wouldn't ruin your wedding, Danny."

"It's hard to predict what you're going to do sometimes, EJ," he said. The smile was still on his face, but it had left his voice. "I just want you to say anything you have to say now rather than later."

I was a little stunned by this. Danny was easygoing, rarely this direct, so I knew it mattered that I was direct back.

"Okay," I said. "I'll admit, when I first heard that you two were getting married, I was a little worried about you. I mean, Mom's . . . Mom. And you're Danny. It's like hearing that Mother Teresa is going to marry Pol Pot. It's a little worrisome."

I laughed at my joke. Danny smiled politely.

"But," I went on, "she seems to have changed a lot. And I've never seen you so happy. So, I guess all I have to say is, congratulations. I really hope you'll be happy."

"Thank you," he said. "I think we will be." He pointed at some planks of wood to our left. "That oak's nice."

"Yeah," I said. "It is." I paused while he stepped closer to inspect the oak, the smile creases around his eyes deepening as he squinted at the wood.

"Danny, why aren't you mad at me?"

He glanced up at me, looking as surprised by what I'd said as I was. "What are you talking about?"

"Well, Mom's getting in her passive-aggressive shots, and Digs has told me he's pissed off. Luke won't look me in the eye, although that is obviously a more complicated situation. But you . . . you don't seem mad. At all."

He smiled. "Do you want me to be mad?"

"No," I said quickly. "No, as a matter of fact, I really appreciate that you're not. But you have every right to be. I took off without so much as a good-bye. I hurt your son. I'm driving the woman you're going to marry crazy. I mean, I've earned a good ass-kicking from you, but you're being so nice to me."

Danny thought about that for a second. "You're right. You do deserve a good ass-kicking. And I was upset with you for a while, EJ. Things were hard for a long time after you left. Your mother, Luke . . . they took a lot of looking after."

I lowered my head, staring down at my scuffed Keds, which looked all the more pathetic against the dull cement floor of the warehouse store.

"But," Danny went on, "look at it this way. If it had been Luke or David, and they had done exactly what you did, what do you think I'd do if they came back?"

"You'd forgive them," I said, without having to think about it. "Instantly. No questions asked."

He nodded. "Right."

"Yeah, but . . . they're your kids. I mean, it's different—"

"No," he said, running one hand over the top of my head the way he used to when I was little. "That's what I don't think you've ever understood, honey. It's not different at all." He smiled at me, then glanced back at the wood and unfolded the paper in his hands. "So, I think four of the one-by-tens oughta do it. You two can use the power saw to cut them down to size. Maybe we get five just in case. I can always find a use for anything left over."

A guy in an orange smock walked into the aisle, and Danny waved him over. Together they loaded all the wood onto the big platform cart and I just stood there, staring and useless. After the guy left, Danny walked over to me and put his hand on my arm.

"EJ? You ready?"

"Yeah," I said, pulling on a smile. "I just hope you don't think you're paying for any of that stuff."

He angled himself behind the cart and pushed it. "I need to get some Teflon tape for the fittings in the guest bathroom anyway, so we'll just ring it all up together. Make it easier on the poor cashier."

"Oh, hell, no," I said, keeping pace beside him. "You're not paying for your wedding gift. I'll get the tape."

He shook his head. "Stubborn as a goat, just like your mother."

"Why does everyone keep saying that?" I asked. "It's really mean, you know."

Danny laughed. We turned the corner, navigated our way to aisle seven, plumbing supplies. I darted into the aisle to grab the tape so Danny wouldn't have to bother navigating that big cart with all the wood into the aisle. I was just turning around to ask him if I had the right kind when he put his hand to his chest and crumpled to the ground.

If you don't give the heart what it wants, it'll keep asking for it. Until it stops.

—Lilly Lorraine as Trudy Mayer in *Heavens to Betty*,
ABC Afterschool Special, April 1976

Chapter Eleven

I don't remember there being any sound in the store; all I could hear was my own heartbeat as I knelt next to Danny, holding his hand, waiting for the ambulance. He kept insisting he was fine, but I could tell by the clammy feel of his hand and the lack of color in his face that he wasn't. While we waited, I kept glancing up at the aisle marker board, reading 7—PLUMBING SUPPLIES over and over again, feeling that if I did that enough, I'd be able to somehow turn back time and this would never, ever happen.

The paramedics came and strapped him to a gurney. I rode in the ambulance with him, his eyes keeping contact with mine over the oxygen mask, telling me that we were all overreacting, it was nothing, he was fine. I held his hand in the bumpy ride over, all the way into the emergency room. Doctors and nurses tended to him and then wheeled him away for tests, and I had to let him go. I stood in the hallway behind the red line they told me I couldn't cross, and watched until they turned the corner and disappeared.

I have no idea how long I stood there, staring. I had the impression of people rushing past me, but I was inside a little bubble that froze when Danny was wheeled out of my sight, and nothing could penetrate the bubble until I heard my mother's voice.

"Danny Greene," she was saying to the nurse at the admitting desk. "I'm here for Danny Greene."

I didn't rush over to her. I knew I should have, but I couldn't bring myself to leave the calm and safety of my bubble. I just turned and watched her from afar, my brain registering that she must have gotten the message I'd left on the house machine.

She really should get a cell phone, I thought from inside the bubble. *How can someone exist these days without a cell phone?*

Mom stood with her arms hugged around her waist, waiting for the nurse to give her information. Behind her, Jess gently rubbed her back between the shoulder blades. Mom leaned forward and talked to the nurse, and then Digs and Luke rushed in. Jess leaned close and spoke to them, and they must have wondered where I was at that moment, because they all looked up and started glancing around the ER.

I darted out of the bubble, past the red line, into the corridor, and leaned up against the wall, my breathing shallow and my heartbeat thready. If it wasn't so pathetic, it would have been laughable, how similar this panic was to another one I'd had so long ago.

I can't do this, I thought, just as I had back then. *I can't do this.*

"Ma'am?"

I looked up to see a tall nurse with blonde braids staring down at me, her eyes kind.

"You're in a restricted area. Are you here for treatment?"

"No," I said. "My . . . um . . . friend was brought in, but . . . there are other people here for him now. Better people. So I'm just gonna . . ."

I hitched my finger over my shoulder, stumbled as I stepped backward over the red line, and glanced around the ER. They were all gone, and as if on time delay, I heard the doctor's voice from earlier echoing in my head, telling me that they'd be moving him to a private room after the tests. Everyone had probably gone to the waiting room on that floor, which made sense. It made sense that they should be there when the tests came back. When the doctor came in and told them that they did everything they could, but—

"Ma'am?" the nurse behind me said. I glanced back at her, and she looked concerned. "Are you all right?"

"Yeah," I said, nodding. "I'm just gonna go sit over there and wait."

I turned on my heel and walked into the waiting room, where I sat for the next seven hours.

It's amazing how numb your butt can get in an ER waiting room. I spent my time re-forming my bubble, watching absently as person after sick person shifted and readjusted, trying to get feeling back in their asses as they waited for their names to be called. I got up and paced every now and again, but I found the bubble was stronger when I was still, so I mostly stayed still.

Then I saw Luke. He was walking down the hall, punching numbers into his cell phone, his face concerned. I swallowed hard, watching him.

Danny was dead. I knew it. Danny was dead and Luke was trying to find me to tell me and if I just stayed still, then he wouldn't see me and I could live for a little while longer in a world that still had Danny in it.

Then Luke stopped suddenly, hesitated, and glanced my way. My heart jumped around in my chest as he stalked toward me, and all I could think was, *No. No, no, no, no, no.*

"Eejie?" he said softly. "Where have you been?"

I blinked hard, regained my focus, and found the strength somewhere to push myself up from my seat. "Um. You know. Here."

His eyebrows knit and he looked around. "We've been calling your cell all afternoon."

"Oh. Yeah. I, uh, I had to turn it off." I motioned toward the wall with a picture of a cell phone with a big red X over it. "Hospital rules."

Luke glanced at the sign, then back at me. "You've been here? All afternoon? It's almost eight o'clock."

I nodded. I must have looked like hell, because there

was no trace of anger or tension in his eyes, only deep concern.

"Hey. You okay?"

I shook my head and my breath caught in my throat. "He's dead, isn't he?"

"Who? Dad?" Luke motioned vaguely over his shoulder and looked at me like I was nuts. "No. He's playing Scrabble with Lilly. He played q-o-p-h on a triple word score and Lilly sent me out to get a dictionary."

"Oh." A cold rush ran over my body and I started to shake. "Oh. Okay. Okay."

I blinked and tears jumped out of my eyes and bounced down my cheeks. A sob escaped me, and I clamped my hand over my mouth. Luke touched me gently on the arm.

"Eejie, he's fine. He has some kind of reflux, which caused the chest pain, and that made him weak for a minute. They're going to keep him tonight for observation to be on the safe side but tomorrow he's going home with a glorified bottle of Tums. He's fine."

"He slumped down." I sniffled and tried to control the rising wave of emotion in my chest, to limited results. "He just . . . he stopped."

"Hey." Luke put both hands on my shoulders. "Hey, it's okay. He's okay."

"He went down," I said, my voice high and squeaky and panicked. "He just stopped. And I couldn't hear anything and I couldn't do anything and—"

"Look at me." His voice was firm and he shook my

shoulders gently as he leaned his face into my line of vision. "He's fine, Eejie. He's gonna be just fine."

"I couldn't handle it, Luke. It was just like before. I was so useless."

I could see in his expression that he was making the same connections that I had between this and what had happened all those years ago.

"Eejie . . . ," he started, but I held my hand up to stop him. There was no way I could talk about that, not now.

"Don't. Please." I waved my hands in front of my face, trying to fight the tears, but all that came out was a pained whine. I knew there was no way I was getting out of there without breaking into full-on hysterics, and I didn't want to do that in front of Luke.

"Danny needs you," I choked out. "You should go."

"And do what?" he said. "Leave you here all by yourself until someone drags you off to the psych ward?"

"Sounds like a plan," I squeaked.

He ran a hand down my arm. "Eejie . . ."

"Please go." And right then, my weakened bubble finally burst. My chest heaved with crashing waves of sobs. Fear and shame and regret and loss ran through me, rattling me at my core, entwined with each other until I had no idea what was killing me more.

Luke pulled me into his arms and ran one hand over the back of my head and down my hair, his good intentions paving my road to hell as the hysteria got a thousand times worse. Someone in the background offered to get me a cup of water and Luke thanked her and sent her away, then kissed me on the top of the head and shushed me, but the tears at that point had become an unstoppable force of nature. After a few minutes, he lowered his mouth down next to my ear.

"Eejie," he said softly, "babe, you're spooking the natives."

I snorted out a half laugh, half sob, and then a fresh wave hit me. I pulled back from him and someone nearby stuffed a tissue into my hand and I swiped with futility at the steady stream of tears running down my face.

"I . . . can't . . . stop," I hiccuped. "I'm trying . . . I'm trying, I swear. I can't—I can't—I can't—"

Then Luke disappeared from the limited field of vision my swollen eyes allowed me. I felt his shoulder connect with my abdomen, and after a rough bounce, I was upside down over his shoulder, looking down at the floor as we headed toward the doors of the emergency room. We passed by the admitting desk and Luke deftly swiped a box of tissues off the counter and handed them behind his back to me.

"Thanks," he said to the nurse as we passed, then turned his head toward me. "Don't get snot on my jacket."

I glanced up at the nurse, a redhead in her forties who seemed nonplussed.

"I'll bring them back," I said lamely.

I swiped at my face with the tissues, my body bouncing to the rhythm of Luke's gait as we made our way through the automated doors out into the balmy Oregon night.

Luke paused at the edge of the sidewalk and I pivoted with him as he looked both ways.

"Okay," I said. "It worked. I've stopped crying." *Mostly.* "You can put me down, Luke."

Luke started across the street toward the parking area. "Not yet."

"Luke," I said through my teeth, giving a casual wave-and-smile to a guy in scrubs who was watching us with a suspicious eye, *"you can put me down now."*

"I know I can," he said, a smile in his voice, "I'm just not going to."

Just as I was about to lose consciousness, Luke set me down on the trunk of a car. I glanced behind me, saw the sign in front of the parking space that read 15-MINUTE PHARMACY PARKING ONLY, and looked down to see a dark blue sedan I didn't recognize.

"Luke," I said, "this isn't your car."

Luke slid up onto the trunk next to me. "Nope. It's not."

"This is temporary parking. They're gonna be back."

"We're not leaving until you're okay."

"Luke, I'm fine. Really." I forced a smile. "See?"

He chuckled. "You are a country mile from *fine*. If *fine* was sunshine, you'd be Seattle. If *fine* was sanity, you'd be Michael Jackson. If *fine* was—"

"I get it."

"—hair, you'd be—"

"I *get* it."

"—Howie Mandel."

I smacked him on the knee. "Are you saying I'm mentally unbalanced?"

"Are you saying you're not?" he shot back.

"No," I relented. "But it's still rude to point out. It's like seeing someone with a hook for a hand and saying, 'Hey, there, Hook Hand. How is it you haven't gouged your own eye out yet? Amazing.' "

"If you see someone with a *hook* for a hand, you should probably educate them on the wonders of modern prosthetics."

"Why? If they want to be all *hook*-handed, why can't they be hook-handed? It's their choice."

He stared at me for a long moment, his head shaking in wonder. "Why the hell would anyone want to have a hook for a hand when they don't have to? They've got fake hands that are practically better than real hands now."

"Really? They do? How do you know this? Are you a fake-hand specialist all of a sudden?" I grabbed his right hand and lifted it up for inspection. "Is this a fake?"

"I didn't tell you I was bionic?" He tightened his hand into a fist and we both stared at it in mock wonder. "Beats the hell out of a hook, I'll tell you that."

"Wow. Can I ask you a question?"

His eyebrows flickered up. "Shoot."

"When you move, do you get those awesome sound effects? Like *ch-ch-ch-ch-ch-chaaaa*."

Our eyes met. "Depends on the move." He lowered

his eyes, allowed a smile and a shrug. "Sometimes. When I moonwalk."

I laughed. "You moonwalk?"

"My talents are strange and varied." His smile widened, and my heart leaped. It was the old smile, the subtle, in-the-moment smile, the one that sprang from genuine feeling and not the forced need to be polite. Suddenly, he was Luke again, *my* Luke, and it was so good to see him that I felt tears springing to my eyes again and quickly looked away.

"Wow. I have really missed out on a lot," I said.

"Yeah," he said. "You really have."

I looked up again and the smile was gone. New Luke was back, and suddenly the reality of the Big Mess I'd Made thickened the air around us. I heard the sound of a throat clearing, and my attention was yanked from Luke to a woman with a pharmacy bag in one hand and car keys in the other.

"Hi," Luke said, waving his bionic hand.

"Um . . . ," the woman said.

"Luke," I scolded under my breath, then hopped off the car and looked at the lady. "Sorry."

"What?" Luke looked from me to the woman, then back at me. "This isn't your car?" He hopped off, buffed the place where his butt had been with his lower arm, then smiled at the woman. "Sorry. She's in treatment. Very severe psychological issues."

The woman glanced at me, then shrugged. "Okay."

She walked over to the driver's side, and I waited for Luke to catch up to me before I started back toward the

hospital. We walked in silence until we got to the eleva-
tors. He hit the up button and stepped back.

"He's in room 405," he said.

"What? You're not . . . ?" I motioned toward the el-
evators. Luke shook his head.

"Dictionary. I'll be back in a little while."

I nodded. "Okay."

He allowed one forced, stretched smile, then turned
on his heel, tucked his hands in his pockets, and ambled
down the hallway, his head lowered. I watched until he
was out of sight, then remembered the box of tissues in
my hand and wandered out to find the redheaded nurse.

I made my way up to room 405 to find that Mom and
Danny had put away their Scrabble game. Danny
laughed and held out his hand to me, making me come
in for a kiss on the cheek.

"This is my hero," he said, smiling. "Saved me from
a near-fatal case of indigestion."

"Danny." Mom's eyes were red-rimmed, but she
managed a small smile. Danny reached his other hand
out to squeeze hers.

"Do I need to bring the doctor back in here to tell
you all it was nothing?"

"Oh, yes!" Jess said quickly, then winked at me. "Dr.
Cummings was—hoo boy!" She fanned herself.

Digs rolled his eyes, motioned to Mom and Jess.
"These two practically fainted when he walked in. You
missed out, EJ."

"Yeah," I said, swallowing hard and forcing a smile.
"I guess I did."

A half hour later, visiting hours were over. Luke hadn't returned, but I don't think anyone was really surprised about that. Digs agreed to bring me and Jess to get Danny's car at the Home Depot, and after some hugs and kisses, we were on our way. Jess kept up the conversation in the front seat with Digs, while I sat in the back and stared out the window, feeling like I'd been hollowed out, left with nothing but a big whistling cavern inside. Although I had to admit, the whistling cavern beat the maelstrom I'd been through with Luke. At least I could breathe through the whistling cavern.

After we switched cars, Jess kept pretty quiet, not saying anything until we were most of the way back to the house. Even then, she was quiet about it, leaving room for me to pretend I didn't hear her.

"You okay?"

I paused for a moment, my eyes on the road and my mind in a million places. I didn't have the energy to lie, but more than that, I wanted to tell her. I wanted to confess, and she was the closest thing to a priest that I had handy, so I started talking.

"A few weeks before I left, Luke's doctor found a . . . thing at the base of his neck. I still don't know what it was, exactly, but the doctors were worried that it might be cancer, and it was close to the spine, and that wasn't good. He had to have surgery to take it out. He was great through it, of course, because he's Luke. He joked about chemotherapy, and how good he'd look bald, and never let it get him down. Or if he did, he sure as hell never let me see it."

I took a deep breath through my nose, exhaled through my mouth, and blinked hard until I could see the road clearly again.

"On the day he was going in to get the test results, I was supposed to meet him at the hospital, but I got there a little early. And as I sat in that waiting room, I just knew. I knew it was cancer, and I saw, in my head, the whole thing. How thin he would become. How much pain he'd be in. How long it would take and how hard it would be. And I knew he would die. I couldn't deal with it." I cleared my throat and forced myself to get out the next part, the real source of my powerful shame. "So I left the hospital and went home."

"Oh," Jess said, and whether the disappointment I heard in her voice was real or imagined, I couldn't tell.

"It turned out to be nothing," I went on. "Luke came home with this great news to find me freaked out and packing. And the thing was, he wasn't even mad. He just got me a glass of wine and sat me down and we talked all night. He said that he understood, and that if the tables were turned, he might have done the same thing. Which was a big fat lie, but . . ." I sighed. I'd never told anyone this story before, and I was bad at it. "And then he asked me to marry him."

"Wow," Jess breathed.

"Yeah. He'd had the ring for a month, but didn't want to be unfair to me, so he waited to ask me. I said yes, but . . ." I swiped at my face. "I mean, how could I love him and still marry him?"

"Well," Jess said, "that's what people do when they're in love."

"I would have screwed up so much bigger, given the chance," I said. "I would have made him miserable and legally bound to the source. Luke . . . God, he just deserves so much better than that, you know? So, I left the next night."

We fell into silence as I navigated the car into Danny's driveway. I stopped the car, then turned to Jess.

"This angeling thing," I said. "You say you can't fix people, because you can't interfere with free will or whatever. But what if someone were to come to you, to directly ask you to fix them? Could you do it then? If it was their will?"

I could feel Jess staring at me, and when I glanced her way, her expression was one of dubious concern.

"So," she said finally, "exactly how are you planning on getting Luke to come to me?"

"Not Luke," I said. "Me."

After a long silence, I felt her hand land on mine, and she squeezed my fingers.

"We'll go out for coffee in the morning," she said. "We should have caffeine for a project like this."

It's hard to just up and change who you are. Not just hard. Damn near impossible. The only other thing you can do is accept yourself for who you are, but what if who you are is unacceptable? What do you do then? You change, I guess. It's either that or throw yourself off the nearest bridge. I don't even know where my nearest bridge is, and if I did, I'd be too drunk to get there, anyway.

—Lilly Lorraine, in a letter to Danny Greene, undated

Chapter Twelve

"So, what kind of person do you want to be?" Jess angled her head down to meet the cappuccino she held in her hands. This time I'd opted to go inside Burgundy's, where we sat in a corner up front, obscured from outside view by the lace curtains in the window, and conveniently to the backs of anyone hopping in for a quick cup to go. The freshness of seeing the real Luke was still with me, and I wanted that feeling to go away before I chanced any interaction with CEO Luke.

"What do you mean?" I asked, picking at my cranberry scone. "Isn't there only one kind?"

She froze in mid sip and stared at me. "What are you talking about?"

"I mean, there're good people and bad people. I want to be a good person."

She lowered her mug. "You think that if the whole world was divided into two camps, good and bad, you'd be in the bad camp? With the baby killers and the puppy beaters?"

I pondered that for a second, then shrugged. "Hadn't thought of it that way. But I know I don't belong with the firefighter heroes and the people who go to Africa to save the tiny, tiny babies."

She snorted with angelic shock. "What could you possibly have done that was so bad?"

I blinked for a moment, wondering if she was being deliberately obtuse, then leaned forward and started ticking things off on my fingers, hoping I'd have enough for the job.

"I'm a loner. I don't like people. I'm not particularly nice to people. I've lived in this town more than any other place, and I don't remember anybody from here, and they don't remember me. I've had exactly three real friends in my entire life—Danny, Luke, and Digs—and I took off in the middle of the night without leaving so much as a note to let them know why I'd left, or even if I'd be back. I'm horrible to my mother, who, despite her mountainous flaws, is trying really hard to connect with me. I abandoned Luke when he needed me most. I completely flaked out on Danny when . . ." I lost my patience and dropped my hands. "Should I get maybe a chart?"

She held up her hands and started ticking off points of her own. "You came out to check on me when my car died."

"Only because that guy from Springfield—"

"Ut, ut! I am not done. Do I look done?"

I wasn't sure if that was rhetorical or not, so I simply broke off a chunk of scone and popped it into my mouth to illustrate my compliance. She continued.

"You helped me when my car died. You didn't call the cops when I kidnapped you. You took me with you to Colorado Springs, pretty much paying for everything along the way, then you drove me the rest of the way to Fletcher. You've been trying really hard with your mother, which is more than a lot of people would do in your case, and you do it not for yourself, but for Danny. That's selfless. Which is a good thing." She sat back and eyed me. "And I think you do like people. I think you just want to disappoint them before they have a chance to disappoint you. You're just a predisappointer, that's all. It makes you a little paranoid, but it doesn't make you a bad person."

"Doesn't make me a *good* person," I muttered.

"Nobody's all good or all bad. Everybody has positive qualities and faults and . . ." She leaned forward, a stunned look on her face. "You seriously don't know this? You *are* thirty years old, right?"

I leaned forward, too. "Don't talk down to me, angel. At least I don't think I'm a mythological creature."

She laughed, sat back, and ticked off another finger. "And you're funny."

"That's a goodness-neutral quality," I said.

She glanced down at her coffee. "Is it too early to put alcohol in this?"

"I drive people to drink," I said, ticking off another point for my side.

"Okay," she said brightly, smoothing the napkin on her lap. "Back to the original question. If you had a completely clean slate and weren't the horrible, terrible, spouting font of evil you seem to think you are, what kind of person would you want to be? Not good or bad; I want qualities."

I opened my mouth and she held up her hand, glancing at her watch. Ah, the sixty-seconds-to-think thing again. Fine. So I sat, and I thought, taking only a brief moment out to flash a quick *What are you gonna do?* smile to a woman who shot a quizzical glance at the angel timing my silence.

"Okay," Jess said, finally lowering her hand. "Go."

"I want to be kind," I said. "Forgiving. Thoughtful. Loyal. Honest. I'll keep funny, but I don't want to be a mean funny. You know. Not funny at the expense of others. I want to notice other people more. Be less self-absorbed. I want to be generous, but not just with money. I don't want to be goody-goody—I hate those people—but just good enough to squeeze into Heaven by a hair. I want to be the kind of person who doesn't give up. I want to be a person who has"—I met her eye for the first time since starting the monologue—"courage."

And then of course there was the part I didn't say: *I want to be a person who'd be worthy of a guy like Luke.*

She watched me for a long time, her eyes narrowing in thought. I knew what she was going to say. That it was impossible. That it was too much to expect. That even if she were a real angel with wings and a halo and a direct line to God and all of His divine power, even *then* she wouldn't be able to pull off a miracle of this magnitude. The truth hurts, but I'd never known Jess to lie, and so I felt pretty sure I knew what was coming.

So imagine my surprise when she leaned forward, smiled, and said, "We'll start with kindness."

Getting fixed by an angel is surprisingly like boot camp. You think you can handle it, and then you're in a brand-new kind of hell you could never have imagined if you didn't have to live it.

Like going shopping.

With your mother.

For bridesmaids' dresses.

"You must be kind to your mother through the whole trip," Jess had said when she sprung the news on me about how we were spending the day, "no matter what she says."

"But—"

"Ut!" She held up her hand. "The whole trip. No matter what. It's one thing to want to change; it's another thing entirely to do it. Plus, bonus, this also contributes to your being the kind of person who doesn't give up when things get hard." She grinned. "Two birds, one stone. How cool is that?"

I decided not to answer. The answer I had in my head was unkind.

"I'm so excited!" Mom said, clapping her hands together as we headed into the Bridal Boutique. That was the actual name of the store. The owner, an impossibly energetic woman named Patsy Frey, was a lot of things, but creative was not one of them. Patsy gasped and clapped when she saw us coming through the front door. I hoped to all things holy that the display was fake, because if it was genuine, it was kinda creepy.

Patsy bounded over to us immediately, giving Mom a big smiley hug and then holding her hand with a well-practiced look of sympathy.

"How's Danny?" she asked, patting my mother's hand.

Mom sighed. "He's fine. He came home from the hospital yesterday and rested, and now he's up and running around like it never happened."

Patsy rolled her eyes as if to say, *Men*, then patted Mom on the shoulder. "How frightening that must have been for you."

"It was," Mom said. "But it's a good thing. Now the doctors will be keeping a sharp eye on him, so I can rest easy knowing that if there ever is anything to worry about, it'll be caught early."

Patsy threw up her hands, celebrating Danny's severe indigestion.

"It's a blessing then!" Her focus shifted to me, her eyes forced into tiny slits by her massive smile. "You must be Lilly's daughter, Emmy. So nice to meet you. You are just as lovely as Lilly described you!"

I glanced at Jess. I was wearing ripped jeans and a faded, oversized orange T-shirt that read, *L'Eggo My Eggo*. I didn't have a lick of makeup on, and my hair was hoisted up into a ponytail I'd thrown on in the car ride over.

Jess raised her eyebrows. Mom cleared her throat. I smiled at Patsy.

"Thank you," I said.

Jess nodded. Mom beamed with pride and put her arm around Jess's shoulder.

"And this is Jess, my bridesmaid." She leaned closer to Patsy. "They're just friends," she said in an attempt at a discreet whisper. Jess and I exchanged kind, gracious smiles, hers saying, *See? It's not so hard*, and mine saying, *My kingdom for a spike I can throw myself on.*

"So," Patsy said, leading us to the big dressing room in the back, "I understand we're in the market for a bridesmaid dress and a maid of honor dress, is that right? Have you thought about colors?"

"Whatever the girls want," Mom said. "I'd just like them to be pretty and comfortable." She tossed me a smile, then moved over to a rack of dresses Patsy had set up for us and started riffling through them. "Although, I was thinking, maybe something in a pale yellow. Maybe peach. I don't know. Something classic, sleeveless. A little Jackie O–ish. And—oh!"

She pulled out a bright pink dress with big puffy sleeves and a massive skirt held aloft by enough tulle to make Little Bo Peep's little sheep-losing ticker give out right there on the spot. I opened my mouth to make a comment to that effect, but Jess put her hand on my arm, so instead, I forced a bright smile.

"So, who gets to try it on first?" I said. "Me or Jess?"

Pick Jess. Pick Jess. Pick Jess. But instead, Mom just shared a smile with Jess and deftly put it back. I shot a look at the angel, who wouldn't meet my eye.

So . . . this was a test. Okay. Fine. I mentally rolled up my sleeves, determined to pass with flying colors. I went to my mother's side and started going through dresses. I'd show them who could play well with others, damn it. I pulled out an ivory A-line and held it up to myself.

Mom's smile dropped. Patsy gasped in horror.

"I'm so sorry," she said. "How did that get in there?"

And she took it from me. I looked back and forth among the embarrassed faces.

"What? What did I do? I was trying." I looked at Jess. "I was really trying."

"I know," Jess said, "but you know it's bad taste to wear white to a wedding, right?"

I blinked. I didn't know. "Why?"

"Because that's the bride's color," Patsy said. "I'm so sorry, Lilly. I really don't know how that got in—"

"You're wearing white, Mom? Seriously? To your eighth wedding? Who do you think you're kidding?"

Annnnnnnnnnnd . . . silence. Mom stared at me, her eyes narrowing, and Jess put her head in her hand and murmured, "Oh, no." Patsy froze, the dress hanging in the air, and I don't think anyone breathed for a while.

Oh, hell, I thought. *Chip, meet block.*

"And—and—and—why shouldn't you wear white?" I sputtered, smiling wider than was either natural or necessary. "This is your day, and white is perfect. It goes so well with your skin tone—and—and—this is the first wedding for you and Danny."

Jess raised her head and looked hopefully at Mom, whose expression softened a touch. Patsy lowered the dress slowly, like a sniper not sure whether the negotiator would pull it off alone or not.

"So it's kind of like your first wedding," I went on. "Which makes white perfect for you and absolutely inappropriate for me." I snagged a light blue number off the rack without looking at it. "This will go well with my eyes, don't you think? I would really like to try this one on."

Mom's face lit up, Patsy breathed again and fluttered about, and I knelt to untie my sneakers. Jess stepped closer to hold the dress for me and whispered, "Nice save."

"Thanks." I stood up and looked at the dress I had chosen. It had this weird wrinkly see-through blue fabric over a layer of white satin with, hand to God, huge blue tulips imprinted on it. I looked up at Jess.

"Oh, God help me," I muttered.

Jess smiled and leaned in. "It could be worse," she said under her breath. "At least it doesn't have a bow on the butt."

The dresses we ended up with were actually okay. They were a dusky blue satin with spaghetti straps, A-lined and knee-length. No butt bows. No tulips. To distinguish me as maid of honor, I got a matching satin drape; I hadn't felt that girly since prom, and I kinda liked it.

Afterward, we went out for hot chocolate. Mom ordered whipped cream and drank half her mug, which impressed me quite a bit. We hurried home to make sure Danny was still alive—he was, and none too amused that we'd worried otherwise—and then we had a nice dinner together in which neither Mom nor I said anything too bad. By the time the day ended, with me, Jess, and Mom enjoying a glass of wine on the back deck, the whole New Me thing seemed . . . doable. For the first time in a long time, I felt hopeful. It was a nice sensation.

If fleeting.

Jess had excused herself to go to bed, and Mom and I were out on the deck by ourselves, nursing the last little bits of our wine. I leaned forward and stared out into the dusky Oregon horizon.

"You know, maybe you guys shouldn't get married this week," I said. "I mean, with Danny's health and all."

"The doctor says it should be fine," Mom said. "And Danny wants to do it. You know how he is when he gets his mind set."

"But getting married is stressful," I said. "There's all that stuff to do. And your trip to Italy . . . I mean, you're putting that off, right?"

"No, actually," she said. "Danny said he still wants to go."

I sat back and stared at her. "So? You tell him no."

"Why? The doctor said it would be fine. It was just—"

"How can it be fine? He collapsed, Mom. In plumbing supplies. He's under too much stress."

"Emmy, the doctor said it was just a stomach thing."

"Caused by stress," I said.

"He's on Prevacid. He's going to be fine."

"So what's the rush, then? Does the wedding *have* to be right now? Can't you put it off for a while?"

"What are you saying, Emmy?" Even in the fading light, I could see how tightly she was clutching her wineglass. "Are you saying that getting married to me is going to kill Danny?"

Fuck.

"No, Mom, I'm just—"

Her eyes narrowed. "I knew it."

"Knew what?"

"This is your way of getting even, isn't it?"

"What are you talking about?"

"You're throwing this at me because of what I said to you. You're trying to make me feel the way I made you feel. I can't believe you would do such a thing, Emmy, honestly."

I opened my mouth to speak, but it took a while for my brain to process what she'd just said to me.

"No," I said finally. "It's really not. And for the record, what I just said to you doesn't even come close to what you said to me."

"You just can't let it go, can you?" She stood up. "Well, I've had it. I'm not going to sit here and listen to you tell me that I'm a poison set to kill the man I love."

"That's not what I said." I shot up off my chair and scooted around in front of her, blocking her way to the house. "I wasn't even talking about you. I was talking about Danny. And I have every right to talk about him. Hell, he was the closest thing to a parent I'll ever have."

She rolled her eyes. "And here we go again. I ruined your life, I'm a horrible mother—"

"Christ!" I yelled, and she shut up. "For one minute in your life could the entire world possibly not revolve around you? Could you for once see far enough past your own fucking nose to give a good goddamn about the people around you?"

"Watch your language."

"No," I said. "You don't get to be my mother now, Lilly. You're lucky I'm even talking to you. And the very idea that you can stand there on your high horse about this after all the things you said to me would be laughable if it wasn't so sad."

She sighed. "Emmy, we've been over this. I said what I said because—"

"There's no reason good enough, Mom. That's what you don't seem to get. Even if all those things were true, even if I was a worthless human being and destined to ruin Luke's life, you weren't supposed to say it. And you know, that'd be fine. I could forgive it. You're human, and if anyone can understand doing something you can't take back, trust me, it's me. But you won't even admit it was wrong. You won't even say you're sorry."

She took a deep breath and her shoulders slumped inward. For the first time in my memory of her, she actually looked old. "I never said you were worthless."

"Who are we kidding, Mom? You've been saying that to me my whole life."

She gasped in shock. "I never, ever—"

"Every time you abandoned me for a man or a job or

a spa weekend with the girls, that's exactly what you said. You missed birthdays and graduations, and half the time you forgot how old I was. You wrote in your memoir that you regretted not aborting me—"

"Emmy, I wrote that thing over ten years ago. And I told you, I only felt that way before I had you. Once I had you I was glad I didn't do it. I've told you that."

"Whatever, Mom. You were the one person in the world who was supposed to give a shit about me, and you never did."

"That's not true," she said weakly. "I was troubled. I . . . I didn't understand what I was doing."

"Fine!" I said. "So say you're sorry."

She slowly raised her eyes to mine, then pursed her lips.

I shook my head. I should have known better than to even ask. I started toward the house, then turned back to look at her.

"You wanna know why I left the man I loved to live by myself in a trailer, Mom? Because when someone loves you, the things you do or don't do . . . they matter. But I didn't know how to matter to someone. I had no experience with it. All I knew was that I never, ever wanted to make him feel the way you made me feel. That's the brilliant legacy of being Lilly Lorraine's daughter. Maybe that'll make it into the next memoir."

Her eyes widened, and her face looked like she'd been slapped, and despite all my efforts to be the New Me, I was glad.

She took a step toward me. "Emmy . . ."

"For the last fucking time, it's EJ." I turned on my heel and headed into the kitchen. I washed and dried my wineglass and put it away, then stalked upstairs to bed without so much as a glance behind me.

"Danny," my mother said at breakfast the next morning, "would you please pass the syrup?"

Danny glanced at me, his eyebrows knitting a bit. The syrup was closer to me, and I was sitting right next to Mom, whereas he was across the table from her. Then his eyes closed in understanding, and he sighed.

"EJ, would you please pass the syrup to your mother?"

I reached for it, but then Mom held up her hand. "Forget it. I've changed my mind. I don't want it."

Jess put her fork down. "Oh, no."

"Oh, yes," I said.

She looked crestfallen. "What happened? Things were so nice yesterday. Why are you two not talking?"

"Oh, we're talking," I said, pouring generous heaps of syrup onto my pancakes, then settling the syrup dish just outside of Mom's reach. "Just apparently not to each other."

"I'm perfectly happy to talk to my daughter," Mom said, turning up the wattage on her smile. "How are you this morning, Emmy?"

I folded my arms and rested my elbows on the edge of the table. "Just fine, Shelley. And you?"

Her lips thinned into a tight line. "That's not funny."

I grinned. "It's actually funnier than you'd think. And since you insist on calling me by a name I don't like, I figured I'd do the same." I pulled my arms back and stabbed at my bacon. "Shelley."

She slammed her fork down and looked at Danny. "She said we should put off the wedding! She said that marrying me was going to kill you!"

I held up my hand. "Okay, now that is some seriously revisionist history—"

"She said that marrying me was too much stress, and that you were sick because of me!"

"Again, not what I said!"

"Enough!" Danny stood up and put both hands on the table. His large frame loomed over us, and I don't know about Mom, but I sure felt like a ten-year-old again.

"I am a man in his sixties who likes his cigars and his whiskey," he said. "It is a damned miracle I haven't had any health problems so far. If either of you thinks that one or the other of you is enough to send me over the edge, then you have no appreciation for the grand specimen of virility that stands before you. I don't mind if you fight. I think it's about damned time you both got all this out and dealt with. But don't use me as a bat to hit each other with. It's one thing I won't have."

Mom and I muttered vague words of apology at Danny, and he nodded.

"Okay, then." He looked at me. "Your mother and I are getting married tomorrow, and then we're going to Italy. If you can drum up the strength to keep your unpopular opinions to yourself for the next thirty-six hours, I'd appreciate it."

I nodded. Mom let out a little self-satisfied sigh, drawing Danny's attention to her.

"And *you*," he said. "If she says that's not what she meant, then take her word and let it go. Hell, if I got wound up over every stupid thing my boys have said to me, there wouldn't be time in the day for me to get any work done."

Mom's smirk faded and Danny sat down. We ate in silence for a moment, then Mom put her fork down and turned toward me.

"Em—," she started, then began again. "*EJ*, I had a lovely time shopping with you yesterday. You were pleasant and funny and you made great conversation."

I glanced up at her. Her eyes were lit like neon signs screaming, *Your turn!*

I dabbed my napkin at the corners of my mouth and angled myself toward her in my seat.

"Thank you," I said. "These pancakes are delicious. You are a wonderful cook."

"Thank you."

We stared at each other with forced smiles.

Danny winked at Jess.

"Eat up, sweetheart," he said. "To deal with these two, you're going to need your strength."

My father abandoned us before I was born. My mother was a shrill stage mother who spent most of my money, then died in a car wreck when I was sixteen. I'm not making a point of this because I want anyone to feel sorry for me. Quite the opposite. From these two, I learned the value of independence at a very young age. It may be an ugly truth, but it's a truth: Needing people is what creates all the misery in this world. At first, the people you love and need might seem to make you happy, but happiness is like milk—eventually, no matter what you do, it spoils. And spoiled milk is no good for anyone.

—from *Twinkie and Me:*
The Real-Life Confessions of Lilly Lorraine

Chapter Thirteen

"Okay," Jess said, angling her head a little to the side as she surveyed our handi-work. There was sawdust in her hair and on her cheek. Between that, the ponytails, and the happy look on her face, she looked about ten years old. "What do we think?"

"I don't know about you," I said, "but I think it's pretty cool."

And it was. We'd surveyed the study and come up with a design that was half reading table, half bookcase. The bookcase part was about two and a half feet tall, with two shelves back-to-back, facing outward—a mini his-and-hers bookcase, essentially. Then we'd bought a nice plank of oak, beveled the edges, sanded it to within an inch of its life, and attached it on top to create the table part. We'd drilled an opening at the back of the oak into which we were going to install a double goose-necked lamp after we stained the wood. It looked pretty neat, actually, and I regretted not taking Jess up on her original offer to build me one.

"Mmmmmm," she hummed. "I don't know. Something's missing."

I stared at it for a moment. "The stain. The lamp."

"No," she said. "Something personal. It's not personal enough."

"You can personalize a bookshelf?"

"Oh, sure. You paint it a certain color, or put designs on it. Sometimes a little stencil detail on the sides . . ." She tapped her foot for a minute. "There's some paint in the cabinet back there . . ."

"I thought we were going to stain it," I said, motioning toward the can in the corner. "That's what that's for, right?"

"Yeah," she said, unsure. "It's just . . . I don't know. It's missing something."

"Well, we've got to stain it. We can't paint oak. Danny will kill us both."

She hummed thoughtfully, tapping her index finger on her lips. "It's definitely missing something."

"I don't think so. It's measured to fit right between the two reading chairs in the study. That's personal."

"Mmmmm, maybe, but . . ." Jess paused, tapping her index finger on her chin. "I just really want it to be special, you know? People like your mom and Danny, they should have special things."

I watched her as she stared at the bookcase, her mind working so hard to get it just right and perfect. I'd been so wrapped up in my own crap that I'd barely noticed how much this seemed to matter to her.

"Thank you," I said quickly. "I mean, you're really going above and beyond, even for an angel."

"You're welcome," she said. "But, you know, I'm happy to do it. I like your family."

"They like you, too," I said, and was surprised to see tears in her eyes when she turned to me and said, "Thank you."

"I'm sorry," I said. "I said the wrong thing. What'd I say? I was trying to be appreciative, you know, to notice other people. How'd I screw it up?"

She laughed and swiped at her eyes. "By not knowing that sometimes, how people react isn't about you." She smiled brightly. "I'm okay. It's just been really nice, being here. It's been a long time since I've felt like part of—"

The door opened, cutting her off, and we both shouted, "Don't come in!" but Digs poked his head around the workshop door anyway.

"Don't worry," he said, stepping inside. "I'm used to women screaming when I walk into a room."

Jess laughed, a little too much, and I glanced at her. All signs of sadness had left her face, her freckled cheeks were slightly rosier than usual, and her eyes sparkled.

At Digs.

Oh, crap.

"Nice job," Digs said, kneeling down by the bookcase to take a closer look. He ran his hands along the smooth oak and gave us both approving glances as he stood up again. "Really nice job."

"Thank you," I said.

He took a step back and angled his head. "It's missing something, though."

"Exactly. See?" Jess gave me a gentle smack on the arm. "Even Digs sees it."

"What do you mean, 'even Digs'?" he said. "I'm sensitive. I have the soul of an artist."

I crossed my arms over my stomach. "What's it missing, then?"

Digs stepped closer, examined the shelf from one side and then the other. "That naked girl silhouette that's on all the mud flaps. You can put one on each side." He straightened up and grinned at us. "Lilly'll love it."

Jess giggled. She actually *giggled*, and at the same time seemed totally unaware that she was quite obviously smitten with Digs. It occurred to me that I should warn her; Digs was a lot of great things, but a safe bet was not one of them, and Jess seemed the settle-down-and-have-babies type. It was disaster waiting to happen.

"We had some permit issues on the worksite today," Digs said, "which means another afternoon of hemorrhaging cash on the worst investment of my young life. I figured the best thing to get my mind off all the money I'm losing is the company of a beautiful woman." He winked at Jess. "So what do you say?"

"Oh, brother," I muttered.

Jess giggled again.

Digs ignored me. "I thought maybe I'd finally take you to that thingy museum we were talking about."

"Oh," Jess said, glancing at me. "Okay. You wanna go to the thingy museum, EJ?"

I was opening my mouth to say, "Sure," when Digs subtly reached behind Jess and pinched my arm.

"Hey!" I said.

He widened his eyes and raised his eyebrows. *Don't cramp my style.*

I widened *my* eyes and raised *my* eyebrows. *Don't mess with my angel.*

He gave me an indignant look. *Who? Me? Never.*

I sighed. *Get out of line, I'll kick your ass.*

"Um . . . do you two want a moment alone to talk?" Jess asked.

"No," I said. "I'm gonna sit here with the bookshelf, try to figure out what's missing. You guys go ahead to the thingy museum. Although, Jess, you're probably gonna wanna . . ." I gestured toward the sawdust on her face, and she laughed.

"Oh, do I have . . . ?"

Digs touched her chin, angling her face so he could check her out, then lightly brushed the sawdust off with his fingers.

"Should I maybe go get cleaned up first?" she asked.

"No way," he said. "Sawdust adds to your charm."

She smiled, and that cinched it for me: The girl was

smitten. I made a mental note to have a talk with her as soon as she got back.

"So, what was the thingy museum again?" she asked as Digs put his hand on the small of her back and led her out. "Was it trains?"

"Now, what's the fun if I ruin the surprise?" Digs said, opening the door for her. "It's got the best thingy display you've ever seen, though, I'll tell you that."

"Stop saying 'thingy,'" I shouted after them. "It's starting to sound dirty and you're hurting my brain."

They laughed and slipped out, and I settled on the shop floor, staring at the bookshelf, trying to figure out what, if anything, was missing. I thought about Mom and Danny. They'd known each other forever, but had lived such different lives. They had been bonded by their childhood, and later, by me, but it occurred to me I knew next to nothing about their recent history. I also had to keep in mind that I was limited to my own artistic abilities, which were . . . well . . . limited. I started rummaging around in the boxes Danny kept from old projects, hoping some material might inspire me. Most of it was stuff like PVC piping and extra bricks from the patio, but then I opened a box full of a mix of colored glass and white ceramic tiles left over from the year he'd redone the upstairs bathroom. I'd helped him with that project, and had accidentally broken so many tiles that he'd snapped up a bunch more at the store, just in case they ran out before the bathroom was done. I smiled and sat down with the box, my fingers tracing lazily over the tiles as I remembered how much fun I used to have doing stuff like that with Danny and the boys. At the time, I'd always seen myself as helping out of obligation to this family that had taken me in for no other reason than just to be kind. Now I realized that I had enjoyed it, and had missed it while living in a big hunk of metal that afforded no real opportunities for home improvement. I grabbed one of the glass tiles, stained a light purple, and held it up to the light coming in from the window.

Then the idea hit me. It wasn't brilliant. As a matter of fact, it was a little dull from all the sentiment and overindulgence and it would probably turn out badly, anyway. But the more I thought about it, the more I knew in my gut how much they would both appreciate it. Especially Mom.

And it was the kind of thing a thoughtful person with courage would do. Plus, I realized with a sudden spark of enthusiasm, it would mean I wasn't giving up on this New Me idea, which was also important, because the thought of dragging my same old sorry ass back to that Airstream made it a little hard to breathe. I'd been avoiding all of this for so long, I wanted some kind of consolation prize for finally facing it all. My ass could still be sorry at the end of all this, but I needed it to be a *different* sorry ass.

Of course, those were selfish reasons, but jeez. Rome wasn't built in a day, right?

So, decision made, I pushed myself up from the floor, brushed off my jeans, and got started.

I was in the driveway, almost finished scouring all the stain and paint and skin off my hands using a deadly combination of Danny's tub o' Goop and the cold-water garden hose, when Luke's silver Prius pulled into the driveway. I hustled to the spout, shut off the hose, and tried to be discreet about tugging at the back of my cut-off shorts to make sure they weren't riding up in the back, as they had a tendency to do.

"Hey," I said, trying to smile.

"Hey." He stopped a few feet away from me. He was wearing a suit, which was acceptable, because it was Thursday, but I was encouraged to see that his hair was not as neatly combed as always. As a matter of fact, the ends were curling out a bit, the way they used to.

He looked good. He looked familiar, like Luke, and my arms ached with wanting to throw themselves around his neck and never let go.

But that would be inappropriate, so I stood frozen where I was.

"Are Dad and Lilly . . . ?" he asked, gesturing toward the house.

"Oh. Yeah. They're in the study, going over the plans for the party tomorrow. Mom keeps calling it a reception, but, I mean, it's really just us, right?"

He nodded, but his brows twitched together a bit, and then he opened his mouth and closed it again, and it occurred to me that maybe I'd assumed too much.

"I mean, just us and dates," I said quickly. "Not that I have a date, but Digs has a date. You know . . . Jess. And I don't know if you . . . actually . . ."

Oh God oh God he's dating he's in love with someone else and I have to watch them goggle at each other oh hell how do I turn and puke in the bushes without him noticing?

"Um, well, you know . . . ," he stammered, then finally met my eye. "Yeah. I have a date."

"Of course you do!" I said with far too much enthusiasm. "And you should. I mean, why shouldn't you, right? But is that going to be weird? I mean, for you? No, not for you, why would you care? For her. Well, unless she doesn't know who I am, which . . . why should she, because really, who am I, right? Nobody. Maybe I just shouldn't go. Would that be better, if I didn't go?"

He stared at me, and for a second I thought I saw amusement flash in his eyes, but decided it must have been my imagination. "Aren't you the maid of honor?"

"Oh. Yeah. Right." I flipped my hand up in the air and the Goop-and-water-soaked rag flew out of my grip and into the bushes behind me. I stared at it for a few seconds, then turned back to face Luke.

"I'll get that later."

"Okay," he said. "I'm just gonna go in and talk to them quickly about something."

"Yeah." *And I'm just gonna drive away and toss myself quickly off a bridge.* "Tell them I said hi!"

I waved, knowing I looked like a big doofus and yet unable to stop myself. It was quite possibly the most awkward and mortifying moment of my life; the fact that it was with Luke, the one person I'd always been totally comfortable with, only sharpened the spike driving that point home. I watched as he gave a small, confused wave back, then turned to go into the house. I willed him not to turn around and look back at me, but of course, he did.

"Claire's not . . ." He smiled and shook his head. "We're just friends. And you . . ." He paused for a long moment, as though warring with himself over whether he really wanted to say what he wanted to say. Finally, he stopped warring and met my eye. "You're not nobody, Eejie."

We stared at each other for a long time, and just as he seemed about to turn away, I blurted, "A woman walks into a bar with a pig under her arm!"

Luke hesitated for a minute, the look on his face a mix of surprise and suspicion that I had finally gone over the deep end, but then one side of his mouth turned up slightly, so I took the opening.

"Yeah," I said. "So, this woman walks into a bar with a pig under her arm, and she dumps it on the bar. The bartender looks at her, looks at the pig, and points to the sign above the bar: 'No Barnyard Animals.' "

Luke's smile tweaked up at one edge. "Because every bar needs that sign."

Judging by the way my heart soared at that moment, you would have thought he'd fallen to his knees with debilitating mirth.

"Exactly. So, the girl says, 'You have to help me. I thought my boyfriend was cheating on me, so I went to the gypsy and asked her to put a curse on the town that, as soon as anyone cheats, they'll turn into a pig. Then I went to his work, he wasn't there, but there was this pig in the supply closet with a naked girl. I need to know if it's my boyfriend. The only cure is to give the pig a boilermaker.'

"The bartender shrugs, makes the drink. The pig slams it down, and then, *poof*, he's a man again. The woman yells in outrage, slaps her boyfriend, and stalks out."

Luke's smile widened a bit. Pure joy shot through me that I was making him smile, and I kept going.

"So, a few seconds later, a guy runs out of the bathroom with a pig in his arms, yelling, 'Oh, my God! Oh, my God! The waitress and I were just doing it in the bathroom, and she turned into a pig!' The bartender, an old hand now, whips up a boilermaker, gives it to the pig. The pig drinks it down, and *poof*, she's a waitress again. The bartender stares at her for a long while, and says, 'This reminds me a lot of our wedding day, honey.'"

Silence. Luke's eyebrows knit for a second, and then, finally, he chuckled. It was the most gratifying thing I'd heard in weeks, and joy bounded through me like a wild pony.

"That's a really bad joke," he said.

"Yeah, I know." I scuffed a Ked against the pavement and shrugged. "I've always had a soft spot for the bad ones."

Luke's smile faded a bit, but his eyes stayed on mine. "I remember." He held the look for a moment longer, then gestured toward the house. "I should really—"

"Oh, yeah, of course." I let out an awkward half

laugh, half snort and tried to pretend it was a sneeze. It was very sad. "Go on in. I have to get cleaned up and everything. So . . . see ya later."

He nodded. "Yeah. Tomorrow, I guess."

"You bet." I gave a little wave, and a moment later he disappeared into the house. I went to the bush, retrieved the rag, and walked slowly through the garage back into the workshop, where I sat and stared at the bookshelf for an hour before darting back inside to get cleaned up.

Love? No one's good at love. It's impossible to be good at love. Unless you're French.

—Lilly Lorraine as Sami Blake in *Parlez-Vous Divorce?*
CBS made-for-television movie, aired March 1981

Chapter Fourteen

Claire.

Her name was *Claire*.

I sat back on my bed and closed my eyes, trying to picture what this Claire would look like, this just-friends Claire. She'd be beautiful, of course, but would she be a slutty, boobs-falling-out-of-the-dress kind of beautiful? Or a smart, sophisticated, touch-of-mascara-and-a-dash-of-lip-gloss beautiful? I clasped my hands together and prayed fervently for boobs. Luke didn't go for that type. Or, at least, Old Luke didn't. Who knew about New Luke?

I glanced at the clock on my bedroom wall; it was a little past eight. I'd begged out of dinner claiming a headache from the fumes of the paint and the stain. I had spent a long time, some three hours, inhaling all

198 Lani Diane Rich

that crap, but my head was fine. At least physically. Mentally, I was messier than an old lady's basement.

I threw my feet over the side of the bed and hopped up, then began to pace. I would be the only one there tomorrow without a date, and there was no way I'd be able to get one by the time we all got to the courthouse at three. Why hadn't I been more social in all the time I'd spent in Fletcher? If I had, if I'd just made some damn friends, I might be able to get out and track someone down and drag him to this thing. As it was, my only chance was sneaking out the window and hitting the Field, a sports bar on the outskirts of town. It was bound to be filled with guys, desperate guys, drunk guys. Pretty much my demographic at that point. I was fairly sure I'd be able to find one who could clean up good by tomorrow afternoon. I walked over to the window, threw it open, and cursed; I'd forgotten that the ash tree I used to climb down had gotten diseased, and Danny had taken it down. Damn it.

Now I'd have to wait until everyone else went to bed. Bonus, the later I went, the more desperate the pickin's. There's always a bright side.

There was a knock on the door, and I jumped and gasped like I'd been caught trying to hide a body. Jess poked her head in.

"You okay?" she asked, giving me a dubious look.

"Yeah," I said, putting my hand to my temple. "Just opening the window for some fresh air."

She smiled, glanced around her in the hallway, and then ducked in and closed the door behind her.

"Oh, my God!" she said in an excited shriek-whisper.

"What?" I asked, my heart jumping at the possibility that she had news that Claire had been hit by a car. Or no, hit by a car was too much. Come down with a plague, any plague, I didn't care which plague. Something that lasted at least twenty-four hours. And was preferably sexually transmitted.

"What you did!" She walked over to me, practically jumping up and down in excitement. "I snuck down to the shop after dinner and it was amazing! The colored glass squares look so beautiful under the light from the lamp! How did you get them to fit so perfectly? And the way they glow—they looked awesome, EJ!"

"Oh," I said, glancing behind me at the window. *It really wouldn't be that far to jump.* "I, um, used the hand-held router to carve out the squares in the wood. Cut out some aluminum to reflect the light back up from underneath. Danny taught me how to do stuff like that when I was younger."

Her eyes widened. "Really? Wow. You've got a talent for it. That's amazing work."

I couldn't help but smile a bit. "Yeah? I was a little worried, you know, because the oak was so nice. I didn't screw it up?"

"No! I love the way the squares are sort of randomly placed, not all in a straight line. It gives it such a fresh, funky feel. And so much of the surface is still the oak. They're really just accents, but it's gorgeous."

"You think?" I could feel my excitement start to

match hers. "See, I knew I'd never be able to line them up right, so I figured, just throw 'em on there and no one will be able to tell. And they're removable, so they can use them for coasters and then pop them out and clean them or whatever." I nibbled on my lip. "I made another set, too, but I don't know. I think maybe it'll be better to just go with the glass squares and forget the other stuff."

"Well, what's the other set?" she asked.

I waved a hand in the air. "It's nothing. I mean . . . just this stupid, sentimental . . ."

Her eyes widened. "You? Sentimental? Seriously?"

I shook my head. "You know what? Forget it. Let's just stick with the glass inserts."

She crossed her arms over her chest and rolled her eyes. "You don't really believe I'm gonna let you get away with that, do you? You're showing me what you did. Now."

I afforded one last glance back at the open window as she dragged me out of my room, but then realized it'd be easier for me to run out to the Field from the workshop, anyway. I could just scooch out through the garage, and no one would be the wiser. Jess led me through the house and down through the kitchen to the back entrance to the workshop.

"Oh, Emmy, are you feeling better?" Mom called from the sink as she hand-dried a glass. "We're going to break out Scrabble in a few minutes if you'd like to join us. I've pulled out the OED in case Danny decides to get fancy again."

"'Qopf' is a word!" Danny shouted from the den.

"Um," I said, but before I could come up with an excuse, Jess called out, "We'll be there in a few minutes!" and she yanked me through the door to the workshop. She turned her back to the bookcase and put her hands over her eyes. "Go ahead."

I stared at her. "Go ahead and what? Hide?"

"No!" She stamped one foot in excitement. "Put the other set in. The sentimental set. I want to see them in the bookcase."

"Look, I really think we should just keep the glass—"

"Oh, for crying out loud, EJ, just do it!"

I walked over to the shelf where I'd put the white ceramic tiles I'd painted earlier that day. My face flamed as I pulled them out and looked at them, and I wondered what the hell I'd been thinking when I mentioned them to Jess. Resigned, I did as instructed.

"You can look now," I said when I was done.

Jess pulled her hands down and turned. I cringed, waiting for her to make some kind of polite commentary, because I knew she wouldn't say out loud that they were cheesy and horrible, which they were. Looking at them at that moment, I couldn't believe I'd ever painted them in the first place. There was no polite commentary from Jess, however, just stark silence. I straightened up and looked at her as she stared, mouth agape, at the painted squares.

"I know," I said quickly. "I told you it was stupid. I used to do these cartoon drawings of people when I was a kid, and . . . I don't know. It seemed like a fun idea at the time, but—"

She held up her hand to silence me and walked

closer, switching on the gooseneck lamp and aiming it at the tabletop. Under the light, the cartoon images of six heads and shoulders smiled out at us. There was Danny, with his round face and confident smile. Digs, in a black T-shirt with a cigarette hanging out of his mouth. Mom, hair pulled back Audrey Hepburn–style, blue eyes smiling, green turtleneck poking out from behind a white apron.

"Oh, my God," Jess breathed.

I couldn't look at them for the embarrassment, so I kept my eyes on my feet. "It was just a thought. We don't have to give them this."

"Look at your mom!" Jess laughed. "You got her smile perfectly. And . . . wow! Look at Luke! With his hair all messy and the flannel shirt! I recognize the eyes, though, and the grin. That's what he used to look like?" She paused and had a sudden intake of breath, pointing to the tile right below Luke, an egghead painting of a blonde woman with spiky ponytails sneaking out from behind her ears. "Is that . . . ?"

"Yeah," I said. "You're in the wedding party. And Mom really likes you. I'm sorry, I hope that doesn't make you feel weird, but hell, you're already as much a part of the family as I am, and—"

She glanced up at me, face beaming. "I think it's wonderful."

I groaned. "It's stupid. Can we just put the glass inserts back and throw these away before anyone else sees them?"

"Over my dead body. These are . . ." She straightened up and stared at me. "Do you have any idea what these are?"

"Deathly sentimental schlock?"

She shook her head and pulled me over to stand next to her, forcing me to look at the table with the ceramic tiles inset. "These were painted by the person everyone else sees but you. The person you really are inside."

I shifted sideways and shot her a look. "Let's not get deep about this. They're just cartoons, Jess."

"No, they're not. They're so much more than that. Whenever your mother looks at that bookcase, she's going to know that you cared enough about her to shuck off that protective shell for a second and allow your heart to express itself. These paintings aren't just beautiful, EJ; they have meaning. You couldn't possibly give your mother a more perfect gift."

Jess gave me her determined look, and I knew I was sunk. I held up the glass squares I'd been holding in my hand. "Can we at least give her these, too? Just a slightly . . . I don't know . . . classier alternative?"

Jess sighed and patted me on the shoulder. "Sure. You bet."

"Okay." I switched off the gooseneck lamp and set the glass squares down, then turned to see Jess staring at me.

"What?"

She smiled. "Thank you."

"Thank *me*? For what?"

"For . . . I don't know." Her smile faded a bit. "I've been having a lot of fun here. It's been . . . nice."

Her eyes got that misty look, and I could see that she was coming close to whatever her Thing was, the place inside her where she wouldn't ever go. I took a breath, and decided that maybe she needed someone to push her the way she'd pushed me.

"Where's your family, Jess?" I asked.

Her face went blank for a moment, as though all expression had been just shocked right out of her, and then she shook her head and looked away. "I don't have one."

"Everybody has—"

"I don't." Her voice was harder than I'd ever heard it, and my face must have looked surprised, because she smiled and squeezed my hand. "I'm sorry. I just . . . I can't talk about that, so I'm going to ask you not to ask me about it, okay?"

"Are you sure?" I said. "You know, I didn't want to talk about any of my stuff, either, but I think it's really helped. And if you need me . . . I want to be there for you."

Holy shit, I thought. *The angel turned me into a real girl.*

"Thank you for asking, though. See? You're not as self-absorbed as you think you are." She smiled again, waving her hand in the air as though shooing the ghosts away. "Ready for Scrabble?"

I glanced behind me toward the door that led to the garage, which would lead outside to my truck and my chance of getting someone, anyone, to be my crutch for tomorrow's wedding.

"You know what?" I said, touching my jeans pockets to be sure I had my keys on me. "I have something I have to do. Rain check?"

"Okay. Do you want company?"

"No, thanks," I said. "It won't take long."

It was a little before nine when I showed up at Luke's door, but at least nine fifteen before I finally got the wherewithal to knock. When I finally did, the door opened almost immediately, and there was Luke. He was wearing his suit pants, but he'd lost the jacket and tie, and his top button was undone. My breath caught in my throat at the sight of him as he crossed his arms over his chest and leaned against the doorjamb.

"You knocked," he said. "I'd have bet cash money that you were gonna turn around and go back."

I blinked. "Wait. You knew I was out here that whole time?"

He motioned over my shoulder. I turned to see a curtain suddenly draw closed in the yellow house across the street.

"Mrs. Pope," Luke said. "She's a Neighborhood Watcher. She called my cell about ten minutes ago. I told her you weren't dangerous."

I rolled my eyes and turned back to him. "So you just let me stand here all that time?"

"Yep."

"Okay. Fine. Whatever. Look, I just came over to say something quickly, then I'll get out of your hair and Mrs. Pope can get back to her *Murder, She Wrote*

DVDs." I waited for him to laugh at the joke, but he didn't. My nerve started to slip, and I began to babble. "So, okay. What I came here to say is . . . important . . . to me, so . . . I'm just . . . I'm gonna say it."

There was a long pause. Luke motioned over his shoulder. "Are you gonna say it now or do I have time to make a sandwich?"

"About Claire," I said, forcing the words out. "I just want you to know, I'm totally okay with it."

He raised his eyes in surprise. "Really?"

"Yeah. I mean, I know . . . earlier today I acted a little weird, but that was just because . . . well. I'm a little weird."

"Right," he said.

"And earlier tonight, I was thinking about going out to the Field to find someone drunk and/or desperate enough to be my date tomorrow, but then I thought, I don't want to be that girl anymore, you know? That insecure, self-absorbed girl who never thinks she's good enough. That girl ruined my life, and I don't want her around anymore." I put my hand to my forehead. "Oh, hell. I'm not making any sense."

"No," he said. "I get it."

I lowered my hand and forced myself to meet his eye. "You do?"

He shrugged. "As much as I ever get what you say. Sure."

"Fair enough. Look, Luke, I want to be someone who can see you be happy and let that be about you. So I'm not going to have a date tomorrow, and that's okay.

I'll probably drink a lot, but you know, that's tradition at Mom's weddings anyway." I took a deep breath. "So, Claire. She makes you happy?"

His eyebrows knit for a second, then he laughed lightly and said, "She's making me really happy right now. Sure."

I blinked. "Okay. I don't know what that means, but it doesn't matter, because this moment is about you. I just . . . I want you to be happy, Luke."

His smile faded. "All right. Thanks."

We stood there, staring at each other, for far too long. The silence mounted between us, and the longer it went on, the harder it was to break. I reached out to touch his hand, but then had second thoughts and drew away just as he started to reach back. We both laughed uncomfortably, and then I stepped back and gave a short wave. He waved back, pushed off the doorjamb, and stood in the open doorway for a long moment before finally closing the door.

"*Ohgodohgodohgod,*" I breathed as I skittered down his driveway to my truck. I opened the driver's-side door and caught movement in the curtains of the yellow house out of the corner of my eye. I shut the door, walked around to face the yellow house, and shouted, "Thanks a lot, Mrs. Pope!"

The curtains fell closed again.

"Big tattletale," I muttered, then got in my truck and left.

"There's nothing more lovely than a wedding," says ex–child star Lilly Lorraine *(Twinkie from* Baby of the Family*). "They make me so happy, and hopeful. A wedding says there's more to be done, to be experienced. Happiness is still within reach on a wedding day."* It's not surprising Lilly's so fond of weddings; she's planning her fifth as of this writing.

—from "Repeat Offenders: Why Marriage and Hollywood Just Don't Mix," by Catherine Michaels, *People*, 18 April 1991

Chapter Fifteen

My mother's wedding day started with a semiformal pajama breakfast featuring Belgian waffles, fresh strawberries, scones, clotted cream, tea, and mimosas. After getting back from Luke's, I'd found a formal invitation laid out on my bed, along with the silk cherry pajamas she'd bought me that first day, a white silk robe, and a pair of silk Chinese slippers to match. When I came down to breakfast, which had been moved from the formal dining room to the back deck in a nod to the nice weather, everyone else was already there. It was wedding party only, though, so I was spared the torture of seeing Luke's lovely Claire in a jaunty negligee. Thank heaven for small favors.

Mom and Danny sat next to each other at the head of the round table, Mom in a pair of bright red oriental-style pajamas, and Danny wearing navy blue silk. Jess was on Mom's other side, wearing a yellow satin nightgown with a coordinated robe over it sporting yellow ducks, which looked really cute on her. Digs was next to Jess in a T-shirt and a pair of flannel lounge pants, and Luke was on his other side, wearing a green sweater and jeans. I raised an eyebrow at him.

"What, no Superman Underoos?" I asked as I pulled out the open seat between him and Danny. "I was so hoping to see them again."

Luke smiled. "You would have, if they still fit."

"Luke got a special dispensation because he has to drive for an hour immediately after this to pick up Claire," Mom said quickly, as though it was no big deal that she knew who Claire was, which of course was information that stopped me short. Not only did she know who Claire was, but she knew that she lived an hour away. So, Luke cared enough about this Claire to drive an hour to see her. He wanted to see this Claire so badly that he was willing to drive—

I took a deep breath. She made him happy. That was all that mattered. Today was about Mom and Danny and Luke and Claire. And everyone who wasn't me.

"You gonna sit down?" Digs asked, eyeing me from across the table. "Or should we just toss chunks of food into your open mouth?"

"Yeah," I said, plunking myself down in the seat. "Sorry. It's a little early for me."

As soon as I sat down, Mom stood up. A single cloisonné barrette held her hair back, and her skin was lovely without makeup. She was beautiful the way brides should be beautiful on their wedding day, lit by a natural glow from within. She raised her glass, and we all followed suit.

"I know it's not traditional for the bride to make a toast on her wedding day," she said, "but I don't care. It's not traditional to get married eight times, either."

I waited for everyone else to chuckle before I even smiled at that one. I planned to be on my best behavior all day, gracious and kind at all times, and not obsessing about Luke and Claire. I snuck a glance at Luke, and he caught me and raised an eyebrow. I reached for my mimosa and downed a large sip.

It was going to be a long day.

"I wanted to let you all know how much it means to me that you're all here today." Mom touched Danny's shoulder with her free hand, and he reached his up to rest on hers. The motions were so natural, you'd think they'd already been married for thirty years. "It's taken me a long time to learn how important family is, but now that I have, I'm so grateful to be able to count you all as mine." Her eyes got misty and she raised her glass a little higher. "That's all."

We all drank and she sat down. We passed around strawberries and cream and coffee. I tried to avoid contact with Luke as much as possible, and with the exception of the few times our elbows connected while passing and reaching, I managed to keep my focus on everyone else. Mostly Digs and Jess, who giggled and teased each other like a couple of kids. I realized at that moment that I'd been so obsessed with my own stuff the night before that I'd forgotten to warn Jess about Digs. I didn't want to ruin her fun today, so that left finding a spare moment to threaten Digs off, which I would be happy to do. The more distractions to keep my mind off of Luke and Claire, the better.

"Oh, look at the time," Mom said, glancing at her watch. "It's almost eleven. The party planners are going to be here to set up the deck."

"Set up the deck?" I said, glancing around. "For what?"

Mom smiled. "The reception."

"I thought that was just us," I said, motioning around the table. I glanced at Luke and cleared my throat. "I mean, mostly just us."

I caught a slight smile at the edge of Luke's mouth as I glanced back toward Mom, and wondered briefly if he was enjoying my discomfort. Which, I guess he had a right to, but still. It was kinda mean, especially after I went all the way to his house last night in an attempt at being a grown-up. The least he could do was give me a little credit.

"Oh, it is," Mom said, "for the wedding. The court-house will only accommodate so many. But you need a few more people to have a real reception."

"Oh," I said, trying to keep the panic out of my voice. It was one thing to be alone while Luke had Claire when I had a limited number in the witness pool; having to deal with that at a big party where I wallflowered it on the fringe was going to be torture. "Out of curiosity, about how many people are you expecting?"

"Oh, I don't know. It's still going to be pretty small." She glanced at Danny. "What was it, Danny? Fifty people at last count?" She shrugged and turned her attention to me. "Although I'm planning for seventy-five. People just don't RSVP the way they used to." She paused at my expression. "I'm sorry, Emmy. Is that going to be a problem?"

"Oh, no. Just curious." I reached for my mimosa glass, draining the last few drops.

Jess cleared her throat. "Well, as long as it's just us now, I was wondering . . . " She shot me a quick glance, then put one hand on Mom's shoulder. "Maybe we could give you your wedding gift now. I took some time to set it up in the study this morning, and I'm just so excited about it. Would that be okay?"

Mom's face lit up and she clapped like a little girl on her birthday. "Oh, really? I'd love to see it!"

"Um, you know, maybe not . . . now," I said, widening my eyes at Jess. "Maybe later. Or tomorrow. Or, you know, when do you get back from Italy?"

But Mom had already hopped up from her seat. The rest of the party followed suit, and I grabbed Jess by the elbow and yanked her back with me.

"What are you doing?" I asked in a harsh whisper.

"I'm sorry, EJ, I'm just so excited. And everyone's here, so they can see what you did."

"Yes," I hissed. "That's the problem."

"It'll be fine," she said, patting my hand. "You'll see."

I trailed behind as everyone went into the study. By the time I got there, Mom was just approaching the bookcase, and Danny was reaching down to switch on the gooseneck lamp.

"Oh, it's so . . ." Mom stopped in mid gasp and stepped closer. Slowly, she knelt down to the bookcase, her fingers reaching out toward the painted tiles, but not touching them, as though she were afraid they might disappear if she did. Danny put one hand on Mom's shoulder and leaned over to look. Digs and Luke shuffled closer as well. The room fell into silence.

The first person to look at me was Luke, his expression a strange mix of pride and stuff I couldn't read. Surprise, maybe. Sadness, definitely. I didn't know if he was reacting to the fact that I'd done this at all, or that I still saw him the way he used to be, but then the pride took over, and his smile widened. I smiled back, then Digs reached out and ruffled my hair like I was a ten-year-old.

"Damn," he said. "That's cool. You done good, kid."

"Thanks," I said, pushing his hand away and smoothing my hair.

Jess let out a little squeal of excitement. "Aren't they amazing? I almost died when she showed them to me last night."

"I, uh, I figured you could use them for coasters," I said. "You can take them out and wash them, and there's also a set of colored glass ones that will fit in, too. They're a lot prettier."

Mom stood up and turned to me, her eyes glistening with happy tears. She walked over to me, put her hands around my face, and kissed me on the forehead. It was an atypically maternal gesture for her to make, the kind of thing I'd wasted my entire childhood wishing for, and it cracked me a little. I blinked hard as she pulled away.

"It's really no big deal," I said quickly, but she shook her head and smiled.

"It's beautiful," she whispered, her voice breaking.

"No." The emotion welled up inside me, cracking me some more. "You should really put the glass tiles in. These are—"

"They're beautiful."

"I'm not an artist," I said. "I'm not talented. I'm not . . ." I sniffled. "The rest of the house is so sophisticated, and this is just kitsch."

"It's the most wonderful thing anyone has ever given me, and if you say one more word against it, I will cut off your alcohol for the rest of the day. Don't think for a moment I won't."

I burst out with a sharp laugh and followed it up with a sob. Hot tears spilled over my hand as I clamped it down across my mouth.

"Oh, dear," my mother said.

"I'm fine," I squeaked, then grabbed at the box of tissues on the desk. "This just happens sometimes."

"Would you like some water?" Jess motioned to both Luke and Digs. "Let's go get some water."

She hurried out, Digs and Luke close on her heels.

Danny reached for me, gave me a quick hug, and kissed me on the top of my head. "I'm gonna leave you girls alone for a little while."

He kissed Mom on the cheek and quietly left, shutting the door behind him. My mother leaned against the desk, shoulder to shoulder with me. "You okay, honey?"

"Yeah." I wiped at my face. "It's just . . . I thought you wouldn't like it. I was prepared for you to be polite. I wasn't prepared for you to actually, you know, like it."

"I see." The room went quiet for a long time, and we stared straight ahead, not looking at each other. "I wasn't very kind to you when you were growing up. I know that. I could explain it. I could tell you that I was afraid you wouldn't like me so I was determined to not like you first. Or that I was afraid that I'd screw it all up, so I decided to end the torture and just fulfill the prophecy. But none of that changes any of the things I've said and done. I know that. All I can tell you now is that . . ." She put her hand to her chest and her voice tightened with tears. "This is the most wonderfully precious gift that anyone in the world will ever give to me, and it means so much to me that you would take the time and effort to paint that . . . for me . . ." Her voice squeaked shut, and tears trailed down her cheeks.

"Oh, hell." I snatched a tissue off the box and handed it to her.

"We're a sad pair, aren't we?" she said.

"Like mother, like daughter," I said.

She pulled back and looked at me. "Do you think we're alike?"

"That's the rumor."

She smiled, then reached up and pushed my hair out of my eyes. "Well. I hope for my sake it's true."

"Why?" I said. "I'm cranky. I'm rude. I have no so-cial grace—"

"Stop it."

I turned to look at her, and her eyes were steely, and a little angry.

"You are my daughter, and I won't have you talk about yourself that way." She paused, took a deep breath, and looked down at the tissues in her hand. "Things were bad for a while, after you left. Really bad. Danny had to come down to LA. Sell the house for me. Drag me back up here like a child. I couldn't . . ." She shook her head. "Then one day, Danny sat me down and asked me, 'Is this the woman you want EJ to find when she comes back?' And it was that day that I decided I wanted to be a mother you'd be proud to have. Someone brave, and smart, and honest. Someone like you."

Our eyes met, and I felt the last of my defenses against her fall away. After all these years, the mother I'd always wished she could be was finally right in front of me, and for the first time in my memory, I loved her without reservation. My face contorted and my eyes overflowed like a damn fountain.

"Oh, damn it, Mom!" I wailed, grabbing more tis-sues. She put her arm around my shoulder and leaned her head against mine, and we both wept and laughed together for a while.

"Our eyes are going to be all puffy for the wedding pictures," she said once we could both talk again.

"Yeah," I laughed, dabbing at my face. "Sorry about that."

"It's fine." She pushed herself up off the desk. "I have some Preparation H upstairs."

I stared at her, hoping to God she was kidding. Judging by the expectant look on her face, she wasn't.

"No," I said. "I'm not putting butt cream on my face, Mom."

"Oh, please," she said, waving a hand in the air. "Don't be so prim. Beauty queens do it all the time."

She started for the door and I followed, tossing my handful of damp tissues into the garbage can as we went.

"Beauty queens super-glue their butt cheeks. I'm not taking advice from beauty queens."

"Honestly, Emmy," she said as we stepped out of the study, "that's twice you've used the word 'butt' in your last two sentences. Could you please find a better word?"

"Oh, I can think of *loads* of better words," I said, and just like that, we were us again. Only this time we were happy about it.

The wedding was scheduled for three p.m. at the county courthouse, about forty-five minutes from the house. Mom and Danny drove in Danny's Explorer while Digs drove me and Jess in his Dodge Dakota.

"So," I said as I poked my head between them from the back seat, "tell me about Claire."

Digs shot me a sideways look. "What?"

"I'm too wiped out to play coy, Digs," I said. "I know Luke has a date, I know her name is Claire, and I just need you to tell me about her so that I'm not going into this thing blind, okay?"

"Luke has a date?" Jess asked. "Why didn't you tell me?"

I smacked Digs on the shoulder. "Come on. Spill. Is she beautiful? She's beautiful, isn't she? And if she's important enough to bring to the wedding, they must have been seeing each other for a long time, right? Are they serious? Dish, Greene."

Digs was quiet for a long moment, and I was about to smack him again, when finally he said, "I don't think so."

"You don't think what?" I asked. "That they're serious? How do you know? Did he say something?"

"No, I don't think I'm gonna *tell* you anything," Digs said loudly over my babbling. "I think this is gonna be too much fun. Although I will say this—getting to watch you today just might make up for the six years you disappeared off the face. I think I'll give you a clean slate after today."

"Oh, my God," I said, slumping back in my seat. "It's that bad? What the hell is she, a supermodel? No, wait. Brain surgeon. She's a brain surgeon, isn't she?"

Digs chuckled, and Jess admonished him quietly, then turned in her seat to face me.

"I can't compete with a brain surgeon, Jess," I said.

Jess sighed and eyed me for a while, her face going serious.

"I don't know if you should be competing at all," she said as kindly as possible, but her point still chafed a bit.

You left him. You created the situation. You made this bed. You must lie in it.

"Right," I said and turned my face to stare out the window. I could see Jess watching me out of the corner of my eye, but after a minute or so, she settled back into her seat up front and we drove in silence the rest of the way.

When you can't take things back, sometimes it seems like the only thing left to do is drink them away. Unfortunately, that doesn't work, either.

—Lilly Lorraine, in a letter to Danny Greene, undated

Chapter Sixteen

Mom met us at the front door of the courthouse and shuffled Jess and me into the women's bathroom, which had a vanity area for the brides who didn't think a courthouse wedding precluded a full tour of hair and makeup.

"Are you sure you can have both a maid of honor and a bridesmaid for this thing?" I asked as Mom zipped me up. "I mean, don't they limit the pomp and circumstance in places like this?"

Mom laughed. "It is limited, honey. Danny has Luke and Digs standing up with him at the podium. Jess will walk down the aisle, then you, and then me, nice and quick, none of that stutter-walking. Then the judge will marry us, and we'll go back to the house and celebrate." She reached for the dry-cleaning bag on the hook.

"Now, Jess, will you help me get into this while Emmy does her makeup?"

Jess grinned. "You bet."

I sat down on the overstuffed vanity stool, opened the makeup bag Mom had coordinated for me, and fished through it for the foundation. "So, where's Claire going to be for all this?"

Jess cleared her throat, and Mom said, "Oh, I don't know. Sitting in the front row, I guess. Now be careful with this part," she instructed Jess, "the zipper always catches at this part of the bag, I don't know why."

I listened as they wrestled with the garment bag, trying to pay attention to my makeup and forget about Claire. Jess was right: I had no leg to stand on with this Claire thing. If Luke was happy, then that was what mattered. Still . . .

"So, what is she, some sort of brain—," I said as I twirled around on the stool, but stopped when I saw my mother.

The dress was amazing. It was ivory satin, sleeveless, with a Sabrina neckline and an accent band of blue-gray silk just below the breast line. The bodice hugged her waist, then flared out, stopping just below her knees. Mom twirled a bit from side to side, then looked at me nervously.

"It's an Eloise Curtis from the fifties. Is it too much? I know it's probably a bit young for me, but—"

"Oh, my God," I said, getting up from the vanity stool. "It's perfect. You look beautiful. Has Danny seen it yet? Because if he didn't have a heart attack the other day, he will when he sees you in this. Do we have a doctor standing by?"

"Just Claire," Jess said quietly, one side of her mouth twitching up. I narrowed my eyes and stuck my tongue out at her. Mom looked back and forth from me to Jess, a slightly confused smile on her face, and then she waved a hand in the air.

"Oh, stop. Claire's not a doctor, and Danny won't need one. He's seen me in it, and he did just fine." She glanced up at the clock on the wall and gasped. "Oh, we'd better finish up. I can't be late!"

"Right," I said, sitting back down at the vanity counter. "A girl only gets married for the last time once."

Mom opened her mouth, then took a moment as if to be sure the comment wasn't barbed. Finally, she smiled. "Why, thank you, Emmy. That's nice."

"What can I say?" I said as I searched through my makeup bag for a lipstick. "I'm a nice girl."

Jess led the way, walking slowly with her head held high to the organ music coming from a boom box next to the podium. I followed her, trying to concentrate on keeping my posture straight, but my concentration was shot as soon as I caught sight of the guys. First was Danny, all round and happy in his classic gray suit. His eyes were locked on my mother behind me, and they twinkled with happiness. I smiled and swallowed against the knot in my throat. Seeing Danny that happy was one of the most gratifying experiences I'd ever have. Next, my eyes drifted to Digs, the oldest son and best man, who had cleaned up quite nicely in a gray suit matching Danny's.

And then, standing behind Digs, was Luke. I was about halfway to the podium when my eyes met his and I held on to the gaze, knowing he would look away soon and the moment would be gone. Except he didn't look away, just kept his eyes on mine and we stared each other down in this weirdly affectionate game of chicken. Considering that I'd abandoned him the day after he'd asked me to marry him, you would think that a moment like this would have been horrifying for both of us, but it wasn't. We smiled at each other easily, comfortably, the way we used to. The closer I got to the podium, the wider I felt my smile grow, and the brighter his eyes got. I wasn't under any delusions that things were all better between us, but I was really proud of both of us for letting the day be about Danny and Mom, and for being able to forget all our crap long enough to give them their happy day.

I was just pondering how grown-up both Luke and I had become when my big toe hit a chair and I yelled out, "Shit!" and grabbed my toe. Mom came up behind me and grabbed my askew elbow as I said, "Sorry, sorry," and then met the eye of the woman sitting in the chair.

"Claire!" I squealed when I saw her. "Oh, my God!"

I bent over and hugged with great affection the old lady with the regrettable black wig who had been Danny's secretary since roughly the beginning of time. I flashed back to all the times she used to sneak us hard candies from her desk drawer when we were kids, and then remembered her retirement party, which had been about a year before I'd run off from Fletcher. "I can't believe it's you!"

"Yes, honey," Mom said from my other side, tugging at my arm. "I told you she'd be here."

"Oh! Right!" I stood up and looked to the judge. "Sorry." Then to my mother. "Sorry."

Mom smiled and took her place next to Danny. The judge started in on his "we are all gathered here" stuff, and I stared down into my simple two-orchid bouquet, sure my cheeks had to be flaming. From behind me, I felt Jess give my upper arm a light pinch, and I shot her a smile and an *I'm such a doofus* eye roll. Then, when I turned back around, my eyes landed on Luke, who was trying to hide his laughter in a cough as he stood behind Digs. His eyes met mine and we smiled amiably at each other for a few moments, and then something shifted between us. Our smiles faded. It wasn't that we were angry, at least I wasn't and I didn't think he was, either. It was more like we had both just banged up against the thick glass wall that remained between us. The judge talked and I don't know that either of us heard a word he said, our attention was so locked on each other. After a minute or so, I took in a deep breath and forced a bright smile. This was my mother's day, and I wasn't going to ruin it by brooding over things I'd broken. Luke smiled, too, and we both looked away just in time to see Mom and Danny be officially pronounced husband and wife.

My mother was a big fat liar with her "oh, maybe seventy-five people" thing. There were easily a hundred and fifty revelers at the reception, spilling off from the huge back deck to the lawn beyond, crowding the parquet dance floor that had been set up next to the band. Two open bars flanked the deck, and Japanese lanterns bathed the backyard in spheres of colored light. Waiters in tuxes wandered the premises bearing trays of hors d'oeuvres and champagne, and by the time the sky turned dusky, I was feeling great enough to head over to the fringe table where Luke was keeping company with Claire. His hot date.

I sat down next to her, kissing her cheek as I did. Claire had always been kind to me when I was younger, and I was ashamed that I had forgotten her enough to make all the wrong connections when Luke had mentioned her.

"Luke," I said, "Mom and Danny are going to do their dance soon, and she wanted to talk to you about something."

"Oh. Okay." He turned to Claire. "Can I get you anything while I'm up? Another Shirley Temple?"

Claire shook her head. "Don't you worry about me. Your girl and I will just sit and chat for a bit."

I opened my mouth to correct her; it hadn't occurred to me that she wouldn't know everything that had happened over the past few years, but I guessed no one had seen fit to bother an old lady with those kinds of details.

"Great," Luke said, giving me a brief nod. *Just play along. It's easier.* "I'll be back in a few minutes."

I smiled, then turned to Claire. "It's so good to see you again."

"Oh, you, too, dear." She reached over and patted my hand. "So tell me, what have you been doing with yourself? I don't think I've seen you since my retirement party."

"Well," I said slowly, playing absently with the stem of my champagne glass, "I've been, uh, traveling. You know. Seeing the world, pissing my twenties away . . ."

She chuckled and nodded toward the edge of the dance floor, where Luke stood talking with Mom. "I would ask you when you're going to make an honest man of our boy there, but I don't like to pry."

She winked and we laughed together. I wondered if there was a way to answer that question while being both polite and truthful. Finally I took a deep breath and said, "If I ever get the chance, you can bet I'll take it."

"Mom?"

I turned and saw a heavyset balding man standing on my other side.

"Oh, Bobby," Claire said. "Is it seven thirty already?"

Bobby. I tried to withhold my shock. The last time I'd seen Claire's son, he'd had hair.

"Hey, Bobby," I said, getting up to give him access to his mother. "How are you?"

He gave me a polite smile as he reached to help Claire up from her seat. "Great. And you?"

He had no idea who I was. Just as well. "Great,

thanks. Claire, do you want me to get Luke so you can say good-bye?"

"Oh, no," she said. "I'm getting tired, and Bobby's in a bit of a rush tonight. Would you say good-bye to everyone for me? And give all my best wishes to Danny and your mom?"

"You bet." I gave her a brief kiss good-bye and watched her go until she and Bobby were out of sight. Suddenly someone touched my elbow, and I turned to see Jess.

"It's about time I found you!" She pulled me by the elbow toward the dance floor. "They're going to start the dance. First it's going to be your mom and Danny, then best man and maid of honor, and then me and Luke."

"Oh," I said, hurrying down with her. "Okay."

We got to the edge of the dance floor just as the band was announcing Mom and Danny. They started in on their song—"You Belong to Me"—and Mom and Danny floated out to the floor amid the cheers of the crowd. Digs settled in next to me and pointed to a petite woman with a headset standing by the corner of the dance floor, next to the band platform.

"See that woman?" he said in my ear. "Her name is Harriet. When she gives us the signal, we need to hot-foot it onto the floor, or her head will explode. Literally explode. That's what she told me."

"Oooh, that might be fun to see," I said, but the woman gave Digs a commanding wave, and he dutifully led me out to the dance floor. We claimed our spot to the left of Mom and Danny, and Luke and Jess moved into the space on their other side.

"Hey," I said to Digs, "I'm glad I got you for a minute. We need to talk about something."

"Oh, yeah?" he asked, his eyes drifting over the dance floor behind me. "What's that?"

"What are your intentions with my angel?"

His eyes shot back to me. "What?"

"Look, Digs, I love you, you know that, but you're about the worst bet any girl can make. And Jess . . . she's . . . I don't know. I think she's a little fragile. I just don't want you doing anything stupid."

His smile faded. "Like what? Like agreeing to marry her and then disappearing in the middle of the night?"

I stiffened in his arms. "Boy, that clean slate sure lasted a long time."

He sighed, shook his head, and smiled. "You're right. Do-over?"

I rolled my eyes. "Fine. Do-over."

"Okay." He twirled me out and pulled me back. "Here's the thing. I like Jess. And I think she likes me. She's leaving for New Jersey on Monday, anyway. How much damage could I possibly do?"

"I don't know. I've just seen what happens to girls when they get around you, Digs. They get all smitten and stupid, and then you break their hearts. It's not pretty, and I don't want it to happen to Jess."

"Look," he said, "I'll handle her with care, okay? But . . ." A slow smile drifted over his face and I felt my mouth drop open as understanding washed over me.

"Oh, my God," I said. "She got to you. Did she get to you?"

He rolled his eyes, and then Harriet of the Exploding Head waved her hand again. Before I could ask what was going on, Danny came over and tapped Digs on the shoulder.

"Time to cut in," he said. "You go grab Jess before Harriet comes after you with an AK-47."

Digs kissed me on the cheek. "Duty calls."

"I know where you live!" I called out after him, then settled into Danny's arms. "Wow. I didn't know we'd be switching partners. How long is this song, anyway?"

"They're doing a special extended version just for this," Danny said. "Harriet thought it would be nice to have us all dance together. New family bonding. Something like that."

"It is nice," I said. I pushed up on my tiptoes and kissed him on the cheek. "Congratulations, Mr. Married Guy."

"Thank you," he said, curling my hand into his chest and giving my fingers a quick peck. "It's a wonderful day. I have a beautiful new wife and a lovely new daughter."

"Well, you've always been the closest thing I ever had to a dad. It's about time we made it official, I guess."

Danny winked over my shoulder, and I glanced to find him sharing a look with Mom, who smiled at me. I gave a little wave.

"So," Danny said, and I turned my attention back to

him. "Your mom and I are getting on that plane tomorrow, and you'll be going to Colorado Springs soon, I guess?"

I nodded. "First thing Monday morning."

He cleared his throat. "You'll keep in touch this time. That's not a request."

"I'll keep in touch." And just like that, my eyes filled with tears. "Damn it. I don't know what's wrong with me. I've been a big crybaby all day."

He reached up and swiped away a tear that had escaped down my cheek. "It's okay, EJ."

"No." I rolled my eyes to distribute the tears, and then smiled at him. "It's not okay. I know that what I did was crap, and I'm so sorry about that. You've never been anything but wonderful to me, and I didn't mean to—"

"Nonsense," he interrupted, squeezing my hand. "That's the past. I'm not mad at you. But your mother's happiness is my responsibility now, and neither one of us is going to be happy if you just up and disappear again. So I'm telling you right now. You can go wherever you want, but you will come back."

I sniffled and did my best to smile. "I'll come back."

"You'll call. And you'll write."

Unable to speak, I nodded. Danny kissed me on the cheek and whispered in my ear, "You're a good girl, EJ. I'm proud of you."

"Oh, jeez, Danny," I said, sniffling. Then, suddenly, Luke was there, tapping Danny on the shoulder at the command of the wedding planner. Danny moved on to

Jess, and Luke put his arm around my waist and took my right hand in his. I was overwhelmed with a thousand whirling emotions I couldn't track, and having Luke's arm around my waist was just about the cruelest trick Fate could have possibly played on me at that moment. I knew I'd break down if I looked at him, or tried to speak, so I simply stared at his tie, willing my wild emotions to tamp themselves back down.

"Hey," he said after a moment, "you okay?"

"Yeah," I said. "I'm fine."

"Then look at me."

Oh, God. "I can't."

"Then you're not fine."

"Luke . . ."

"Look at me."

"No."

"Am I going to have to throw you over my shoulder again?"

"Damn it, Luke."

"I'll do it. Don't think I won't."

I knew he would. So I pulled together every bit of strength I had left and forced myself to meet his eye. He stared down at me, and I up at him, and it was like everything else in the world stopped. Our dancing slowed until we ceased movement altogether. His arm tightened around my waist, and our clasped hands curled in between us as the strength to hold them out seeped away from us. My heart began to ache on every beat, and his face looked as pained and conflicted as I felt.

A fast rock beat slammed into us, making my body

jolt with the shock of it, and people flooded onto the dance floor. Keeping his hand tight on mine, Luke led me away, down the slope of the backyard, out to the dirt path that circled the lake. We were quiet as we walked, hand in hand, until the cover of the trees obscured the sight if not the sound of the party. A minute later, he stopped and turned to me. It was too dark for me to read his expression, but I knew exactly what he was feeling, because I was right there with him. Being together was so natural for us that it was a constant fight to keep ourselves separated, yet the very idea of opening that door again, of battering down the glass wall between us, was terrifying on so many levels that we just stood there, fingers entwined, barely breathing.

It felt like an eternity that we were frozen there, unwilling to move closer and unable to walk away. Then Luke slowly raised his free hand and touched my face. His breathing was rough and I knew he was struggling. I didn't know what to do to make it easier. Kiss him? Run away? Both seemed equally selfish, so I went with the theme, chose the one I wanted more, and shifted closer to him. His fingers extended into my hair and I tilted my face upward. He released the hand he'd been holding and reached up until both of his hands were cradling my face. I kept my arms at my sides, afraid that the feel of him under my fingers would send me over the edge, but I moved in again until I was as close as I could get without our bodies touching. I could feel his breath, a sweet mix of champagne and heat, on my neck as he lowered his face closer to mine, and then, finally, kissed me. The feel of him, the taste of him, overwhelmed my senses and I grasped for him, my hands sliding up his chest to his face, his hair, my fingertips drinking in as much of him as they could while the glorious moment lasted.

Then, just as suddenly as it had begun, it stopped. Luke pulled back, leaving my lips cold. I stumbled back a bit as he released me, feeling dizzy and trying to regain my balance.

"I'm sorry. I shouldn't have . . ." He ran his hand through his hair and sighed heavily. "This is my mistake, okay? I just—"

"I love you." The words were out before I could stop them, and I was so weakened from the emotional battering I'd been withstanding all day that I had no defenses left, which was okay, as they were useless, rotten little bastards anyway. I looked up and waited until he allowed his eyes to meet mine before I spoke again, and when that happened, I took a deep breath and plowed forward with every last bit of courage I had left.

"I love you, Luke. There has never been a moment in my life when I didn't love you. Even when I left. Even while I was gone."

"Eejie . . ." His voice was rough and shaken, and if I had any pity in me, I would have stopped there, but I was on a speeding train, and there was no stopping it. I grabbed for his hand. "I left because I was stupid and scared and weak. I would give anything, Luke, *anything*, if I could just go back and do it differently. I need you to know that. I'm so sorry."

The silence was long and unbearable. His hand was

limp in mine, and finally, I released it. Even in the dark, I could see how stiff his stance was, as if he were bracing himself against a wind that threatened to knock him down. My head became fuzzy from the intensity of the emotions running through my system, and I ran out of steam to keep talking. Instead, I simply stared at the ground, and some minutes had passed before my brain registered that Luke had left me there, alone on the dirt path in the woods.

It's at this point in my story that I must confess, I have no idea how to keep a man. I know how to get one; I'm very good at that. But keeping one is still a bit of a mystery.

—from *Twinkie and Me:*
The Real-Life Confessions of Lilly Lorraine

Chapter Seventeen

"Where's Luke?" I asked when I found my mother holding court with a bunch of women from the ladies' auxiliary.

"Oh, hi, honey," she said, looking surprised. "I don't know. I think I saw him go into the house. Are you okay?"

"No," I said, then turned and ran up the deck into the house. People were milling about inside, and one or two might have said my name, but I ignored them, rushing through the crowd, looking over their heads for the familiar messy mop I knew and loved. I cut through the house to the foyer by the front door, where I found Luke with one hand on the door handle, giving a large woman in an orange caftan directions to the bathroom. The woman left and I stepped out into the foyer. Luke saw me, closed his eyes, and cursed under his breath.

"Go back to the party, Eejie."

"No." I held his eye and stepped closer in defiance.

He shook his head and shut the door. "See, it's crazy, because I can hear myself saying the words, and yet, it's almost like you don't understand them."

"I'm being a pain in the ass, I know it, but Luke, there isn't time for me to be polite. I'm leaving on Monday."

His eyes widened, and then he let out an angry huff. "Of course. Of course you are."

"Well . . . what did you think? That I was going to just live here? Forever? With my *mother*?"

He ran his hand over his face. "I didn't think about it. I try not to think about you, Eejie, as much as humanly possible. Makes life easier."

"I know I screwed up. I threw everything away, and even treating me like this, you're giving me better than I've earned, but I have to tell you how sorry I am, and that I still love you."

"Why? Why do you have to tell me that? Do you know what that does for me? Nothing. It's all about you and relieving your conscience or . . . whatever. Well, I'm not here to make you feel better about it, Eejie. I don't owe you that."

"Fine. You owe me nothing. Big deal. What I deserve, what you owe me . . . that's all just about being polite. Screw polite. I'm too tired and desperate to be polite. This may not be fair, but it's the truth, and you have to face it. I love you. I never stopped. You need to know that."

He went quiet, kept his eyes on the floor for a while,

then finally shot me a look. "Fine. Now I know. What do you expect me to say?"

"I don't know," I said, giving the anger bubbling within me full rein whether I could justify it or not. "Maybe you could recognize how hard it is for me to say this to you. Maybe you could . . . I don't know. Smile. Remove the pole from up your ass. A small gesture, sure, but it'd be a start."

He advanced on me, his frame towering angrily over me as his words scratched past me. "So, tell me how this works, Eejie. You come back after six years, tell me you still love me, and we're supposed to . . . what? Pick up where we left off?"

I crossed my arms over my chest and didn't step back, keeping my face in his. "Did I say that? No. But, hell, Luke, I don't know. I don't know how to do this, but I can't leave without letting you know that one word from you would keep me here."

He nodded, tucked his hands in his pockets, and stared at the floor again. I wondered if it had some kind of hidden cheat sheet for this kind of thing, but when I glanced down, it was just a floor.

"I'm sorry, Eejie," he said finally. "I don't know how I'm supposed to respond to all this."

I took a deep breath. I was already in for the penny, might as well go for the pound. "Maybe admit you still love me, too?"

He raised his head and I could tell by the look on his face that I had said the exact, perfectly wrong thing.

"Admit that I love you?" he spat, his eyes lit with

fury. "Love isn't the issue. Do I love you?" He threw his hands up. "Hell. Probably. I'm probably that stupid, sure. But I'm not stupid enough to jump back into this with you. It took me two years to recover from you leaving like that. Two years, Eejie. I was a fucking wreck. And now I'm on my feet and I'm fine—"

I snorted. I couldn't help myself. And since I'd already said the exact, perfectly wrong thing, I figured, what did I have to lose? Nothing that wasn't already out of my reach, anyway.

He stared at me, eyes narrowed, thoroughly pissed. "What did you say?"

"I said, 'Snort.' You are not fine. You are not within shouting distance of fine. If fine were water, you'd be the Sahara. If fine were sensitivity, you'd be Simon Cowell. If fine were—"

"Get to your point, Eejie."

"My point?" I held up my fingers and started ticking. "You take business meetings on Sunday mornings. You wear suits. All the time. Not just for special occasions."

"It's been six years, Eejie. Enough time for at least one of us to grow up."

I raised my hands up higher and continued ticking off my fingers. "You comb your hair down. Your date for your father's wedding was an octogenarian. You never laugh. Hell, it's like pulling teeth just to get you to smile. When was the last time you cracked a joke, Luke?"

His mouth tightened into a thin line. "Are you seriously suggesting I tell you a joke right now?"

"Not me, necessarily, no. But, someone, yeah. Sometime. I mean, I assume you didn't have a humorectomy while I was gone. So where the hell are you, Luke? You used to be fun, you used to smile, now you're all suits and meetings and Oh-I've-got-a-date-named-Claire—"

"Hey, you jumped to that conclusion all on your own," he said. "I didn't lie about anything."

"But you didn't rush to clear it up, did you? You liked that it bugged me."

"Yeah. Right," he said, the sarcasm thick in his voice. "Because everything in my world revolves around you? Not anymore."

I crossed my arms over my chest. "Great. So if you're so fine, prove it. Tell me a joke."

He stared at me for a long moment, then huffed in anger. I raised an expectant eyebrow. He just stared back.

"Here, I'll even get you started," I said. "Two men walk into a bar—"

"Fuck you," he muttered, then turned on his heel and slammed the front door so hard it rattled my teeth. I stared at the door for a while, feeling what strength I had left seep out through my toes. It was a perfectly wrenching end to a perfectly wrenching day, and the idea of ever moving from that spot was too much to even contemplate.

"Well, you're working some miracles today."

I pivoted in my spot to find my mother standing in the hallway behind me.

"Yeah," I huffed. "I'm nothing if not a little ray of sunshine."

"I'm serious," she said, walking up behind me. "I haven't heard Luke say an angry word in five years, and he just *cursed* at you, sweetheart. This is wonderful."

"No," I said, staring at the doorway. "It's not. He's so angry, and he has every right. I should stop trying, save us both the pain. He's never gonna forgive me."

My mother's hand settled on my shoulder, and she leaned her head against mine.

"Never say never, sweetheart," she said. "You only fail if you give up."

I had stopped taking my mother's advice somewhere around the time that she told me that strong women only need to eat once a day. I was eight. For most of my life, ignoring my mother had been a wise choice. But with New Lilly, the slate was clean, so when she grabbed my keys off the front hall table and handed them to me, I decided to give Mother-knows-best another shot.

I arrived at Luke's house about twenty minutes after he'd left the reception, then spent another ten minutes sitting outside in my truck, wishing I'd changed out of my wedding finery. It's hard to fight for the man you love while wearing satin. But, finally, I accepted that going back was impossible, so I had no choice but to move forward. I got out of the truck, forced myself step by painful step to make it to Luke's door, then pounded relentlessly on it until it opened, pausing only to glance behind me and give a quick wave to Mrs. Pope.

When the door opened, I had to do a double take. Maybe I couldn't turn back time, but Luke sure could. He had one of his old flannel shirts on, a solid burgundy one I remembered him wearing a lot back when we were still together. Underneath, he was wearing a Black Crowes concert T-shirt and an old pair of jeans. His hair was Old Luke messy, and in his hand he had a half-empty beer. I couldn't help it; I laughed.

"Wow," I said when I was able to get command of my voice. "Dig you."

His face was hard, still angry. "What do you want, Eejie?"

"I want to talk."

"We've talked." His face softened a bit and he shook his head. "I don't want to fight."

"I don't want to fight, either," I said. "Please, just let me in. I need to talk to you."

"About what? About what happened six years ago? We can't talk that away, Eejie. It's done. We're done." He sighed. "Just . . . go home."

I didn't know whether he meant home with Mom and Danny, or home back to my Airstream in Colorado, but before I could ask, he'd shut the door in my face.

I stood there for about five minutes, staring at the front door that should have been mine, knowing that behind it was the man who had been meant for me. I had thrown so much away, though I'd never known exactly how much until that moment, and it filled me with such an all-consuming fury that I didn't even care that I'd only gotten what I deserved.

I reached for the door handle, opened the door, and stepped inside. The only light was coming from the stairwell, so that's where I headed.

"Luke!" I called. "Luke!"

I got up to the second-story landing and one of the doors opened. Luke stood in it, staring at me.

"Like a damn dog with a bone," he muttered.

"I'm not giving up," I said. "I can't."

"Sure you can, Eejie," he said. "All it takes is for things to get hard. I'll start working too much, or we'll have a baby that cries too much or doesn't like you enough or reminds you of your mother. Whatever. Something will spook you and you'll run. So let's just head that off at the pass now. Go home."

He turned and went into his bedroom. I followed.

"I can't tell you that that won't happen," I said, "because you won't believe me. I know that, and I understand. I do. But if you'd just give me a chance—"

He turned on me. "A chance to do what? To finish me off this time? Do you have any idea how hard . . . ?"

He trailed off. I shook my head.

"I'm sorry," I said.

"Sorry? Jesus, Eejie. I slept on a fucking couch for two years, just in case you came back and lost your nerve before you made it to the bedroom. I sat in that apartment for *two years*, waiting. Digs told me I was crazy, but I knew. I *knew* you were going to come back. I knew you couldn't leave me. Maybe someone else, but not me. Not us." He ran his hand through his hair and sighed. "It took me two years to get up and start my life again, and now that I've done that, you want me to just pick up with you like it never happened."

"No," I said. "Not like it never happened. Like it'll never happen again."

He stared at me for a long time, and I could see the fight leaving his face. His eyes filled and he swiped at them, then shook his head and said only, "Don't."

"I'm so sorry." I tried to fight the tears; I didn't want this to become about me, but I couldn't help it. I was already emotionally overwrought, and seeing Luke in that much pain would have brought me to my knees on a good day. I took a step closer to him, reached up to touch his face. "I screwed up. I can't go back and fix it. I know that. But I can't leave you again, either."

He wrapped his fingers around my wrist and pulled my hand away from his face, his eyes heavy-lidded as he looked down at me.

"I think you should go," he said.

I stepped closer, and his grip loosened on my wrist. "I can't."

I snaked my hand up again, this time resting it on the back of his neck.

"I can't," I whispered.

His eyes met mine and we stared at each other for a long time. I could see myself in him, and could feel him in me. It's one of those things that happens when you grow up with someone. I think it has something to do with how children are so vulnerable and malleable, that the souls of the people you love at a young age become part of yours. Luke and I had loved each other since the age of five, and standing so close together at that moment, I think we both knew we'd never love anyone else the same way. He took me into his arms and rested his forehead against mine, and we strengthened each other and weakened each other at the same time.

"Goddamnit," he whispered, then leaned in and kissed me, his arms grasping at me as though I might disappear if he didn't hold on tight. We came together so hard our teeth clicked, but neither of us cared. We tore at each other in desperation, buttons and zippers becoming objects of such damning frustration that we ended up cursing and biting and scratching our way to the bed. Everything was frenzied, like a movie played at high speed, and it hurt not to have his hands on me, so much that I whined when he paused to put on the condom. I don't think I took a full breath again until he was inside me, and then things escalated so quickly that I couldn't think or breathe or see. All I knew was that we were together again, and it was the first time in years that I'd felt anything even approaching peace.

We spooned for a while afterward, his large frame covering me as a warm breeze came through the window, until we were both ready to go again. The night passed in waves of sleep and sex. We didn't say a word to each other, just pretended we were still who we'd been, all those years ago. It was nice pretending, although as I stroked the back of his hand as it rested flat on my belly, contemplating the inevitability of sunrise, I knew there would be a lot of shit to wade through, and then only if he let me. I knew that, for him, this could be just his way of getting the good-bye he'd never gotten the first time, and that was fair. He deserved that good-bye, and if I was forced to leave him again, I'd need it, too.

I shifted in the bed and angled my head to look at him in the dim, predawn glow. His eyes flickered a bit, then opened wide as though he was surprised the night hadn't all been just another in the series of dreams I was pretty sure we'd both been having since the day I left. He reached up and touched my face, and I could see the conflict in his eyes, but I knew he'd never tell me the truth, which was that sex was one thing and forgiveness another. If I wanted to trap him, I knew all I had to do was curl up in his arms, say I loved him, and tell him how happy I was that we were back together, and that would be it. He would stay with me forever, even if it meant never being sure I'd be there when he got home at the end of the day. He would stay with me because he loved me, and because he was the kind of man who could never have sex with a woman who loved him and not treat it like a promise.

"Good morning," I said quietly. "I'm gonna go now."

He nodded, but his eyes were still conflicted. He wanted me to go, and he wanted me to stay, but I couldn't do both. I shifted out of his arms and gathered my dress up off the floor. I slipped into it in silence, then turned to him.

"We shouldn't drag this out," I said, "or make it any more painful than it has to be. I'm going to leave for Colorado Springs on Monday, unless you ask me not to."

He sat up, pulled my vacated pillow behind him, and leaned against it. "So it's on me?"

"Sorry, babe. Can't be helped. I know what I want."

He stared down at his fingers, interlocked over his bare stomach. "And what if I can't give you an answer by Monday?"

My heart ached at the thought of it. "If you can't give me an answer by Monday, I think that's an answer."

I stood in the doorway, staring at him, loving him so much that all the muscles in my body hurt. Of course, that could have been the sex, too. I smiled lightly and tapped the doorjamb with my hand, then used it to pull myself away.

I was really proud of myself. I didn't start crying until I was halfway home.

A breakdown is the one thing other people can always see coming. Yet, the person who has it is always surprised. At least, I know I was.

—Lilly Lorraine, in a letter to Danny Greene, undated

Chapter Eighteen

I had hoped that at six forty-five in the morning, my walk of shame wouldn't have witnesses, but after I gently clicked the front door shut, I turned to see Mom standing behind me.

"Oh!" I said, putting my hand to my chest. "Jeez, Mom, you scared me. What are you doing up so early? I thought you didn't need to leave for the airport until ten."

She put one hand on my shoulder, and I could see how tired she was. Her eyes were sad, and my entire body tightened in alarm.

"What is it? What happened?" I grasped at her hand. "Is it Danny? Is he okay?"

"Danny's fine, sweetheart. Come into the kitchen. We can talk there."

She turned and led the way down the hall, and when I came into the kitchen, I saw Danny and Digs sitting at the breakfast bar, each of them staring down into a mug of coffee. Digs was a mess. He was still wearing his suit from the wedding, although with the tie loose and the collar unbuttoned. He shook his head when he saw me.

"Where were you?" he said. "We tried calling you on your cell phone, but it went to voice mail."

"And Luke's phone I guess was shut off," Mom said, a simple statement, not commentary. I hadn't noticed anything about Luke's phone, but considering how badly he didn't want to hear from me last night, that would have made sense.

"What happened?" I looked around from one face to the other, noting which one was missing. "Where's Jess?"

"She's upstairs," Danny said quietly. "In bed."

"Is she okay?" My nerves, already jangled, shrieked for relief. "Will somebody kindly tell me what the fuck is going on?"

Mom exchanged a look with Danny, then started down the hallway. I glanced at Danny and Digs, then turned to follow her, all the way up the stairs to the guest bedroom. Before opening the door, she put a hand on my shoulder.

"If she's sleeping, don't wake her. And whatever you do, don't touch her. It upsets her too much."

"Upsets her?" I whispered. "What happened?"

"We don't know," she said, and opened the door.

The shades were drawn, so even though the sun had

fully risen, the room was still dark. In the middle of the bed, Jess lay on her side, on top of the covers with her bridesmaid dress spread out around her like a tremendous deflated balloon. I walked around, pulling a chair up into her line of vision, and sat down. Her eyes were open, if not terribly focused.

"Hey," I said softly. She blinked, but otherwise made no response. It was as if I wasn't even in the room. A chill of panic crept down my spine, and I leaned forward, taking heed of my mother's advice not to touch her, but wanting to get as close as I could anyway.

"Jess? Hey, sweetheart, are you okay?" Stupid question, of course, but "Are you comatose?" while possibly more appropriate, didn't seem too kind.

There was nothing from her. I spoke to her a few more times, each time saying something equally as lame as "Are you okay?" but got no response. Finally, I gave up and went back downstairs, stomping my way into the kitchen.

"What happened?" I walked around and hit Digs on the shoulder. "What did you do to my angel, Digs?"

"I don't know," he said, shaking his head. "I kissed her. That's it, I swear. We were having a nice time. She was fine. We went for a little walk, and I kissed her, and she freaked out."

"She ran off," Danny said. "We had search parties out looking for her, and finally someone found her huddled in a ball down by the lake. I picked her up and carried her in." Danny's eyes met mine and I could see that he was shaken. "She's a tiny little thing, but it was a

chore, EJ. She kicked and screamed and cried like someone had ripped her heart out on the spot." He let out a
heavy breath. "It was heartbreaking, I'll tell you. Took
your mother the better part of the night to calm her
down."

I looked at Mom. "Why didn't you come get me?" I
asked quietly.

She shook her head. "What could you have done?"

"She could have told me what was wrong!" Digs
said. "What the fuck, EJ? You give me this 'fragile' talk
like maybe she's a little sensitive. You didn't tell me she
was . . ." He trailed off, unable to come up with a word
to describe Jess's current state.

"I didn't know," I said. "I mean, there's something in
her past, something she won't talk about, but I don't
know what it is. That's why I told you to be careful with
her, Digs."

"I *was* careful!" He slammed his fist down on the
counter. "I just kissed her. That's all. She was smiling
and happy one second and the next, it was like—*boom.*"

"Okay, okay," Danny said, patting Digs on the shoulder. "Let's all calm down. This isn't anyone's fault.
But . . ." He exchanged a look with Mom. "We need to
decide what we're going to do."

I glanced back and forth between them. "What do
you mean, what we're going to do?"

Digs shot Mom a look; obviously there'd already
been some sort of discussion. He pushed back from
the breakfast bar and went off to sit on the couch in
the den.

"What? Just tell me. What are you guys thinking?"

"Well," Mom said slowly. "Honey, she's not responding to anyone. She did get up last night to go to the bathroom, which I think is a good sign, but I don't know if she'll eat. I think maybe we should call Dr. Travers—"

"Oh, hell," I said. "You think she needs a shrink?"

Mom's face registered surprise, and she sighed. "I think, honey, she might need a hospital."

"What?" I stared at her. "No. No. It's only been, what, a few hours?"

"Look," Danny said, his voice strong and calm and I loved him for it. "Let's give it a little time. See what happens, okay? Hell, she might even come down in a few minutes asking for a heaping plateful of Lilly's famous Belgian waffles. Right?"

Mom and I looked at each other, neither of us hopeful. I sighed and ran my hands over my face. "I don't want to leave her up there by herself. I'm gonna get cleaned up and go sit with her for a bit, okay?"

"Okay, sweetheart," Mom said. "I'll make some tea and bring it up in a while. I've got a really nice lemon green tea. With a little honey, I think it'll be very cheerful."

I smiled and squeezed her hand. "Thank you." I turned to head upstairs, then stopped and spun back to face them. "Oh, God. Italy. I was going to drive you to the airport. Maybe, um . . . can Digs . . . ?"

Mom shook her head. "We're postponing the trip."

Danny looked a little surprised at this, but I could tell by his expression that he approved. Mom glanced from one of us to the other, then huffed in indignation.

"Don't look so shocked," she said. "This girl brought my daughter back to me. I'm not leaving this house until she's dancing a jig on the front lawn." She twirled around and grabbed the teakettle off the stove, then shooed her hands at me. "Go on and get showered, Emmy. We've got work to do."

I took the first shift, sitting with Jess for seven hours. Mom brought the tea up, but Jess didn't even blink when we asked her if she wanted any. I opened the blinds sometime around noon, but she just shifted over to her other side to shield her face from the light. I tried to get her to change out of her dress at one point and made the mistake of touching her on the shoulder. She shrank violently from my touch, and wept inconsolably for an hour straight until she fell asleep. A little after three, Mom came in and told me to go get some rest. She sat down in the chair with a pile of women's magazines and read them out loud, starting with ten tips for a sexier, sassier you.

I stepped out into the hallway and leaned against the wall. I had never been so exhausted in my life. Even though all I'd done all day was sit and watch her, I felt like I'd been pushing a boulder uphill for hours. My muscles were weak and my mind was brittle. I slowly made my way downstairs to the den, where I found Digs sitting on the couch, staring out the sliding glass doors to the deck. He had gone home, showered, and changed clothes, but he still looked as much of a mess as he'd been that morning. He noticed me after a moment, gave a brief nod, then continued staring. I sat down next to him, and we communed in silence for a while until Digs finally spoke.

"Did I . . . did I do this to her?" he asked. "I've never forced myself on a woman, ever. And I didn't force myself on her last night, I swear. All I did was kiss her, but I feel like I raped her or something."

"Digs, stop." I shifted over closer and leaned my head on his shoulder. "It's not you, babe. I don't know what it is, but something in her was already broken when I met her. If anybody did anything wrong, it's me. I should have pushed her, made her tell me what it was. There were a few times when I could have, but I didn't."

I felt him nod slightly, then he kissed me on the top of my head.

"I'm here for the duration," he said. "I don't want to sit up there with her. I don't want to upset her again. But I'm here. You need anything, just say the word."

I smiled and pulled back, patting his hand. "Where's Danny?"

"In the study, I think," he said.

I pushed myself up from the couch. "Get some rest, Digs. Eat something. You look like shit."

He chuckled. "If that ain't the pot calling the kettle . . ."

I let out a weak laugh and started down the hall toward the study. I knocked lightly and poked my head in to find Danny sitting at his desk. He waved me over and I padded in.

"Hey," I said.

"Hey," he said. "How's our girl?"

I shrugged. "Not good."

Our eyes met and he nodded. "Well, we'll just get Lilly cooking and the wonderful smell will bring her out of it. You'll see."

I smiled and felt a strong rush of love for this stout man and his interminable optimism.

"You hired a detective, right? To find me?"

Danny leaned back in his chair and nodded.

"I need him to find her family, or some friends, maybe," I said. "There's got to be some people out there wondering where she is, and they should be the ones making decisions about hospitals and stuff like that. I've got money in my savings. I can pay for it."

"Stop it," Danny said, dismissing me with a wave of his hand. He reached for a legal pad and pen and handed it to me. "You write down what you know about her, and I'll make the call."

I took the pad and jotted down everything I knew about Jess, then handed it to Danny. He read it quickly and sighed, then reached for the phone. I started for the door, the information I'd just written down traveling circles in my head.

Jess Szyzynski.

Mid to late 20s.

Drives a white Toyota.

I hoped that detective was very good. He'd have to be.

I was napping when Luke showed up with takeout Chinese food. The smell woke me and I traipsed downstairs to find the three guys eating out of containers in the den. I was so worn out that seeing Luke sitting in Danny's leather La-Z-Boy caused only a subdued jolt to my system. I plunked myself down on the couch between Danny and Digs and reached for a napkin and an egg roll.

"Any change?" I asked Digs.

"Lilly's still up there," he said. "She tried to get Jess to eat some soup a little earlier, but . . ." He shook his head, his eyes dull and tired.

"She hasn't eaten anything at all?" I asked.

Danny patted me on my knee. "She took a little water earlier. And if I know women, it's a small jump from water to cheeseburgers." He winked at me. "She'll be better tomorrow, I think."

I picked at the egg roll in my hands. "And if she's not?"

Danny's eyes met mine, then darted to Luke. I glanced back and forth at them and knew that some planning and discussion had been going on. I didn't know what was wrong with Jess, but despite the fact that a hospital seemed at this point like the reasonable, maybe even the responsible, solution, my gut said no. Jess was a person who listened to her internal guides, but they weren't working right now, so I owed it to her to listen to mine, and they were screaming against the hospital. I didn't have the energy to argue about it now, though. At the moment, no one was pushing hospitalization. I'd fight that battle when I got to it.

"I'm gonna go give that detective another call," Danny said, then got up and headed out to the study.

"Well," I said, leaning forward to get up off the couch. "I'm gonna go relieve Mom."

"No," Luke said. "Dad and I are taking the night shift."

I stared at him, unable to process what he was saying. "But . . ." All I could think was, *What's it to you? You hardly even know Jess*, but that seemed both ungrateful and insensitive, so I blurted out, "You've got work, don't you?"

He shrugged. "Nothing that can't be put off or handled by the crew in the office."

Our eyes locked and after a long, painful moment, he smiled. It was a sad, resigned smile, but I was in no position to be choosy.

"You eat something and get some rest," he said, pushing up from the recliner. "Dad and I will wake you guys up if there's any change."

He walked around behind the couch and touched me lightly on the shoulder as he passed by. I reached my fingers up, just grazing his before he moved on down the hallway. I watched him go, then looked back to find Digs staring at me with a mock-disgusted expression.

"What?" I said.

"You do know he's your stepbrother now, right?" he said, a light smile tracking at the edges of his eyes.

"No, he's not," I said, breaking off a piece of egg roll and popping it in my mouth. "If the children are adults who have already had a relationship before the parents ever got together, it doesn't count."

"Whatever," he said, digging his fork into his sesame chicken. "You big freak."

I laughed and punched him lightly on the leg, and then we fell into exhausted silence and ate.

It was a horrible day, the day I realized that I wasn't one of those nurturing, capable mothers who would instinctively know the right thing to do. All I was was a woman who'd had sex, and gotten caught.

—Lilly Lorraine, in a letter to Danny Greene, undated

Chapter Nineteen

I woke up at six the next morning, hopped out of bed and shuffled off to check on Jess. Danny was sitting in the easy chair next to her bed, his face turned thoughtfully toward the window. He didn't seem to notice me until I sat on the arm of the chair.

"Any change?" I whispered.

He shook his head. "She slept the whole night through. She should wake up and come out of it soon."

For the first time, though, his eyes had lost their typical hopeful glimmer. I glanced at Jess. Her face was deeply shadowed, and though she'd always been tiny, she looked downright small and fragile, like a sick child.

"My turn," I said, patting him on the shoulder. "You go get some sleep."

"Not yet," he said. "You get cleaned up, have some breakfast. Your mother is downstairs making you something right now, and she's going to need you to eat, so you go down and do that, hungry or not. I'll be fine until you're ready."

I leaned down and kissed him on the top of the head.

"Thanks, Danny," I whispered. "You're the best dad God ever made, you know."

He smiled at me, and I pushed off the chair and left the room. A few moments later, I came down into the kitchen to find Mom cooking like a madwoman. There were eggs, bacon, waffles, pancakes, and cinnamon rolls, and, as if that weren't enough, sausages were sizzling in a pan on the stove. She wiped her hands on her apron when she saw me and poured me a cup of coffee, which was ready and waiting for me by the time I made it to the breakfast bar.

"Expecting company?" I asked, staring at the spread.

"Cooking soothes me," she said, turning to grab a plate from the cupboard. "Besides, when Jess comes out of it she's going to be hungry. Poor thing hasn't eaten since . . ."

She trailed off and our eyes met briefly, then she heaped scrambled eggs and bacon onto the plate.

"Please eat," she said quietly, placing the plate in front of me. "Even if you're not hungry."

"I'm starving," I lied, pulling the plate closer and digging in. I took a big bite of eggs and my stomach railed against it, but I broke off a piece of bacon and stuffed it in my mouth anyway. "Thanks, Mom."

She smiled, took the sausages off the heat, and leaned both hands against the counter. I ate slower because I didn't imagine my immediately throwing up her food would make her feel better, and I'd made my point, anyway. She let out a big sigh.

"Something happens to you when you have a child," she said. "You think you have a grip on the world, that you can handle whatever life has in store for you. And then this little person shows up and you would throw yourself in front of a train for her without even thinking. And every time anything happens to any child, anywhere in the world, in your head, that's your baby. Every tragedy in the world, for a few seconds at least, it's yours. It's exhausting and frightening, and some people . . ." She paused and took a deep breath, and when she spoke again, her voice cracked. "Some people just aren't strong enough for it."

I put down my fork. I knew what was coming. It was odd, considering how badly I'd wanted to hear it for so many years, that I just as badly wanted her not to worry about it now.

"Mom—," I started, but she talked over me.

"Dr. Travers never told me not to apologize. That was a lie."

I blinked. That wasn't what I was expecting. Once again, Lilly Lorraine had surprised me. "Okay. Look, maybe now isn't the time for—"

"I was scared. It was all I had left, the only thing I had that you still needed. If I gave it to you, and you didn't forgive me, I'd have nothing left. It would be over."

She paused and I tried to think of something to say, but I couldn't. She grabbed a tissue from the box on the counter and went on.

"And then I sit up there in that room with that sweet girl, and I think, 'What would her mother want to say if she knew her baby was here like this?'" She turned her face to me, her eyes red-rimmed and weepy, but her mouth set in firm resolve. "I'm sorry."

"Mom, it's—"

She leaned forward, reaching one hand out toward me on the counter. "No. Emmy, I'm sorry. I'm truly, truly sorry."

I patted her hand and pushed off my stool. I grabbed a plate from the cupboard and filled it, then walked around the breakfast bar, set it down next to mine, and pulled out the stool next to me.

"You're forgiven," I said. "Now sit down and eat something. You're too damn skinny."

She laughed, snatched another tissue from the box on the counter, and swiped at her face, then sat down next to me and took a bite of eggs.

"So, these are supposed to be my fat and happy years, huh?" she asked.

"Yep." I grabbed a cinnamon roll off the platter in front of us and put it on the edge of her plate. "Get cracking, Lilly. You're behind the curve."

It was about ten o'clock that morning when Luke came back from the private detective's office with the information about Jess. I knew that whatever the news was, it was bad. I could tell by the tone of the muffled voices that drifted up to the guest room from the foyer. I pulled my legs up to my chest, waiting for the news to come to me. A few minutes later, there was a knock on the door. I got up to find Luke and Danny standing in the hallway, their faces grim. Danny put his hand on my shoulder and guided me out, stepping wordlessly into the room and shutting the door behind him. Luke's face was tight and he stared down at the folded piece of paper in his hands. He finally raised his eyes to meet mine and then handed me the sheet.

I unfolded it to find a photocopy of a newspaper clipping from the *Forster County News* in eastern Michigan, with the headline MISSING WOMAN FOUND:

A woman reported missing last week has been located, authorities report.

Jessica Marinello Szyzynski, 25, failed to show up for work at the Pinkerton Public Library in Pinkerton Township last week, causing a panic among her coworkers. Szyzynski had been suffering from a depression since her husband and baby son were killed in the pileup on I-196 last summer, and there had been fears of a possible suicide attempt.

"She was a foster child," her supervisor, Elizabeth Masters, said. "She has no family. Tim and little Matty were her whole life. When they died, something in her just shut down."

Workers and patrons from the library pooled

their money to hire a private detective to locate the woman.

"She was always such a sweet and happy girl," said library patron Sandra Coolidge, 83. "We all love her dearly."

The private detective found Szyzynski staying with a friend in Two Trees, Oklahoma. She sent the following message to the *Forster County News* and requested we print it for her:

"Dear Friends,

"I am so deeply sorry for any worry I might have caused you, and I am sorry I couldn't say good-bye to you all. Thank you for everything. I'm safe; please don't worry about me."

"At least we know she's safe," said Masters. "We're just glad that nothing terrible has happened to her. Well, nothing else."

I checked the date on the article; it had been written almost three years earlier. I folded the paper up and handed it to Luke. I looked up at him, but couldn't say anything. I mean, what could I say? It was worse than I could have imagined, and I wasn't prepared for that. I had thought she was like me, that she had done something dumb and abandoned people who loved her, people we could fly out to see her, people who would save her through their sheer loving presence. But there was no one. I felt numb but anxious about what was coming, like the moments between when you break your arm and when you actually feel it.

"Thanks," I said, and turned toward the door to Jess's room.

"Eejie," I heard Luke say, but I continued on into the room. Danny opened his mouth to say something, but if he did, I didn't hear him. A moment later, as I sat in the big chair staring at Jess's face, I heard the door click shut behind them, and it was then that I started to cry.

Much of that day blends together in my memory. I remember refusing lunch and dinner, and I remember the light growing dimmer and dimmer until I was sitting in the dark, but I don't think I had any reliable consciousness of time passing. It felt like seconds, and it felt like days. All I could see was Jess's face, and all I could think was, *What if it were me?* What if Luke and I had stayed together, and had a baby, and what if . . . ? My stomach turned just thinking about it. I couldn't even wrap my mind around what she had been through and I wanted to reach her wherever she was now, but I couldn't. All I could do was sit there with her and make sure that she wasn't alone, so I was determined to do that. On occasion, Mom or Danny would come in and ask to relieve me, but I refused. I'm not sure if at that point I was much more responsive than Jess. I know that by the time they sent Luke in, the room had been dark for a while.

He came in and turned on the small desk lamp, which didn't add much light to the room, but still made me squint. He shut the door behind him and stood next to it for a while. I kept my eyes on Jess, who had rolled over in the bed so her back was to me, but I watched her body carefully to be sure she was still breathing. She was. Shallowly, but there was movement.

After a minute or so, Luke walked over to me and knelt down next to my chair.

"Eejie," he said, his voice registering just above a whisper, "you've been in here for ten hours."

I shrugged, keeping my eyes on Jess. Luke leaned over, trying to get into my eyeline, but I just closed my eyes.

"Hey," he said. He touched my face and I opened my eyes and looked at him. He looked tired and worried and his hair was its old, beautiful mess and I didn't even care.

"Lilly made some food. It would really mean a lot to her if you would go down and eat something. I'll stay with Jess, okay?"

"No," I said. "She's going to wake up soon, and I need to be here when she does."

Luke glanced behind him at the bed, where Jess lay motionless except for the slight movements of breathing. He turned back to me.

"Babe, look. Dad and Lilly need to talk to you about that."

Alarm shot through me. "What do you mean?"

"It's been two days, Eej. She hasn't eaten. She . . ." He shook his head. "You need to go down and talk to Dad and your mom. I will come and get you the second she moves, I swear."

I stared at him as the cold realization washed over me: They wanted to put her in a hospital. She didn't have any family to make the call, so it was down to me. I was going to have to convince them not to do it, and I didn't know how to do that, especially because all logic stated that we should have called the hospital that first morning. But my gut was screaming no, and Jess believed in that, so I had to believe in it, too.

I slowly pushed myself up from the chair. Luke put his hand on the small of my back and guided me to the door. I glanced back at him and he gave me a small, encouraging smile.

"I'll be here," he said.

I felt weak, my muscles shaking, as I walked down the stairs. The lights in the house seemed uncomfortably bright, and when I came into the kitchen, Danny, Digs, and Mom descended on me. Danny walked me to the breakfast bar and sat me down on the stool, Digs put a blanket around my shoulders, and Mom poured some broth into a mug and slid it in front of me. I got a few sips in before Mom said, "Emmy—," and I said, "No."

"EJ," Danny said. "There are doctors there that can help her."

"I know." I took a sip of the broth, then set the mug down. "I know. There's not an argument you can make that I don't agree with."

Mom reached across the breakfast bar and touched my hand. "Honey, she could die."

"She will die, if I send her to a hospital. I don't know how I know that, but I just know. Jess, she . . . she follows her gut on everything. And I'm all she has right now, I have to do that for her. And my gut just says no. No hospital."

"Okay," Danny said, his voice strong and soothing and fatherly. "Okay, then. No hospital tonight." Mom opened her mouth and Danny held up one hand. "*To-night*. But, EJ, sweetheart, if she's not eating by tomorrow morning . . ."

I raised my eyes to Mom's. She held them for a long moment, then slowly nodded. I couldn't nod back. I just knew she couldn't go to a hospital. I felt that the only thing keeping her here at all was us, and how much we'd all grown to love her in such a short time. It didn't make any sense. I knew she needed food, I knew she needed care, I just couldn't agree to it.

Except I had no choice. At a certain point, she was sure to die at home, too. Didn't matter where you were if you weren't eating.

"Okay," I said finally. Mom's shoulders slumped in relief. "I'll just get her to eat, then."

I picked up my mug of broth and started for the stairs. I had no idea how I was going to get Jess to drink it. As a matter of fact, I was pretty sure I'd fail, but trying was the only thing I had left in my arsenal, so I was going to try. I could hear footsteps behind me, but whether it was just Mom or all three of them, my brain was too addled to distinguish. I opened the door to Jess's room and Luke stood up instantly from the chair and walked over to us. I could hear him and Danny talking in low tones behind me as I knelt by the bed, but I couldn't hear what they were saying.

"Jess?" I said, my voice wavering. "Jess, honey, I need you to wake up now. You need to eat something, okay? Just a few sips of broth, that's all, and then you can sleep again. Can you do that?"

She didn't respond. I stared at her waist, looking for the movement of breath, and it was a while before I saw it. It was so shallow, as if at any minute, it would be time to just stop. I glanced up to see Danny, Mom, Digs, and Luke standing in a line, looking at me. I had to do something. I had to do *something*.

I just didn't know what. And if I didn't figure it out soon, she would die.

"What do I do?" I asked. My eyes locked with my mother's. "I don't know what to do. She has no one but me, and I don't know what to do. She always knows what to do, and I . . ."

It was then that my mother stepped forward, her movements forceful and confident. She put her hands on my shoulders and pulled me up, walking me over to stand with Danny, who put his arm around me. I leaned my head on his shoulder and watched as my mother crawled in the bed with Jess. She snuck one arm under Jess's head, and nudged her up until her face was resting on Mom's shoulder. The dirty satin of Jess's dress shifted on the bed as my mother pulled her into her arms like a life-size rag doll.

"Mom . . . ," I said, but I trailed off when I saw Jess's eyes open suddenly, as if she'd been slapped awake. She howled as though my mother had lit her on fire, but Mom didn't move, just tightened her hold. Jess kicked and struggled, but was so weakened by the days of not eating that ninety-eight pounds of determined Lilly Lorraine were just too much for her. Then, as suddenly as she'd come to, her entire body went slack.

For a second, I thought maybe she'd passed out or died, and I stopped breathing myself. Then a sound came from her throat, a hard knot of a sob, the kind of sound you expect to hear when someone's been punched in the gut. I took in a breath and Danny tightened his hold on me. Then Jess began to wail like nothing I'd ever heard. She wept with long, racking sobs that shook her body, my mother, the bed. My mother smoothed her hands over Jess's ratty hair and made comforting mom noises, but still Jess cried and writhed like she'd been cracked wide open. I cried with her, and Danny held on to me, stroking my back and my hair, telling me it would be okay. He motioned for Luke and Digs to go, and they silently did as instructed.

Mom cuddled Jess as though she were a small child, holding on to her, whispering words of encouragement and pride into her ear, selflessly giving every bit of strength she had to this motherless girl. She didn't cry a single tear, just held on to Jess and was a mom. The mom Jess never had. The mom *I* never had. But still, there she was, fixing the impossible, saving Jess's life, saving me. I leaned against Danny, felt him strong and solid next to me, and a bone-deep relief flowed through me. This was what it was like, I marveled, to have parents who would catch you, no matter what. This was what it was like to be loved so powerfully that it even transferred to the strange little angels you brought home with you. This was what it was like.

After a while, Jess's wails quieted into soft weeping, and still my mother held on to her. A little while later, Jess fell asleep again, but her breathing wasn't as shallow as before. Her chest rose and fell like someone who had a hold on life, and I felt hopeful again. Mom extricated herself from under Jess, wrapping the blankets around her. Jess took a deep, grief-stuttered breath, and then sighed and rolled over, still passed out. Danny and I stepped into the hallway and waited. A few seconds later, Mom clicked the door gently shut behind her and led us all downstairs to the kitchen, where she started to toss out orders like a drill sergeant.

"Danny, I want you to gather some fresh queen-sized bedding from the linen closet. Digs, I need you to go out and get chocolate—ice cream, cookies, truffles. Whatever you can find."

Digs opened his mouth to protest but she held up her hand.

"Don't argue. You want to help Jess, you'll get ice cream." She turned to Luke. "Luke, we need something clean and fresh for her to wear. She's a size six petite. Go out and get some basic T-shirts, sweatshirts, jeans. Just make sure you buy them for comfort, not fashion."

Luke shot me a look. *Fashion?* I offered him my strongest smile, which was still pretty weak.

"You can go to the Target in Troutdale," Mom said, misinterpreting Luke's look of puzzled amusement as not knowing where to shop.

"Mom," I said, "Jess has clean laundry here."

"Clean, yes," she said. "But not new. She needs

things that are new, fresh. When she comes out of this, she's going to need to start over again."

Her eyes locked with Danny's, and I could see by his face that they'd been through this before. About five years ago, I guessed. She took a deep breath, clapped her hands.

"Hop to it, boys," she said. "The Queen has spoken. Shuffle off."

They dispersed, and Mom headed to the pantry. "I don't have any homemade stock on hand, so we'll have to use store-bought, but I've got everything we need for a hearty vegetable soup. Let's see. Macaroni and cheese, mashed potatoes . . . Good. Good. We'll need some protein, though." She came back from the pantry, arms full, and dropped her cache on the counter, then opened the freezer. "Oooh, roast chicken. By the time this is thawed and cooked, she should be ready for it. Perfect."

She pulled out a big frozen bird and moved it to the refrigerator to thaw. She grabbed two aprons off the hooks on the wall and handed me one.

"You can start with the carrots. Wash 'em, peel 'em, and chop 'em, and then I'll tell you what you can do next."

I grabbed the bag of carrots. "Mom, how do you know she'll come out of it? I mean, I think maybe she's better, but how do you know?"

"I'm a mom," she said, smiling. "We know these things." She grabbed a peeler from the counter and handed it to me. "Now get to work. She'll be down soon."

Luke and Digs returned with the goods, and Mom immediately shuffled them back to the front door.

"Too many people are going to overwhelm her," she said. "When she wakes up, it should be just me and EJ." She squeezed Digs's hand. "I'll have Danny call you with updates, and we'll let you know as soon as you can come back and see her. Okay?"

Digs nodded, then pulled Lilly in for a hug. I leaned against the wall in the hallway and watched, amazed at how small Digs seemed in that moment. It was funny; I'd always been conscious of being a fatherless girl, but I'd never thought much about what it had been like for the boys to grow up without a mother. I'd had Danny at least, but as Digs held on to my tiny mother for strength, I realized how much she had to offer them, even as adults.

I glanced at Luke to find him watching me as intently as I'd been watching Digs and Mom. I smiled lightly and he smiled back and then looked away. Mom hustled them both out the door and we went back into the kitchen, where we played Scrabble at the table with Danny, pausing the game only to fold Jess's new laundry. At ten thirty I was just about ready to throw in the towel and head to bed when I heard a small voice from the hall behind us.

"Hi."

I turned and there was Jess, haggard and worn in her bridesmaid dress, but walking and focusing on her own power. Mom hopped up from the kitchen table and wordlessly pulled out a chair for Jess. Danny smiled, but didn't say anything as he beelined for the linens that were lying in wait on the couch in the den, quietly doing as he'd been instructed by the Queen. He disappeared upstairs to clean out Jess's room, and Jess dutifully sat where instructed. Mom put a mug of broth in front of her with a handful of saltines and a glass of water.

"Eat slowly, sweetheart," she said as she sat down next to her. "But eat."

Jess allowed a small smile, then dipped her spoon into the broth and sipped delicately, staring down at the Scrabble board.

"Who played 'qaid' on the triple word score?" she asked.

Mom huffed. "That was Danny. I didn't think it was a real word, either."

"No, it's a word," Jess said, clearing her throat. "I, um . . . I used to work at a library, and we would play when it got slow. That was one of my standby words."

I sat back in my chair, realizing that this was the first specific piece of information Jess had ever volunteered about herself or her background. I glanced at Mom, who gathered up the pieces to set up for a new game, chattering with Jess about nothing in particular. There was a lot about all this that I didn't understand, but I knew Mom did, and I was happy to lean on her to run the show. I was more than happy. I was relieved. By taking care of Jess, she was taking care of me, too, and it was a wonderful feeling to be able to relax, knowing that she had my back.

We played a game and ate soup and Jess smiled twice

before being sent upstairs to shower, change into fresh clothes, and go to sleep. She hugged us both before she left, and when she walked away, she looked stronger already. I put my arm around Mom's shoulder and leaned my head against hers.

"You done good, lady," I said. "For such a tiny little thing, you're pretty amazing, you know that?"

She reached up to her shoulder and patted my hand.

"Yes," she said quietly. "I know."

This letter doesn't have a joke. I'm sorry. I can't tell one now. I'm too depressed. I'm in Utah, and I've been crying so long I'm bone dry. I'm still huffing and sobbing but nothing's coming out, which is good. I'm out of tissues.

It's now ten months since I left, and it's too late to go back, and I miss you. I miss you so bad my eyelashes hurt, and I can't move my toes. I used to think that I'd get over this, that eventually I'd be better, and it would all be all right. But it's never going to be better, is it? At least not for me. Hopefully for you. It's hoping that things are better for you that's keeping me from going back right now. Well, that and the guy in the lot next to mine. He's playing guitar, really badly. And singing. And he has no idea how bad he is, and it's so scary. I'm listening to him, and I'm thinking, That's how bad I was. I was that bad. *But I loved you as much as that guy loves his guitar. More, actually. If he loved the guitar as much as I love you, he'd put it away, because he's just making the poor thing suffer.*

—Emmy James, in a letter to Luke Greene, undated

Chapter Twenty

Jess and I spent most of that week padding around the house, eating chocolate and watching old movies and sitting on the back deck talking. She talked a lot about her life, about her husband and son, and while she still got that distant look on her face when she did, she got through it. She didn't cry nearly as much as I would have expected; it was more like she was just sweeping her head clean of things that had been locked in a sunless room for too long.

"Digs feels really bad," I said the following Sunday night as Jess and I had our usual after-dinner tea on the back deck. "He thinks he did something wrong."

Despite having been invited back to see Jess a number of times by my mother, Digs hadn't stepped foot in the house. I think he was waiting for Jess to tell him it was okay first, which was unusually sensitive for Digs. When the whole week had gone by without Jess mentioning Digs, I thought it was time to say something. I didn't want to pry, but it had been not prying that had allowed things to get as bad as they had, so I went for it.

"Oh, no," Jess said, her eyes widening as she looked at me. "It's just . . ." She shook her head and stared out into the horizon. "When Tim and Matty died, I didn't want to live, you know? But I'm Catholic. Suicide has never been an option for me. So I prayed to God every night to take me in my sleep, but He didn't. Which kind of irritated me."

"Oh, I totally get that," I said, laughing lightly.

She smiled a bright, full smile. "Thought you would. So, anyway, I decided, Fine, God, if you won't listen to me, I'll just stop living. I'll give my life to other people, to their problems, their lives. And for a long time, that really worked out well. But everything here . . . spending time with you and your family . . ." She paused, blinking rapidly. "I started to love you guys. I mean, who wouldn't, right? I'm telling you, the second Lilly grabbed the chef's knife and hacked off that hunk of cheese, I was hers forever."

We cracked up at this, but then the laughter subsided, and she went on. "And then I, uh, I started to really like Digs. He's just so funny, you know? And smart. So when he kissed me, and I was really happy for that moment"—she took a moment, her lips trembling a bit—"I was happy for myself. I was happy in a world that didn't have Tim and Matty in it, and I wasn't prepared for that. It had never occurred to me that something like that could happen. It was like all the pain I'd been pushing aside for all this time just whooshed down over me, and I shut down." She swiped at her face, went quiet for a moment, then said in a small voice, "Can you tell Digs that for me? That it wasn't his fault? That I'm so sorry?"

I reached out and patted her hand. "Let me tell you something about being sorry," I said. "It's always better coming directly from the source." I glanced at my watch. "Which gives you about fifteen hours to make a very important phone call."

She nodded. "Okay. I'll call him in a little bit."

We sat in silence for a while, then I said, "Are you sure you don't want to come to Colorado Springs with me?"

"I have to pick up my car in New Jersey," she said.

"Well, it'll still be there in a week," I said. "We can grab the Airstream and you can kidnap me again. It'll be fun. Like old times."

"That would be fun, but no. My flight takes off so soon after your parents' flight to Italy. It's just easy for you to drop us all off at the airport tomorrow, and then . . ." She angled her head and looked at me. "Then I guess you'll be going?"

"Sometime around noon tomorrow," I said.

"What about Luke?"

I shrugged. "He knows I'm going. He knows all he has to do is say the word, and he hasn't. So, I'm going to accept that. The important thing was that I did it, right? I told him how I felt. It may be over, but at least it's over the right way this time, and that matters, right?"

She smiled. "Right." She pushed up from the chair. "I'm gonna go call Digs. Wish me luck."

"Luck," I said. She walked off, leaving me staring at the Oregon horizon, wondering why, if I'd done the right thing, I felt like such total crap.

It still wasn't technically stalking. After Jess got off the phone with Digs, she mentioned that he and Luke had gone out to shoot some pool—which made me happy, shooting pool is an Old Luke activity—and then she went upstairs to finish packing. I sat on the back deck for a while, and once the sun started to go down, I had a flash of inspiration and knew exactly what I needed to do. So I got in my truck and drove.

I parked down the street a bit, in a place where I could see Luke's house and not be immediately detected by Mrs. Pope. I sat in the truck for probably an hour. His car wasn't there—no doubt Digs needed a designated driver after the week he'd been through—so I felt safe just sitting there, staring at our dream home.

His home, I corrected internally. *His home*.

I reached underneath the passenger seat and pulled out the box of stationery. I flipped open the top, lifted the drawer, and riffled through the fifty-odd letters I'd written over the six years we'd been apart. As best I could recall, there were one or two direct ones in there, but most of them were jokes, all of which had meaning that Luke might or might not get. Hell, if I'd opened and read them right then, I might not have gotten them all, either. When I wrote them, I'd intended for Luke never to see them, but it had been important to write them anyway, just as it was important for me to write this last one. I pulled out a sheet of paper and an envelope, closed the box, and began to scribble.

Dear Luke,

The letters in this box belong to you, so I thought I would finally make sure you got them. I want you to know that it's all okay. I'm okay. I'm not upset with you for making the choice you had to make. I respect it, and I understand, and it's okay. I already said that, didn't I? I've been repeating myself a lot lately. Sorry.

Anyway, I'll be back for Thanksgiving, if Lilly lets me disappear that long, and I hope to find you happy when I return. Just do me a favor. Stop it with the neat hair and the Sunday business meetings. You're too young for that shit. For my part, I will consider living in something that doesn't have wheels, but I can't make any promises. Baby steps and all that.

I want you to know that I genuinely wish you well. Oh, and, if you are dating a non-octogenarian when I come back, I promise to handle it with all my usual grace and decorum. I realize that's probably not comforting, but it's all I've got, and I give it to you.

I want you to be happy, Luke. That sounds like typical end-of-the-relationship bullshit, but it's really true. Giving you this box helps me with that, you know? I guess it's my way of saying good-bye, to all of it. Finally. Aren't you proud of how grown-up I am? Well, you should be, damn it. I'm giving up my hook hand. That's gotta count for something, right? But if you can do nothing else for me, do this—find what makes you happy, and make it yours. For my part, I'm going to try to do the same.

I guess that's it, although I do have one last thought for you.

A priest, a rabbi, and a duck are building a time machine . . .

The next morning, I took Mom and Danny and Jess to the airport in Danny's Explorer. Danny drove for the ride over, while Mom angled herself to face me and Jess in the backseat and elicited multiple promises from Jess to write and call frequently, and visit for every major holiday or have a damn good reason why not.

"And the only acceptable reasons are hospitalization or traveling out of the country," she said. "No other excuse will do, do you hear me, young lady?"

"I hear you," Jess said, and she and I exchanged a cheerful eye roll, then Mom pointed a finger at me.

"The same goes for you, too," she said. "I will hunt you down again if I have to."

"Don't I know it," I muttered, and Jess and I giggled like a couple of teenagers in the backseat.

I drove slowly on the way back to Danny's, alone with my thoughts. I wasn't particularly excited about Colorado Springs, but I wasn't sure where else I would go. I had the whole country open to me, but there was nowhere else I'd rather be than here in Fletcher.

Of course, that was impossible. I hadn't left that box of letters on Luke's porch for nothing. I was grown up, and I was moving on, damn it. Even if it killed me. But it would take a day or so to get to Colorado Springs, and when I did, I could always throw the dart again, and let the Universe guide me where She wanted me to go. Maybe I'd hunt Jess down and we could angel together. It didn't seem like such a crazy idea to me now.

I was halfway down the driveway when I realized I'd left my cell phone inside. I hopped out of my truck, leaving it running while I rushed to the house and snatched my phone off the half-moon table, being careful to lock the door behind me. I had just stepped out of the house when my peripheral vision registered a figure standing next to my truck. I gasped, froze where I was, and stared, not believing my eyes.

He was wearing a dark green flannel shirt, jeans, and workboots. His hair was messy, curling at the ends and beautiful. He had his hands tucked in his front pockets, but didn't move. For my part, I didn't move either. I was afraid if I did, the mirage would vanish, and I wanted to hold on to it as long as I could.

"Hey," I said finally.

He nodded. "Hey."

There was another long moment of awkward silence, then he started toward me. My heart beat faster with each step he took, until finally he was standing right in front of me, close enough to touch, and I felt kinda dizzy.

"I was just on my way," I said lamely, motioning toward the truck.

He glanced at it, then back at me. "Yeah. I guessed."

I motioned behind me toward the house. "Um, Danny and Mom are already gone, if you were coming by to say good-bye to them."

He shook his head. "No. That's not why I'm here. I actually, um . . . I got the box."

"Oh, yeah," I said, wringing my fingers in my hands. "I figured leaving it on your porch was a good way to get it to you."

"Yeah. It was."

Another long, awkward silence, and I felt as if my heart were being ripped out of my chest. Why the hell was he doing this to me? Didn't he know that I had said my good-bye last night? What did he want, for me to break down weeping in the driveway? Which, I realized, was exactly what was going to happen if I didn't get out of there immediately.

"Well," I said, "I have to go."

He looked surprised, but then nodded and stepped back out of my way. My heart sank as I realized that he wasn't there to stop me from going. God only knew why he was there, but if it wasn't to stop me, then I didn't care. I turned around and started toward the truck, my eyes welling as I did. Which was okay. Once I was in the truck, he wouldn't see—

"Eejie."

I stopped where I was, my back to him. "Luke. Just

let me go. Please. My ass has been kicked enough, trust me, you don't need to add your footprint to the—"

"Two guys walk into a bar."

I twirled around to face him. *"What?"*

He started toward me, his gait strong and determined. "Two guys walk into a bar . . ."

"Goddamnit, Luke. Don't mess with me. Not today. It's just mean."

He kept coming. ". . . and the first guy says, 'Hey, bartender. A round for the house. I just asked the woman I love to marry me and she said yes.'" He stopped about a foot away from me, his eyes dark and earnest. "And then the second guy says, 'I want to buy a round, too. The woman I love left in the middle of the night and disappeared for six years.' And the bartender says, 'What are you buying a round for? That's not good news.' And the guy says, 'Yeah, it is.'" Luke smiled and reached up to touch my face. "'Because she came back.'"

I stared at him for a long time, pretty sure I understood what he was saying, but unable to fully trust it.

"Really?" I asked, my voice shaking.

He smiled. "Really."

A tear tracked down my cheek and he wiped it away with his thumb, then leaned in and kissed me gently. I put both hands on his face and kissed him back, then threw my arms around his neck. He laughed and lifted me off my feet in a happy hug. When he set me down again, I grabbed both of his hands in mine.

"Well, crap," I said. "I have to go get my stupid trailer now."

"Okay." He put his arm around my waist and walked me to the truck. "Let's go."

"Um . . . all right," I said, then noticed when we got to the truck that a familiar beat-up army-navy duffel was sitting in the bed with all my stuff. I glanced over at him. "I see we're pretty sure of ourselves, aren't we?"

He grinned and raised his eyebrows at me.

"So, this Airstream of yours," he said as he pulled the driver's-side door open for me, "is it gonna fit in my driveway?"

"No," I said, "but it'll fit in this driveway."

Luke laughed. "Oh, Lilly's gonna love that."

I put my arms around his waist and pulled him to me. "Yeah, I know. Is it bad that driving her nuts still kinda makes me happy inside?"

He put his hands on my shoulders and kissed me. "I'll cut you slack on that one. Some habits are tough to break."

"Yeah," I said, smiling. "Thank God."

About the Author

Lani Diane Rich is a wife and mother living in upstate New York. She's held lots of odd jobs—including working as a convenience store clerk for a while—during her professional lifetime, but she loves writing the best because it's the only job she's allowed to do in her pajamas. It's all about the fringe benefits. She would like to thank everyone who bought this book, and gives extra thanks to anyone taking the time to read the bio. You people are obviously exceptional; Lani hopes you feel good about that.

You can find Lani at her Web site and blog (lanidianerich.com); listen to her on the weekly podcast she hosts with award-winning author Samantha Graves (willwriteforwine.com); and read about her adventures in collaborating with Jennifer Crusie and Anne Stuart (dogsandgoddesses.com).